Binding De

Kiki Archer

Title: Binding Devotion
ID: 21441385
ISBN: 978-0-244-63248-9

K.A Books *Publishers*

www.kikiarcherbooks.com

Twitter: @kikiarcherbooks

Published by K.A Books 2013

Author photograph: **Ian France** www.ianfrance.com

ISBN: 978-0-244-63248-9

For everyone who has supported me.
You know who you are.
Thank you.
This is for you.
xxx

CHAPTER ONE

"Just shove it in, sweetie!"

"I'm trying."

"No. Not like that! You have to shove it in and out quickly, or it won't work."

"That's what I did."

"No! Shove it in harder!"

"I can't. I'm all flustered," said Melody, turning to look at the woman waiting impatiently behind her. "You try!" she said.

Zara ignored the command and slipped her fingers under the back of Melody's loose blouse, reaching around for her target. "No, sweetie." She squeezed roughly. "My hands are too busy."

Melody gave a frantic glance up and down the carpeted corridor. "Stop it! Someone will see us."

"They will if you don't open that door!" urged Zara, increasing the pressure.

"What am I doing wrong?" puffed Melody, deliberately twisting her upper body and shaking herself free from the clamping fingers. She focused her attention, re-reading the diagrammatic instructions on the back of the shiny plastic card.

Zara ignored the warning and bit Melody's exposed neck. "You, sweetie, need to relax."

"Zara, please! Will you just let me focus?!" Melody turned the shiny card over, held it against the slot and pushed down firmly. The metal box of room 223 made a reassuring click and the illusive green light finally flashed.

Zara halted her teasing bites. "It's green! Push the handle."

Melody used her left shoulder to force open the heavy hotel room door. "And we're in! Not that you've been much help!"

"You love it," moaned Zara, pushing her conquest into the dimly lit room and pinning her against the wall. She kissed her full on the mouth and used her fingers to unzip the top of the fitted work skirt. She pushed down on the waistband and watched as Melody's skirt fell to the ground.

Melody was about to kick off the skirt, when she froze at the sound of applause. She glanced around the small room, relieved to see the flicker of the television. "The TV's on," she said.

"So?" gasped Zara, in-between her heated exploration.

Melody tried to edge sideways along the wall to get a better look.

"Get back here," commanded Zara, pulling at the buttons on Melody's gaping work blouse. "They always leave the television on in these rooms." She exhaled in success and yanked the blouse wide open, immediately pulling down at the black lace bra and exposing Melody's super-enhanced breasts. "I've been waiting for these all day." She thrust her head into the cleavage and sucked a huge muffled breath through her nostrils. "You've got incredible breasts, sweetie."

Melody craned her neck once more and squinted at the television. "I bet you say that to all of your women."

"No. Just you." Zara reached down and pulled at the complicated hosiery, unable to unhook the expensive garter. "What's this bit attached to? Give me a hand, sweetie."

"With what?" Melody was still transfixed by the quiet television.

"Your suspenders. They're sexy, but I can't find the hooks." Zara looked up at her distracted conquest. "Melody, come on! I'm in a tangle here!"

"Sorry, it's..." Melody scanned the basic room for the remote, "...it's the debate."

Zara stood bolt upright and swivelled to look at the television. "Well that can go right off then! Where's the remote?"

Melody kicked off the skirt that was still lying in crumpled heap around one leg, and shuffled to the bedside cabinet. "Got it. Let's just turn it up for a second."

"You've got to be kidding me?" Zara's tone was sharp.

Melody pressed the soft rubber volume button and sank down onto the hotel room bed. "No, she's brilliant, and it looks like she's winning."

"I didn't want to watch the debate, sweetie. If I wanted to watch the debate, I would have gone over to the studios and watched the debate. But I didn't. So I haven't. I chose to be here with you instead." Zara pulled her poker straight black hair over her left shoulder and lifted her nose. It was one of those habits that everyone was aware of apart from herself. "Now turn it off, please."

Melody turned up the volume once more. "Just give it a second. They're onto the marriage bit." She nodded officiously, pulling her double-D cups back up around her breasts and trying to look serious. "This is important for all of us."

Zara tutted and turned herself towards the bright screen, not wanting to watch, but drawn in all the same. The articulate debate host was addressing the bright eyed young woman on her left. "So, Andi, are the Church right to be so vocal in their disapproval of gay marriage?"

The petite blonde woman, with a trendy pixie haircut and pretty features, smiled politely. "Can I just ask, once again, that we call this equal marriage, not gay marriage?" The woman's tone of voice was soothing, yet firm. "And no, the Church continues to harm what's left of its already tarnished image, with this constant preoccupation with gay issues." The banner flashed across the bottom of the screen: *Andi Armstrong – Proud Unity© – Chief Executive.* The pretty woman continued to talk. "Under the current proposals, the Church will not be asked to play any part, whatsoever, in the new marriage laws. The new laws will simply extend the right of marriage to all members of society." Andi Armstrong paused and looked directly into the camera with a confidence and self-belief that evoked trust and support in her army of enthusiasts. "Marriage strengthens society, so logically this is a positive move." The young woman waited for the clapping in the studio to subside and focused, once again, on the lens. "It's illogical for the Church to suggest the introduction of equal marriage will destroy the very foundation of marriage itself. It just doesn't make sense." Andi Armstrong lifted her hand to the host to indicate that she wasn't quite finished, and made her final impassioned point. "Allowing people to fulfil their desire to commit to one another, is a good, just, and righteous addition to the laws of our Great Britain."

Zara slammed the button on the side of the widescreen television, muting the rapturous applause. "She's always doing that crescendo thing with her voice. It annoys me." She crossed her arms. "And her eyes always look like they're about to pop out of their sockets when she does her spiel of: *'I've been married to my wife for seven years and our committed relationship is outliving many of our straight counterparts.'* Yada, yada, yada."

Melody shook her head. "She's inspirational."

"Well, why aren't you at the debate then, sweetie?" mocked Zara, narrowing her eyes and betraying the annoyance well hidden by her latest bout of Botox.

Melody stood up and seductively stroked her own chest. She spoke slowly. "Because *you*, suggested that *we,* should get *this,* out of our system before we end up exploding at work." Melody smiled. "But actually, I quite fancy exploding all over your CEO desk, boss."

Zara pulled her long black hair over her left shoulder and lifted her nose. "I'm not sure I'm in the mood anymore."

Melody raised her knee and sank a black stiletto heel onto the bed. She parted her legs and licked her finger slowly.

Zara went to roll her eyes, but stopped midway with a jerk of her head, suddenly spotting something unexpected. She stepped backwards, bent down and squinted. "Melody! You're wearing peepholes?"

"Of course," smiled Melody. "I know you like to get straight to the action, so I thought I'd make it easy for you."

"Nothing about chasing you has been easy, sweetie," said Zara, lunging forwards and thrusting her hands greedily between the parted legs. "But I'm going to make it worth my while."

Melody grinned, aroused by the sudden rush of power. "And it'll be worth mine too," she whispered.

****

Andi Armstrong raised her tall glass of Champagne and chinked it cheerfully against the outstretched tumbler of orange juice. "To us," she beamed. "No, to you," she laughed. "No actually, let's toast to the impossible task of finding your replacement!" She smiled widely and sipped thirstily, feeling an immediate release of stress and worry. The debate was over, the sound bites were good, and she could finally relax - for a moment. Monday morning would come and the preparations would begin for her appearance on Question Time. She paused and pushed the intruding thoughts to the back of her mind, wanting to enjoy the current feeling of liberation and accomplishment.

Andi placed her Champagne glass back down and smiled at the friendly but exclusive surroundings, enjoying the buzz of the fellow diners and the temptations of the deliciously aromatic smells. She turned to her dinner companion and sighed. Her friend was fanning her face and sipping from her tumbler of orange juice; looking all together rather uncomfortable.

Stella was her PA, and very best friend, having worked together for the past eight years, taking what was originally a small group of like-minded campaigners, to what was now, the huge success of the nation's number one lesbian, gay, bisexual, and transgender, campaigning and lobbying group: *Proud Unity.*

Andi felt a pang of compassion and was overcome with gratitude. "Oh Stella, I can't thank you enough. Look at you! You're about twelve months pregnant and here you are, taking it to the wire with me. I don't deserve you and I'll certainly not find a good enough replacement for you."

Stella sighed and tried to arch her back. Every single movement hurt. From her ankles to her neck, she felt a dull pain, and the posh restaurant's minimalistic style of chair was not helping. Patting her huge baby bump, she forced a smile. "I wouldn't have it any other way, Andi."

"No, but I bet Sandy would."

"Sandy? Who's, Sandy?"

"Exactly! Your wife must curse me."

Stella smiled. "Actually, Andi, she adores you. Just like I do, and just like the rest of the liberated female population do."

"Stop it."

"Seriously, you were great today."

Andi waved her hand dismissively. "I'm just doing my job."

"Well thank you."

"Stop it, you dafty. We're here so I can thank *you*!" She smiled. "So thank you for all of your hard work. You've been the best PA I could have hoped for." Andi glanced towards the restaurant's entrance and checked her watch. It wasn't quite 7.00 p.m. She turned her attention back to her heavily pregnant friend. "So just how much have we cut into your maternity leave then?"

"Four weeks."

Andi frantically shook her head. "Four weeks? Are you mad?"

Stella shrugged her shoulders and grinned. "It's okay. I'm not due until Tuesday."

"This Tuesday? Four days to prepare! Sandy is definitely cursing me."

Stella laughed. "Well I think your wife curses me too. She reminded me that I'd already sent a reminder about the reminder for tonight."

Andi lifted her eyebrows. "You're great at reminders and she needs it. Her schedule's a nightmare."

"That makes two of you then," smiled Stella. "You're a match made in heaven."

"We are, actually," nodded Andi, sweeping her short blonde fringe to the left side of her forehead. She took another sip of Champagne. "And can you believe it's been seven years since our wedding?"

"It's still the most beautiful wedding I've been to." Stella grinned. "They should have covered it in *Hello*. Oh, I forgot, they did!"

"We had a tiny picture in the back of the events section and that's only because of-"

"Yes, we know, your wife and the multi-million pound FTSE 100 Company she almost owns." Stella drained the last of her orange juice. "But the picture did cover at least a page."

"The picture was not a page! And she doesn't own the company!"

Stella knew how to tease her boss. "You're a popular power couple though, aren't you?"

"Stop it, Stella! You know I hate talking about this."

"You're like the UK's Ellen and Portia, only younger."

"I wish," laughed Andi.

"Well, your hair's definitely rocking the Ellen *do*."

Andi ran her fingers through her short blonde locks. "I like it cropped."

"So do your legion of fans."

"Seriously, stop it!" blushed Andi. "I'm just a happily married campaigner, living the dream."

Stella winked. "You're a hot campaigner, with a hot wife, and a Champagne lifestyle."

"Oh please! It's been non-stop and it will continue to be non-stop until equal marriage finally becomes law." She lifted her glass and smiled. "And anyway, this is the first drop I've had since-"

"Since last Saturday at the *Who's Out* Awards. I saw the pictures in *Fierce* magazine. You guys looked incredibly glam!" Stella noticed the approaching dinner guest and burst into a teasing smile. "And here she is now! Let me check my watch ... what's this? She's on time!" Stella did a quiet drum roll on the table. "It's the wife herself. It's Mrs Andi Armstrong."

Andi's wife rolled her eyes and spoke. "And always pleased to be in her shadow. Am I not even worth addressing by my own name now?"

Stella smirked. "No, I think Mrs and Mrs Andi Armstrong suits you guys best."

Andi stood up and kissed her wife on the cheek. "Stella's being cheeky. She's officially signed off from work today and she's seeing how far she can push it." Andi pulled out the padded chair for her civil partner of seven years and reached for the bottle of bubbly. "Come on. Tell us all about your day. I'll pour you a Champers."

Stella tapped her finger on the table and frowned at Andi. "I don't think so! I think your good wifey here should be asking you all about *your* big day."

"Give me a chance," came the eye rolling reply.

Stella leaned forwards, she couldn't help herself; she was proud of her boss. "She smashed it! Your wonderful wife smashed it! She hit those bigots right out of the studio! Their arguments looked pitiful compared to hers!"

"I know. I watched it."

Andi's eyes lit up. "You did?"

"Of course I did. But I did worry that you were going to sing *Rule Britannia* at one point."

Andi blushed. "I just get so fired up."

Stella lifted her glass in support. "And so you should! Look at you, Andi. You're the model lesbian, demonstrating the perfect example of how wonderful…" she winked, "…and potentially fruitful…" she winked again, "…in maybe a couple of years…" she did a triple wink and an exaggerated nudge, nudge, "…how wonderful and fruitful a same sex marriage can be."

Andi couldn't help but smile. "I like fruit." She waited for her wife's reaction. It was always the same when they had the *children* chat. She watched hopefully, but as her wife pulled her long black hair over her left shoulder and lifted her nose, she knew what was coming.

"Not yet, sweetie," said Zara, draining the remnants of her glass.

CHAPTER TWO

"Was it the fruit comment?" Andi spoke quietly to the back of her wife's head.

Zara shifted slightly on the backseat of the black cab, but continued to stare out of the cold window at the glowing London skyline. "You clearly tell her everything, don't you, sweetie?"

"Stella?"

Zara suddenly twisted around. "Yes, *Stella*. She's spent more time with you over the past seven years than I have." Zara shrugged. "I hate the idea that you dissect our relationship with her."

Andi reached across the leather seat for her wife's hand. She spoke softly. "You know that's not true. Stella's my PA. She has to be with me non-stop."

Zara removed her hand and narrowed her dark brown eyes. "So you do then? You've told her all about our *children chats,* I take it?"

"I wouldn't quite call them *chats*, would you?" Andi thought back to their last discussion, which had quickly turned into a heated row. There was no way she would ever admit such a thing to Stella. "I haven't actually." She turned to her own window and watched as Hyde Park flashed past on their left. Their cab was heading quickly through Mayfair and up towards the prestigious area of St John's Wood. Andi tried to sit it out, but the sight of a young couple giggling and cuddling up for warmth on a damp park bench made her turn back around to her wife. "I'm sorry. I shouldn't have made the fruit comment." She couldn't help it. She was well aware of Zara's ability to hold a grudge and knew the solution to all of their problems was often found in her own ability to admit defeat and offer an unequivocal apology.

Zara nodded. "Thank you. It felt like a dig and you know I don't like being shown up."

Andi frowned sympathetically. "Oh Zara, I never meant to show you up. I was just on a high from the debate today and I thought I'd be cheeky. I shouldn't have said it in front of Stella and I'm sorry." She reached out and squeezed her wife's knee. "I know you're not ready to start a family yet and I should respect that. I really am sorry."

Zara inhaled an exaggerated breath and nodded. "Thank you. But please don't do it again."

Andi stared at her wife with sincerity. "I won't. I promise."

Zara looked away. "Okay, fine." She turned back to the window and shivered. "Please stop looking at me with those fiery eyes of yours."

Andi smiled. "But I love you, I can't help it."

"I know you do, sweetie. Come on. We're home."

The black cab pulled into Wellington Place and Zara quickly paid the fee, shuffling along the leather seat and out onto the pavement after Andi. She called to her. "Wait a minute. I want to show you something." Zara caught up with her wife and took her hand, turning them back around and checking for traffic. She walked them across the road, dodging the moonlit puddles, and came to a standstill directly opposite their house. "Look, sweetie." She stood behind Andi and looped her arms around her tiny waist.

Andi puzzled, but enjoyed the sensation of the touch. "It's our house," she said, "from the other side of the road."

Zara started to sway their bodies together. "Remember when we were standing here, all of those years ago, wondering if we should even dare to entertain the idea of securing this place."

Andi smiled. It actually felt like yesterday. Zara had brought her blindfolded, in the back of a cab, to this exact point. She had held her from behind, as she was now, pulled off the blindfold, and started to talk. *"It's one of the finest houses to come on the market on the west side of St John's Wood. It's a grade II listed, semi-detached, period house."* Zara had been overcome with excitement, jumping the pair of them up and down. *"It's got five bedrooms, two reception rooms, it's even got a garden. Plus it's private and secluded, yet close enough to Abbey Road with its gastro pubs, Italian deli's and Spanish Tapas bars."* Andi had looked up at the beautifully tall, cream bricked house, and burst into tears.

"Of course I remember," said Andi, pressing her cheek gently against her wife's.

"We have everything we've ever wanted, sweetie. Why spoil it with children?"

Andi stopped the swaying and turned to face Zara. "You've never said never." She paused. "It's always been, not yet."

Zara pulled her hair over her shoulder. "Oh face it Andi, we can't have kids. Look at our lifestyles. Where in the world would they fit in?"

"We'd get a nanny."

Zara lifted her nose. "And I'm paying for that as well, am I?"

Andi shook her head and turned away, stepping off the pavement and starting her lonely journey back across the damp road.

"Well I do, don't I?" Zara had started to shout. "I pay for everything, while you go off and do all of your charity appearances and pro bono stuff. It's the same old story. I do the work and you get the glory."

Andi walked through the tall white pillars and stepped up the short path, reaching their shiny front door and sliding her key into the lock. She twisted with force and pushed open the heavy door, feeling completely frustrated. She paused and turned back around to look at her wife, still standing on the opposite side of the road. All marriages went through rough patches. It was one of the things that sorted the wheat from the chaff. Those who believed in marriage from those who didn't. Those who wanted to succeed from those who gave up all too easily. She looked at Zara, still pouting on the pavement, and prayed to God her wife was one of them.

Zara suddenly shouted, "I'm sorry!"

"What?" gulped Andi, almost under her breath. She turned and walked slowly back down the path and out of the white pillars.

Zara trotted across the road, causing her poker straight hair to sway from side to side. "I said, I'm sorry." She rushed forwards and enveloped Andi in a full bodied hug.

The contact felt wonderful. Just like it used to. "It's fine."

Zara looked to the floor. "I've had a hard day. The stocks are down. We're having issues with our biggest client and I'm just a bit strung out. I feel like I only ever get to spend time with you at social events, and I miss you." She kept her eyes on the pavement. "I'm sorry, Andi. You didn't deserve that. Forgive me?"

Andi squeezed her even tighter. It was more of an explanation and apology than she had ever hoped for. "Forgiven and forgotten," she said smiling, taking her wife's hand and leading her up the path and towards their handsome home. She pushed open the black door and flicked on the lights, gently illuminating their spacious hallway into a warm glow.

Zara clipped over the dark parquet flooring, hung her designer jacket on the antique coat stand and kicked off her red bottomed Louboutin heels. "Straight to bed?" she asked with a hint of suggestion.

Andi sat down on the velvety chaise longue next to the door and began to unzip her favourite black boots. She tilted her wrist and checked her watch. "I feel dreadful saying this, but I do just need five minutes to check the Twitter feed, and then I'll be up."

"Seriously?" snapped Zara. "After what I've just said? After the apology I've just given you? You're still going to go and check on your bloody Twitter feed?"

"Oh Zara, you know I have to. It's work. We have to get an idea of the public response to the debate."

"I'll give you my public response," spat Zara. "It was painful." She made her way to the bottom of the open staircase and clung on to the oak banister, staring angrily back at her wife. "It was painful to see you fighting for the marriages of other people when you clearly don't give a shit about your own."

Andi leaned back in shock. She felt winded. Knocked off guard. Zara could be cold sometimes, a bit mean even; but never vindictive. This was a new low. She sat still and tried to compose herself. "You know me better than that." Andi paused, trying to take in the enormity of the accusation. "I married you for life, Zara." Coughing lightly, she spoke with more force. "I've said I'll be up in five, and I will."

"Don't bother," came the harsh response.

****

Andi pulled her cream leather chair into her home office desk and clicked her computer back to life. All of her regular pages flashed up. Email, Twitter, Facebook, LinkedIn, and Proud Unity. She decided to leave the thirty two emails that were flashing, waiting to eat up the precious little time she could afford, until the morning, where they would still be waiting for her, in her inbox, along with another thirty two new ones at least. Twitter was different. Twitter couldn't wait. @iProudUnity and @iAndiArmstrong received so many mentions, that if not checked regularly, would disappear into the ether forever. She clicked onto the Proud Unity feed and scrolled through the tweets, quickly noticing that someone had already been through the bulk of them and posted polite replies, thanking them for their support and pointing them in the direction of the Proud Unity website. Or alternatively stating that Proud Unity followed a no-exceptions policy of reporting offensive tweets to the police. "*Stella,*" sighed Andi under her breath. "*What on earth am I going to do without you?*" She smiled and switched users.

Her personal page flashed up with 867 new interactions; a record high. Today's debate had been well publicised as a means of kick starting the government's twelve week equal-marriage consultation period, and Andi realised that a huge proportion of the LGBT community, and that of the Church, would have been watching. She started to scroll through the messages, posting brief replies to important tweeters, such as supporting MPs or campaigning celebrities, who had praised her on her sterling performance. In her eyes, every single tweet was important, no matter who sent it. The fact that people had taken the time to show their support and offer their personal congratulations, continued to mean the world to her, and always would. But she had fast learned that a personal reply to all was simply not possible. She stopped at the message from @iJohnElton. It read:

Check in the dictionary under the words: Courage, Fearlessness & Balls. They all say @iAndiArmstrong #EqualMarriage.

Andi let out a silent scream. John Elton, the real John Elton, with a blue tick next to his name, had tweeted *her*. She pushed away from the desk, sending her chair skidding backwards on its wheels. She was about to jump off and run upstairs, when she stopped, suddenly remembering the look of disgust on Zara's face. Would this make things worse? Would this confirm Zara's suspicion that she was indeed in it for the fame and stature? Andi sighed, remembering how excited they both used to get in the early days when she received a three lined mention in the local paper, or a vague recognition from someone in the street. She smiled at the memory. It seemed a lifetime ago. Pulling herself back into her work desk, in her private office, she pressed the retweet button instead.

Andi rubbed her eyes and tried to focus. Maybe Zara was right. Maybe this could wait. Maybe it should wait. People knew she was busy, and they never expected a reply, always replying back, once more, to say thank you to her for the reply to their reply. She decided to do what she hated and send a general tweet of thanks. She composed it carefully.

To everyone who's tweeted. Thank you. This is a battle we'll win together, with unity, pride and justness on our side. #equalmarriage.

She pressed the blue tweet button and rolled her shoulders, resigned to the fact that she was once again in the wrong. Zara was right. She needed to slow down. Show her wife that she was, and always would be, her priority. She reached down to turn off her computer, suddenly noticing a new interaction flash up.

Beth @iWatchThemFall -Time u @iAndiArmstrong got what's coming 2 u. Self righteous bitch. #NastyPayback

CHAPTER THREE

Zara and Andi were gently making their way through Regent's Park, strolling arm in arm towards the Honest Sausage Café. They used to make the short walk from their home every Saturday morning, eagerly anticipating a hearty breakfast in the welcoming, and deliciously aromatic, old-fashioned eatery. They would enjoy the buzz of the early morning joggers, and smile at the love struck couples passing slowly by. But today it felt different. Today it was muted. The walk was pleasant enough and the contact felt good, but there was something missing; a strange distance between them. Andi looked towards the huge boating lake and decided to try again. "How deep do you think that lake is?"

Zara straightened her hair. "Regular lake depth? I don't know."

"It's only four feet deep."

"Is it, sweetie?"

Andi could tell that Zara wasn't really interested, but at least she was trying to engage. "I read about it a while ago. I guess we haven't made this walk since then."

Zara shrugged her shoulders inside her expensive shearling coat. "We've been busy."

"I know," accepted Andi, hoping it wasn't a dig. She pointed at the lake "Apparently one winter's day in the eighteen sixties, there were over two hundred people on the ice, walking, skating and playing, when it gave way." Andi looked up at her wife to see if she was paying attention. "All of them plunged into the lake. Forty were killed, I think."

"Cheery," nodded Zara, keeping her eyes on the open parkland ahead and the trees that were still bare after the unusually harsh winter.

"Yes, so they drained it and reduced its depth to just four feet, before reopening it to the public."

"Thank you for that useful nugget, my darling."

"Oh Zara, what's wrong?" Andi pulled on the linked arm. "Are you still cross with me from last night?"

"I've never been cross with you. Just frustrated."

"With me?"

Zara exhaled, misting the cold air. "With us."

Andi stopped walking and looked to the wooden park bench. "Talk to me then. Please, let's just sit down, and talk. We're a married lesbian couple, we're good at talking."

Zara pulled her faux fur collar tighter around her neck. "Sweetie, it's February. It's cold. I'm hungry."

"Do you love me, Zara?"

Zara shifted on the spot. "What a ridiculous thing to ask. Of course I love you."

"Well sometimes you don't act like it."

"What do you want me to do? Bow down to you like one of your crazy fans. Constantly tell you how brilliant you are and how lucky I am to have you?"

Andi rubbed her own shoulders, trying to fend off the cold. "Once in a while might be nice."

"I told you last night that I loved you."

Andi looked up at the dark eyes staring down at her, unsure if it was anger or hurt she could see. "Only after you accused me of using you for your money and being some sort of glory hunter."

"Did I call you that?"

Andi became conscious of a passing female jogger and lifted her eyebrows at Zara's slightly raised voice. "Not exactly," she whispered

"So don't put words into my mouth then," said Zara, loudly. "I'm a 39-year-old business woman. Not a 12-year-old school girl."

"I'm sorry, I'm sorry, I'm sorry. The last thing I want to do is argue. It's the first Saturday we've had off together for ages, and I want it to be great."

"Well stop being so needy then." Zara offered a smirk. "You're the great Andi Armstrong, the powerhouse of women's lib. What would people think if they saw you now?"

"It's a good job I recognise your sarcastic side," said Andi, gently nudging her wife and starting their slow walk once again. "But sometimes, I still don't know how to take you."

"You can take me anyway you want," smirked Zara, "but my preference is from behind."

"Oh be serious, will you!" Andi finally found the eye contact she had been looking for. "You know I love you." She kept staring at her wife. "And I'm not needy. You know that. I just really love you, and I really love you loving me. We both have crazy work schedules, and things can get tense sometimes. But I love you." Her amber eyes were honest and wide. "You know that, don't you?"

"I know you do, sweetie, and maybe I was a bit insecure like you when I was-"

"I'm not insecure."

"Well maybe I was a bit needy like you, when I was twenty nine." Zara paused. "Actually no, scratch that, I'd already made my first million and was busy reaching for the top rung of the ladder at work. Not to mention busting the balls of all of those men on the way."

Andi laughed. "So what did you see in me?"

"You were my young whipper-snapper. I wanted to know I'd still got it."

"Was that all?"

"Oh, Andi, I'm teasing you." Zara broke the eye contact. "You know what happened. We fell in love. We were smitten with one another." She shrugged. "You remember how it was?"

"I remember how you wooed me." Andi smiled. "You sent me flowers every single day for a month." She shook her head in remembrance. "Every single day. But you know I only agreed to a date because I thought I was developing hay fever, right?"

"Touché!"

Andi smiled. "I thought you'd like that one." She laughed. "But remember how you used to ring me every couple of hours just to say hi?"

Zara rolled her eyes. "What a waste of time and money."

"Stop it! We were love's young dream."

"Yes, I guess we were."

Andi frowned. "Were?"

Zara looked at her wife. "Oh Andi, stop questioning things. I love you just as much now as I did then. But we got married. The focus shifts. It's not all love notes and spontaneous surprises. We've grown up. We're concentrating on our careers."

Andi smiled. "I loved your spontaneous surprises. Remember the time I arrived home and you were standing in the hall with a suitcase and a sombrero?"

"How could I forget? I ended up with Dysentery."

Andi looked down and kicked a broken twig from the path. "It was a great holiday. You know it was."

Zara lifted Andi's chin with her finger, drawing their eyes together. "We *always* have great holidays." She smiled. "Stop worrying. We're fine. We work. We always have done and we always will do."

Andi nodded. "Yes, it does work, doesn't it?"

"It does, sweetie." Zara laughed. "You save the world and I pay for it."

****

Andi took a bite from her hot sausage sandwich, feeling warmth both inside and out. The atmosphere in the café was always fantastic, with locals and holiday makers mixing nicely and chatting about the uniqueness of the place itself, the Honest Sausage Café. She felt an extra special glow, thanks to the gentle kiss Zara had placed on her lips as they had entered. Zara had always been hard to read, but Andi had attributed that to their age gap and the high profile nature of Zara's job. Spending her days securing multi-million pound deals for her Investment Company, G-Sterling, and working with some of the biggest players in the industry, only to return home to her, who must seem rather dull and insignificant in comparison. It was love though. It always had been.

Andi smiled at her wife as they enjoyed their breakfasts. "I don't think there are many honest sausages out there, do you?"

Zara swallowed too quickly and started to cough. She took a shallow breath, checking her airways were clear. "You always tell that joke when we're here and I never laugh at it, sweetie."

"You're meant to say: *'well it's the only sausage getting past my lips.'*"

"Am I?"

"Yes, can't you remember?"

"No."

"It's true though, isn't it?"

Zara put her warm, sausage filled baguette, back on her plate. "What?"

"Men and their..." Andi looked around the cosy café and hushed her voice. "...Men and their tiddlers. They're not honest are they? None of them!"

Zara narrowed her eyes. "Ooo, what have we here. The ever so diplomatic Andi Armstrong, being controversial and stereotypical."

"I know, but it's true! Lynda's left Eddie." She took a bite of her warm sandwich.

"Lynda Farrington?"

Andi chewed carefully and swallowed, delicately wiping a smudge of ketchup from her bottom lip. "Yes. She found out about his affair."

"They got married after us, didn't they?"

"Exactly. We're proving those critics wrong. We're the ones strengthening society."

"Oh, no, not another speech, please." Zara covered her ears. "How was it anyway?"

"What?"

"Your precious Twitter feed. The one that prevented our night of passion."

"You prevented our night of passion by sleeping in the spare room."

Zara flicked away the comment. "Come on, sweetie. I'm not going to give you another chance to tell me."

Andi laughed. "If people didn't know you, they'd think you were awfully mean."

"I am. It's one of my best points."

Andi lifted her steaming mug. "What would you call your humour style? Deadpan?"

Zara actually laughed. "I'll give you that one, sweetie. That was funny. Come on. Tell me. How was it?"

Andi took a long sip of the rich hot chocolate, savouring the sweetness as it trickled down her throat, wondering whether to start with the positive or the negative. "The majority were great. One in particular from John Elton."

"THE, John Elton?" Zara was trying to furrow her brow, but nothing really moved.

Andi smiled and nodded. "It was indeed!"

"Oh wow! You should have told me!"

"It didn't feel right, you were in the spare-"

"Okay, sweetie. Line drawn." Zara fanned her face. "But seriously, wow! You should invite him to the next charity do. Could you imagine the pictures?"

Andi lifted the white napkin from her lap, patted her mouth, and placed it on her empty plate, which she slid into the centre of the table. "Yes, maybe. Anyway, he tweeted, as did a few high profile MPs."

"Ooo, look at you."

"You asked, Zara."

"I know. I'm teasing. Come on, who else?"

"Annie."

Zara's dark eyes widened and her lips started to crease at the corners. "The bi-sexual singer?"

"Yup."

"Oh wow, sweetie. It really was a big deal then?"

"You know it was," smiled Andi, teasingly rolling her eyes.

Zara drained the last of her black coffee. "Did you get the usual crap from the bigots?"

"Well actually, there was one particular tweet that got me a bit worr-"

"Zara! Hi!" Melody Fickler strode, tits first, up to their table. "I thought I saw you!" She looked down at Andi. "Oh my goodness, I'm so excited! Please tell me you remember me?"

Andi smiled at the heavily made up woman. "It's Melody, isn't it?" They'd met a couple of times at Zara's black tie events and Andi recalled her being slightly sycophantic on those occasions too.

"Yes, yes, it is!" Melody nodded eagerly. "I'm thrilled to see you guys. I've heard Zara mention this place a billion times, so I thought I'd check it out. But I never dreamed I'd have the pleasure of bumping into you here!" She looked around at the beamed ceilings and open fire. "It's rather cute, isn't it?"

Andi smiled, warmed at the thought of Zara sharing personal tit-bits with her work colleagues. "Would you like to join us?" she asked politely.

"Really? Wow, I'd love to!" Melody grabbed a spare wicker chair and scraped it next to Andi's. "I'm sure I said it last time, but I really am a huge fan!"

"I paid her to say that," said Zara, keeping her face straight.

"You didn't," giggled Melody, playfully bashing Zara on the shoulder. "You need to pay me extra, or start to give me a few more perks." She widened her eyes at her boss.

Andi tilted the handle of her empty mug. "Drinks anyone?"

"Black coffee," came the joint response.

****

Melody waited for Andi to disappear around the corner of the counter, before turning to Zara and slowly shaking her head. "You're worse than I imagined."

"I'll take that as a compliment, sweetie."

"Come on then. What's so important that forced me north on the Northern line, west on the Central line and then north again on the Bakerloo?"

Zara lifted her nose. "I detest the tube. Please get a cab next time."

Melody frowned. "From Clapham? Now I know you're taking the piss."

"Far from it, sweetie. I need you available."

"For what?"

Zara reached under the table and grabbed Melody's thigh, riding her hand higher until it reached the warm spot between her legs. She squeezed. "For this."

****

Andi let out a small gasp, quickly watching with apprehension as the drinks on her tray sloshed dangerously close to the rims of their oversized mugs. She tightened her grip, nodded politely at the fellow apologising customer, and completed the short walk back around the corner of the counter to the table by the fire. "Sorry, I just got nudged," she said as she arrived. "There might be a couple of drips."

"Who cares!" giggled Melody, patting the seat next to her own. "Sit yourself down and tell me what it was like going up against that monster in the debate!"

Andi frowned. "You watched it?"

Melody plumped up her breasts as she spoke. "Of course I did!" She nestled in closer. "I'm not a lesbian, you know me, as straight as they come, tie your husbands and sons up, and all that!" She paused, lowering her voice. "But you're the closest thing I'm going to get to a celebrity friend."

Andi shifted uncomfortably in her seat.

"Well, I mean acquaintance, obviously." Melody maintained her eager look, wiggling her defined eyebrows for Andi to begin.

Andi gently blew some steam from her mug of hot chocolate, glancing over the rim at Melody, whom she assessed as naturally pretty, and certainly not in need of the shovel-load of makeup currently heaped onto her face. She wondered if Melody presented herself this way at work too. "I think it went quite well," she said.

"You *think*?" Melody looked shocked. "Didn't you see the Twitter feed? You got rave reviews!"

Andi took a tentative sip of her drink, thrown by the level of familiarity. "I didn't realise you followed me on Twitter?"

Melody plumped up her breasts once more, as if trying to move them into Andi's eye-line. "Are you kidding? Everyone at work follows the boss's wife."

"They don't bloody follow me though, do they?" said Zara, twisting her body to the side and crossing her legs.

Andi leaned out and rubbed her wife's thigh. "I like your twice monthly tweets. They're ... oh, wait a minute." She stopped at the sound of her chirping phone and reached under the table for her bag, quickly locating the noise and silencing it with gusto. "Andi Armstrong is on a day off!" It rang again. This time she caught sight of the caller name. "Oh, hang on, it's Stella. I better answer it. She might be giving birth."

"*Why would she be calling then*?" mouthed Zara, as Andi answered the phone.

"So, am I an auntie yet?" she grinned into the receiver.

"*Auntie*?" mouthed Zara. "*Are you two related?*"

Andi turned her back on Zara's distraction and listened carefully. "Oh sorry ... Oh right, okay I'm listening ... He called you? I'm so sorry about that ... Right ... Well thank you ... Okay ... No, it's fine ... No, thanks, Stella ... Yes I will ... It's fine ... It's fine ... You did the right thing ... I'll make sure they remove your number as my contact point. Now get some rest! ... Yes, yes ... Don't worry ... I'll be there as soon as I can."

"And there we have it," smiled Zara as she watched Andi hang up. "Life with the wonderful Andi Armstrong who said she was on a day off."

"Are you okay?" Melody asked. "You look flustered."

Andi dropped her phone into her bag and pulled her coat from the back of her chair. "She's not in labour, but there has been a delivery at work. Our police liaison officer's been called." She frowned, perplexed. "I didn't quite catch it all, but it seems Jerry, from the front desk, signed for some post and packages this morning, but when he went to move them upstairs, he noticed a foul smell."

"What sort of smell?" Melody was wide eyed.

"I'm not quite sure of the details, but due to the nature of our work we have to alert the police about any unusual deliveries."

"And what's this got to do with you?" asked Zara with her arms crossed and her face straight.

Andi stood up. "The package was addressed to me."

CHAPTER FOUR

Andi pushed open the door to exit the Honest Sausage Café and was engulfed by a blanket of cold air, which didn't help the shiver of regret and annoyance that was rushing through her body. The timing couldn't be worse but her duty couldn't be helped. Yes it was Saturday, yes it was a day off, but things like this had to be dealt with. She pulled her coat collar up around her neck and headed south towards Regent's Park tube station, certain it wouldn't take long.

Zara drained her hot coffee, adding to the heated thrill that was already searing through her stomach. The timing couldn't be better and her urges couldn't be helped. Andi's early exit had made her own plan of escape completely superfluous. She pulled on her shearling coat and told Melody to do the same, guiding them quickly out of the café and hurrying them west through Regent's Park, aware they didn't have long.

Andi raced down the steps of the tube, towards the crowd of people who were filtering through the turnstiles, swiping and cursing, and swiping again. She reached for her oyster card and chose the smallest queue, checking her watch and thinking of Zara. Five stops to Waterloo, ten minutes tops. Half an hour with the police liaison officer, and back home for one o'clock. She pressed her card against the large yellow circle, dismayed by the pitiful balance displayed on the screen, annoyed at the further delay this would cause. She pushed through the metal barrier and headed left, reaching into her bag for her purse and joining the oyster card top up queue. She sighed with frustration, mentally adding an extra fifteen minutes to her journey time. Poor Zara, she thought, shaking her head with dismay.

Zara walked Melody briskly around the outer circle of the park, past the boating lake, and out towards St John's Wood. Ten minutes to get home, half an hour of games, and the obligatory ten minutes of down time before she could politely ask her to leave. She looked at her watch. She could be done by one o'clock. Poor Andi, she thought, desperately trying to disguise her delight.

Andi boarded the escalator that was heading down to the underground station. She stood to the right and was brushed and nudged by the faster travellers who were whizzing past on the left. She needed a moment to plan. She remembered the wonderful delicatessens next to work. Some nice wine and a beautiful meal, heaped with apology and calls for forgiveness. It would be fine, she reasoned, moving left into the fast lane, hopping down the final few stairs and racing quickly to the platform on the right. She squeezed onto the heaving train.

Zara turned into Wellington Place and picked up the pace, tasting the thrill of seduction. She needed a plan. She'd keep it contained, confined to the front of the house and the informal reception rooms. That would be fine, she reasoned. Not betrayal; just compensation. Compensation for Andi's desertion. She squeezed her fingers inside her black leather gloves, excited by the illicit deception.

Andi bent under an outstretched arm and shuffled to a pull-down seat next to the door, glad of the stable position before the surge of people at Oxford Circus. The train raced to a jerky stop and the doors sprung open again. People stepped out and bodies rushed in; pushing and shoving and squeezing too close.

Zara clicked the key in the lock and pushed open the door, pulling Melody inside and kicking it shut. She lifted Melody's arms to the wall and kissed her hard, moaning as she pressed their bodies together, feeling the heat spread between their legs.

Andi fanned her face. The air was clammy and the smell was nauseous. A mixture of that distinctly metallic, tarmac-like, tube smell, combined with the overpowering stench of perfumes and stale body odour. It was difficult to swallow. She turned to the scratched plastic window and watched as the darkness of the tunnel rattled by.

Zara observed the aroused glow in Melody's eyes as she kissed her deeper and caressed her harder, unbuttoning her shirt and sucking her neck, consumed by her rich perfume and soft skin, enjoying the rush of air as she pulled the shirt free; throwing it carelessly to the floor.

Andi braced herself as the door sprung open and another gust of stale air raced in. She held her breath. One final stop and she'd be there.

Zara moaned in arousal as the roles were reversed. Her turn to be pinned and caressed, squeezed into submission. She held her breath. Not long now and she'd be there.

Andi squeezed off the train and worked her way through the strange lull of the white bricked tunnels, up towards the surface and the clean, fresh air. She emerged from the ground and breathed deeply, pulling her coat in tight and staring anxiously at her tall work building and the daunting task ahead.

Zara loosened their remaining items of clothing, freeing herself from all other distractions. Manoeuvring their passion towards the black velvet chaise longue and staring greedily at Melody's naked body and the appetising task ahead.

Andi pushed open the door of the glass fronted building and headed down the steps, towards the usually welcoming front desk, this time tainted by the sight of a uniformed officer and his serious stare.

Zara pushed Melody onto her back and straddled her stomach, staring once more into her fervent eyes, before twisting herself around and seeing her moistness. She bent her head and lifted her bottom, feeling kissed while kissing, and licked while licking. Both taking the other and moving in time.

Andi offered the pleasantries and listened with care, quickly guided to the package and its offensive contents.

Zara followed the rhythm and moved with intent, sucking and grinding, and bringing them close.

Andi walked to the package and bent her head forwards, gasping in horror and recoiling in shock.

Zara pressed herself forwards and arched her back up, gasping in pleasure and shaking in shock.

"Fuck." groaned Andi.

"Fuck." moaned Zara.

Neither fully aware of the enormity of the moment.

CHAPTER FIVE

Andi walked through the two white pillars and up the short path to their home. She reached into her bag for her keys and fumbled with the lock, finally twisting the correct key and pushing their glossy front door ajar. The two bulging bags from the wonderful delicatessens were weighing her down and making it difficult to fully open the door. What made it even more difficult was the sudden twang of the thick metal door chain as it pulled taut. It jolted her and her shopping backwards, causing the heavy black door to bang shut again. Andi sighed, completely at wits end. She had been as fast as she could, but it had literally been one thing after another. She placed the bags on the front step, adjusting them slightly so they wouldn't fall and spill their contents. She looked at her watch. Zara must be fuming. She put her key back in the lock, twisted, and pushed open, more carefully this time. She pressed her mouth into the gap. "Zara, I'm back. The chain's on." She listened carefully.

Nothing.

She pressed her face between the door and its frame and raised her voice. "Zara, the chain's on. Could you let me in, please?" She heard a definite scampering of feet. "Zara?" She used her toe to keep the door ajar and squeezed her arm into the space, looping it up and feeling for the catch. She'd tried this before, never to any success and she wondered, once again, why she thought she'd be able to override a security system specifically aimed at stopping people doing just this. She tried all the same, patting her hand on the opposite side of the door and stretching in vain for the catch. Andi screamed out in shock as something grabbed her wrist. The grasp was firm but her initial alarm quickly subsided as she paused in recognition, slowly aware of what was happening. Someone was pushing something into the palm of her hand. She smiled and pulled her newly released arm back out into the cold. She opened her palm and looked at the scrunched up note. She flattened it out and started to read, hearing the thump of the chain banging free against the inside of the door. Andi studied the note.

To my wonderful wife,

I love you, no matter what. (Even when you leave me stranded alone on a Saturday)

Now follow your cute little nose. xxx

Andi lifted her bags of shopping back up off the step and pushed open the door, pleased to be out of the cold and inside their wonderfully aromatic home. The smell was rich and warming; a hearty greeting of bay leaves and thyme, simmering gently with winter vegetables in a beef and red wine bourguignon stew. Andi knew the smell. It was one of Zara's specialities. She smiled with relief, dropping down onto the black velvet chaise longue and releasing the bags. She unzipped her boots and wiggled her toes, finding it hard to resist the temptation to lean back on the long chair and close her eyes. She rubbed her thumbs into the smooth velvet in an attempt to push herself back up and continue her task of undress, but paused as her left thumb hit a rough area. She looked down at her treasured chaise longue and spotted a small glistening smear. It reminded her of a snail's trail. She licked her thumb and rubbed the offending mark, repeating the action a couple of times in an attempt to revitalise the smooth fabric. It didn't really work, so she made a mental note to add it to her *'jobs to do around the house'* list; the one that was already impossible to remember and long overdue.

Andi gave herself that final push up and took off her coat, hanging it on the old fashioned coat stand and reaching back down for the bags. She shuffled across the warm parquet flooring, down the wide hallway, praising once again their decision to add under-floor heating to all of their downstairs rooms. She used her left shoulder to push open the kitchen door and smiled widely at the image in front of her. Zara was standing at the white Aga oven, lightly stirring the simmering pot of stew. Her apron was tied tightly around her middle and her long black hair was pulled into a loose pony. She was wearing her cosy joggers, hooded top and bootie slippers. It was exactly how Andi loved to see her. Comfy, relaxed and seemingly stress free.

A pang of regret hit Andi hard. "Oh Zara, I'm so sorry. What did I ever do to deserve you?"

Zara looked over her shoulder and smiled. "No, I'm sorry. I should have come with you, sweetie. No one likes dealing with the police on their own."

Andi frowned. "Don't be daft. I wouldn't have let you come." She placed the two bags onto the huge kitchen table and smiled. "Anyway, it looks like you've been busy."

Zara tapped the wooden spoon against the side of the ceramic pot and placed it in the black bowl next to the Aga. She walked around to the other side of the table and encased Andi in a full bodied hug. "I should have come with you. I'm sorry. You know me. It didn't even occur to me until you were long gone."

Andi felt her shoulders relax. She exhaled heavily. "This is why I love you, Zara." She looked up at her wife's make up free face, naturally rosy from the heat of the cooking. "You look beautiful."

Zara tutted and moved backwards. "No I don't, sweetie, I look old."

Andi pulled her back in, wanting to savour the moment. "This is when I love you the most."

Zara pulled away and marched defiantly back to the stove. "Enough! I'm almost forty, my Botox needs a top up, and I've started to sag."

"Not that I've noticed," grinned Andi, chasing her back around the table and laughing as she caught her from behind. She held onto her wife's waist and nuzzled into her back. "You look cute in your hoodie and joggers."

Zara couldn't help but smile. "You're so soppy, Andi Armstrong."

"I know, but you love me."

Zara twisted around in Andi's arms and looked down at her wife's wide eyes. "I do." She smiled, stroking the short blonde fringe to the side of Andi's forehead. "But I'm not sure if I've made you feel guilty enough yet for deserting me."

"Did you get stuck with Melody?"

Zara maintained the eye contact. "No. I have to be honest, I've actually had a lovely day. I had one more coffee and then I came back here, had a bath and spent the afternoon relaxing," she tilted her head in the direction of the simmering pot, "and then of course slaving over this hot stove."

"You could make that dish with your eyes closed. It's your speciality and you know it's my favourite, so thank you. You're very thoughtful."

"You didn't say that last week when I was getting told off for," she paused, "what misdemeanour was it?"

Andi smacked her wife's bottom and grinned. "That was last week. This is now. And right now you're being incredibly thoughtful."

"See, I do learn! And now I'm going to ask you to take a seat and tell me all about your afternoon." Zara gave herself a congratulatory smile and nod of the head, before pulling out one of the padded black chairs from under the table and signalling for Andi to sit down. She reached for the almost empty bottle of red wine, warming by the stove, and poured the remainder into a glass, placing it in front of her wife.

Andi looked flabbergasted.

Zara pulled out another seat and angled it so their knees were almost touching. "Seriously, Andi. I should have offered to come with you this afternoon. I was walking home on my own and I realised that it was a perfect example of me not thinking and me not showing you that I love you."

Andi took a long sip of the rich red wine and shook her head. "No, this afternoon showed me how *you* are right and how my work *does* always get in the way of everything. I understand why you get so frustrated with me and I can only apologise for having such a demanding job. I'm the one who's sorry."

Zara took her hand and squeezed it softly. "You can't control your job, but I can control my behaviour."

Andi laughed. "What's happened?! Please bring back my hard faced wife! I miss her quick witted put downs!"

"Forgive me?" said Zara.

"Oh stop it."

Zara gave the hand a final squeeze and jumped up to fetch another bottle of red. "I'll remind you of that next time you're moaning about my thoughtlessness!"

"You, thoughtless? Never!" Andi laughed, relieved at the turn of events and warmed by the spark still present between them. She took another sip of the wine, enjoying the relaxing sensation that each slow mouthful brought. "Well, I thought *I* was being thoughtful." She signalled to the two bags full of goodies from the delicatessens. "I didn't imagine for one minute that you'd be cooking, so I bought a load of cheese, patés and crackers."

"...And olives, and caramelised cashews," Zara was lifting the extortionately priced items out of the bag and placing them on the table, "and quails eggs and bilinis."

"Starters?" suggested Andi.

"We're not all naturally tiny and slim like you, sweetie. You'll be asking me to get lipo next if I eat all of these."

"What do you mean, next?"

"Botox first, lipo next."

Andi gasped, enjoying the teasing. "I never told you to get Botox!"

Zara twisted the lid on the almond stuffed olives and popped one into her mouth, enjoying the smooth saltiness and textured crunch. She swallowed and tried to frown. "Yes you did. You said you thought the age gap was looking more noticeable between us."

"Stop it, Zara."

"You did, sweetie."

Andi sighed. "No I did not. Come on, sit down. Let me tell you about the latest crazy, bigot stalker, we have at Proud Unity."

Zara touched the front of a bespoke worktop drawer, causing it to slide open on command. She lifted out a black and white chintz bowl, which, like the rest of their crockery, matched the theme of their kitchen, from the black and white floor tiles to the white Aga and black hard stone sink. "She's not called Melody, is she?"

Andi laughed. "Did you notice that too?"

"Of course, sweetie. She was practically pushing those dreadful fake tits right up your nose."

"She seems harmless enough. I can't quite picture what she does at your firm though."

Zara emptied the olives into the bowl and returned to her seat, taking a sip of wine and pausing in thought. "She's actually quite a ball buster."

"Really?"

"Yes, but she only busts them after she's bonked them."

Andi pulled a face. "Ooo, nasty image!" She placed her wine back on the table and looked at her wife. "I've had a really frustrating afternoon."

"Come on. I'm listening. Let it out."

"Really?" asked Andi.

"Yes, but don't drag it out and don't be all dramatic about it."

Andi ran her fingers through her short blonde hair and couldn't help but smile. "I think a box of offal and a note saying: '*Shut it, Armstrong*,' is dramatic enough, all by itself, don't you?"

Zara smirked. "*Shut it, Armstrong*?"

Andi laughed. "I know. But it really was disgusting, and it stank! Poor Jerry was in a real flap, asking if I wanted a lift home and telling me to keep an extra special eye out."

Zara popped another olive into her mouth. "Just a random sicko, or something more sinister?"

Andi waved away the suggestion, "Don't be daft. It's that same old bunch of bigots, using anything they can to try and knock us off kilter. They're working their way through the hierarchy and it just happened to be my turn. Did I tell you that Janet had the word *sinner* scratched onto her car last week?"

Zara tutted. "And criminal damage, that's not a sin?" She took a large gulp of wine. "That's what gets me the most. The hypocrisy of these people."

"I forgot that your nickname was Saint Zara."

Zara lifted her nose. "I'm serious. They're a joke, and so are the police! They don't care about a box of offal! They're just covering their own backs."

"I know, I know, but it's all sorted now. I'm just sorry it took so long." Andi paused, inhaling the wonderful smell of her wife's famed beef bourguignon. "You didn't see any weirdos lurking around the butchers when you bought that beef did you?"

Zara smiled. "No, only a vicar standing at the counter writing a post-it note that said, '*Shut it, Armstrong*.'" She coughed. "I doubt it's related though."

CHAPTER SIX

Andi sat up in bed and adjusted her plush eiderdown pillow, angling it so she could rest without any pressure on her stomach. Zara's beef bourguignon dinner had been wonderful, as had the starters and desserts, contributed from her visit to the delicatessens, and now both she and Zara were relaxing in a satisfied, if slightly uncomfortable, state of contentment. She watched as Zara reached into the bedside cabinet drawer. It was the same every evening. They would get washed, changed, and ready for bed, side by side, before getting comfy and reaching for their alternative evening's entertainments. Tonight, Andi had the files of the two candidates shortlisted for her recently vacated personal assistant role; and Zara, as always, had the remote. Andi watched as her wife snuggled into the luxurious pillows and cushions, triumphantly pressing the red button and making her nightly statement.

"This is the best thing we've ever bought," announced Zara as the widescreen television slowly appeared out of the bottom of their bed. It whirred upwards, before making its final clunk, signalling that it was in position and ready to be fired into life. Zara pressed another button and the screen lit up with a complicated menu of choices.

Andi realised that she had no idea how to get the thing going, but then again, wondered when she would ever find the need. All too often she spent her time in bed reading through files, or preparing speeches, or grabbing whatever bit of time was left from the day to finish things off, before waking up and starting the process all over again. She smiled as her wife selected the latest episode of Rizzoli and Isles. "You know I love this, Zara! It's going to distract me."

"Good," said Zara, turning up the volume.

Andi shook her head and opened up the first brown file, nodding at the high rise television. "That, is the worst thing we've ever bought."

"You loved the bed."

Andi lifted her eyes. "Yes I did. It was a wonderful surprise to arrive home to this huge, bouncy, super-king-sized piece of luxury, perfectly matching the regal-ness of our sprawling bedroom." She frowned. "But then you had to go and press that button and transform it into the latest state of the art home cinema."

"Actually the latest version has surround sound, with speakers implanted in this headboard." Zara tilted her head backwards against the expensive brown leather. "Do you think we should upgrade?"

Andi laughed. "Get back to Jane Rizzoli. Look, she's showing her stomach again."

"Ooo, let me freeze frame." Zara paused the picture. "Come on, sweetie, put that work down. We've had a lovely evening. Watch this with me?"

Andi passed one of the brown files over to her wife and smiled. "You tell me who to appoint as my PA and I'm there."

Zara took the file and flipped it open. "Go for the one with the biggest tits."

Andi tutted. "They've only got head shots."

"Okay, go for the sexiest one."

"Which one's that?" laughed Andi, lifting up her photo of candidate number one, Elizabeth Burns.

"Well it's not her!"

"Don't be rude." Andi studied the photo. "I actually think she's got nice eyes."

"Oh, I love you, my wife. You manage to find the good in everybody." Zara grabbed the photo of Elizabeth. "Her eyes are far too close together and she's got a mono-brow. Not to mention the tomb stone teeth and crazy orange hair."

Andi read the headlines that Stella had put together and thought back to the briefing she had been given on both candidates. "The panel seemed to like her and she's got an impressive CV."

"But it's not her CV you'll be looking at every day, is it? It's those peg teeth."

"You're a cruel, cruel, woman."

"No, I'm not. I'm just honest." Zara pulled herself up and adjusted her pillow. Propping herself against the brown headboard and reaching for Elizabeth Burns's CV. She scanned the details. "She's straight."

"I know." Andi edged in closer and followed Zara's tapping finger to the personal statements section.

"She says, '*My husband and I are keen to show our support for our LGBT comrades.*' That, is a definite no right there!"

Andi frowned. "Not everyone who works at Proud Unity is LGBT."

"Yes they are, sweetie. And anyway, *Elizabeth Burns*, seems far too hung up on her own academic prowess."

Andi took the sheet and returned it to the folder. "It's a CV, you have to sell yourself. And why are you giving Elizabeth Burns that posh voice?"

Zara lifted her nose. "She sounds up herself."

"Right, switch the television back on. Your input is not helping me!"

Zara smiled. "No, I'm enjoying this. Let's look at the other lady."

Andi dropped Elizabeth Burns's file to the floor and snuggled into Zara's shoulder. "They've both obviously got something about them. They're the final two."

"And you haven't met them yet?"

"No. Stella and Janet did the first two rounds of interviews, and said both candidates would be perfect for the role. It's just a case of deciding who I'd prefer. I'm actually quite excited about Monday. They're arriving at nine and I have the whole day scheduled in to interview them."

"What on earth are you going to do for a whole day?"

Andi grinned. "You know me. I like to keep things interesting and unique."

"Stella's trying to stitch you up with old mono-brow over there." Zara flicked through the papers in the second file and lifted out the photo. "Ooo, but you might be onto a winner here." She turned the picture over and read the name scribbled on the back. "*Pippa Rose.*"

Andi laughed. "Now why has Pippa Rose got a seductive voice?"

"Look at those dark brown eyes, they're practically begging for bed."

Andi took the photo and studied it closely. "She looks clean cut, fresh and smiley ... with quite a cute dimple in her right cheek."

Zara snatched it back. "How can you summarise this alluring, dark eyed siren, with that mass of curly brown *come to bed hair*, as fresh and smiley?"

Andi reached over and took the summary sheet, reading Stella's headlines quickly. "She's quite young."

"Even better," moaned Zara. "How old exactly?"

"Twenty two." She scanned a couple more points. "And she doesn't seem to have an awful amount of experience."

"I can help her with that."

"Stop it, you dirty old woman!"

Zara spun around onto all fours and pretended to grab a handful of hair. "I'd take her from behind, pull that mass of bouncy brown hair into a pony and ride her all the way to heaven."

Andi collected the papers and folded them back away. She dropped Pippa's file to the floor. "It's a good job you're married because your seduction style's not a winner."

Zara lifted herself onto her knees and stuck out her chest. "That's what I miss about you."

"What?"

"Your hair. Since you've had it cropped there's nothing to hold on to anymore."

Andi lifted herself onto her knees, mirroring her wife's position. "You could always look into my eyes as we make love instead?"

Zara pushed her wife backwards, sending her down onto the bed. "No, that's far too boring. I like it spicy. Now turn over."

Andi looked up and spoke softly. "Come here."

"What?"

"Just come here." Andi reached out and beckoned her wife to come down on top of her.

"What?"

Andi reached out for Zara and gently pulled her down, enjoying the feeling of her weight on top of her. She looked into Zara's dark eyes and stroked her cheek. "Let's make love. Just like this. With you on top, looking into my eyes."

Zara glanced away.

"Zara, please, look at me. Make love to me."

"Okay, hang on." Zara rolled off Andi's body and reached above the bedside cabinet to flick the light switch off. The room plunged into darkness, softened only by the gentle glow of the paused television. Zara picked up the remote and accessed the digital menu, selecting the recorded programmes from her favourite channels. She scrolled down the extensive list and finally pressed play.

A busty blonde women burst into life, giggling and moaning and almost swallowing a huge plastic dildo.

"Oh Zara! Turn this off! This isn't what I meant."

Zara placed the remote back on the bedside cabinet and propped herself against her pillow. "It's a new one. I recorded it yesterday."

"I don't care! It's disgusting. Look at it. Eugh! It's clearly made for men. Come back here and make love to me."

Zara wriggled out of her pyjama bottoms and kicked them to the floor. "I will, I will, but look, there aren't any men in this one, only women." She pulled off her top and glanced at Andi. "Get naked then, sweetie."

"I know it's just women, but look! How many lesbians spend time in bed giving blow jobs to their dildos?"

Zara straightened her hair. "Don't be such a prude."

"I'm not! This just doesn't do it for me." Andi glanced at the screen where the woman was now squeezing her own tits and begging for a big fat cock.

Zara kept her eyes fixed on the action. "Look, here comes the other woman."

Andi laughed in frustration, "Yes! With a giant, king kong, strap on, on!" She narrowed her eyes and winced. "Eugh, that looks painful!"

"*She* seems to be enjoying it," moaned Zara with wide eyes.

"Lesbians don't even do that."

Zara bit back. "And how would you know? You're hardly an experienced lady lover."

Andi swallowed the insult and tried a different tack. "Because, my darling, lesbians..." She straddled her wife and pinned her arms to the side, "...do this." She kissed her gently and hoped for a response.

Zara tilted her head out of the embrace. "At least take your top off so I can see your tits."

Andi pulled up her vest top and dropped it to the floor. She leaned backwards and displayed her breasts. "Better?"

"Getting there," smirked Zara. "Now spread my legs and kiss me roughly."

Andi watched as Zara's eyes lifted over her shoulder and back onto the screen. "You are so demanding, aren't you?"

"Yes I am, but you love me, sweetie."

Andi shuffled down the bed and parted her wife's legs. "For some strange reason, I do."

"Show me then," said Zara, wrapping her legs around Andi's back and pulling her head in close.

Andi glanced up and got one final look at Zara's eyes, fixed in arousal on the television, before feeling her face pressed into position by her wife's impatient fingers.

CHAPTER SEVEN

Andi was sitting at her desk in the Proud Unity offices, going over her carefully selected interview questions and trying to imagine how she might answer them if they were ever put to her. She smiled. Today wasn't about knowledge, or intelligence or aptitude for work. Elizabeth Burns and Pippa Rose had beaten over two hundred other applicants to this morning's final round, having already demonstrated all three. Today was about creativity. It was about their ability to think on their feet and react to the unexpected. Their ability to remain calm and considered. Their ability to approach everything with a smile. Andi smiled to herself. She had to like them.

Tapping her papers into a neat pile on the desk in front of her, Andi glanced at her office clock. Almost nine. She was actually feeling quite nervous herself. Stella would be such a hard person to replace, but it had to be done. Stella had made it perfectly clear that she would not be returning to work until all of her children were in formal education. This baby was the first of a planned three, so Andi had advertised the job as full time and permanent. She glanced at the clock once more. Two minutes to go. Janet would bring them in and make the proper introductions, whereupon she would explain the format of the day. She pulled the small pocket mirror from her desk drawer and checked her reflection, quickly wiping a fallen eyelash from her cheek. She nodded at herself, fully aware that the candidates had to like her too.

The knock was loud and the door was opened with gusto. Janet strode into the office and threw her arms out in presentation. "So here we have it. Andi Armstrong's office and the wonderful woman herself. May I introduce you to the Chief Executive here at Proud Unity, Mrs Andi Armstrong."

Andi stood from her seat and made her way around to the other side of the desk, slightly embarrassed by the fanfare. "Not quite necessary, Janet, but thank you, all the same." She looked at both candidates, suddenly taken aback by Pippa Rose's natural beauty. She glanced away, feeling short of breath. "I'm really nothing special."

Janet clapped her hands. "Ladies, if you get the job, that's your first task."

Andi frowned.

"Improve your boss's perceived level of self-importance. She's a real mover and shaker is our Andi."

Andi noticed Elizabeth Burns nodding in sombre agreement, so she smiled in response. She then looked at Pippa Rose who seemed to be distracted by the purring coffee machine.

Janet continued. "Proud Unity is now the largest LGBT campaigning organisation in the UK, thanks primarily to the work that Andi has done lobbying-"

"Janet! That's quite enough, thank you! I'm sure Elizabeth and Pippa are fully aware of what we've *all* accomplished here at Proud Unity over the past few years."

Elizabeth nodded again.

"She's self-deprecating as well," smiled Janet, "not to mention kind, and caring. She's basically the best boss you'll ever work for."

Andi finally caught Pippa's attention and smiled. "Please, let's take a seat and have a coffee. I'll explain the format of the day, and as you can probably gather from Janet's informal manner this morning, today is no longer about the formalities." Andi signalled towards the cluster of soft chairs next to the large office window. "I've been told that you both excelled in the first two rounds of interviews and proved that you're more than capable of doing the job itself." She smiled at Elizabeth who had taken a seat and was now nodding with her hands clasped together in her lap. "One of you might even be over qualified for the post." Andi quickly looked back at Pippa. "But both of you showed a real aptitude for problem solving, organising, communicating-"

Janet chimed in from the coffee station. "Brilliant computer skills, both of them."

"Thank you, Janet. So I'm confident that you can both do this job with your eyes closed. But what I *want,* is for you to enjoy this job, and the only way that's going to happen is if we work well together."

Janet joined them with a tray of freshly poured coffees and placed them on the table next to the milk, sugar, and plate of cream filled biscuits. "There she goes again! I don't think I've ever met anyone who doesn't get along with Andi!"

"Yes, thank you, Janet." Andi signalled for the women to help themselves. "What I mean, is that today is probably more of a mutual assessment. Can we see each other working in a very close proximity, for a very high proportion of each working day? I want to understand your personality. What makes you tick? What motivates you? How you handle difficult situations? How you handle difficult questions? How we would potentially rub along together?" Andi noticed an immediate glint in Pippa's eye and an immediate shift in Elizabeth's body weight, suddenly realising how that might have sounded to two women of opposing sexual orientations. She felt her cheeks redden and tried to avoid Janet's raised eyebrows and cheeky grin.

****

Andi had eaten her lunch at her desk, pleased for the half hour's reprieve. Janet had taken the two candidates down to the canteen for a small buffet, giving her time to mull over the events of the morning and adjust her afternoon questions accordingly. Both women had performed well in the group sessions, showing co-operation, flexibility, support, and leadership. There was hardly anything between them. Her only niggling concern was Elizabeth's slight stuffiness and Pippa's slight over familiarity; neither of which would actually impair their ability as her PA. She took one final look at her question sheet and glanced at the clock. One thirty.

The knock was immediate.

Andi watched for any movement of the door handle. It stayed still. "Come in," she shouted.

Elizabeth Burns walked into the office with her brown leather handbag still fixed to her side, clutching onto the strap like a form of life support. "Hello again," she said.

Andi stood from her desk and indicated to the hard backed chair positioned opposite her, in front of the imposing desk. "How was lunch?"

Elizabeth took a seat and slid the handle of her handbag down her shoulder, pulling it tightly into her feet. "Wonderful, wonderful. Yes, very nice."

"Great, well let's get started because you still have the final written assessment to do this afternoon and I don't want to keep you too late."

"No problem. I'm looking forward to it."

"The written assessment?"

Elizabeth nodded. "I'm a SPAG fanatic and I pride myself on producing high quality pieces of work."

Andi couldn't help but notice the wiry orange hair that had started to ping free from the tight bun, giving Elizabeth the look of an electric shock patient. She smiled to herself, aware of the nerves and hoping the next half hour would actually put Elizabeth Burns more at ease.

"So," said Andi. "If someone wrote a book about you, what do you think the title should be?"

"About me?"

Andi nodded. "Yes."

"Why would someone write a book about me?"

"Hypothetically. What would the title be?"

Elizabeth frowned as if not quite comprehending the question. "I've always liked Wuthering Heights."

Andi decided to go with it. "Okay, why?"

Elizabeth shrugged, as if slightly embarrassed. "I guess it's the love story. The passion between Heathcliff and Catherine."

A vision of Stella at the karaoke warbling the words to Kate Bush's classic came to mind and she smiled, tempted to sing the brilliant lyrics. *'Heathcliff, it's me, I'm Cathy, I've come home again.'*

"But I detest that dreadful Kate Bush song."

Andi coughed, glad she had only hummed it in her head. "Oh right, okay. Well I have a related question here." She paused and met Elizabeth's eyes. "What makes you angry?"

Elizabeth started to tap the palm of her hand with a long, thin finger. "Lying. Deceit. Pretence. Adultery. Cheating." She paused as if conscious of her sudden outburst. "I just get angry when people don't behave as they should."

Andi smiled, trying to relax her. "That's fine. I asked the question and that was a great answer."

Elizabeth nodded and returned her hands to her lap.

"Okay, if you could trade places with any other person for a week, famous or not, living or dead, who would it be and why?"

"It has to be Jesus, doesn't it?"

"Does it?"

Elizabeth nodded. "Of course. You'll find most people say Jesus."

"Do they?"

"Yes, who wouldn't want all of the answers in an instant?"

Andi paused. This session was meant to be a light hearted insight into the candidate's true personality, but she didn't fancy being drawn into a deep and meaningful debate with Elizabeth Burns. "Anyone else?"

"My dog, Mimi. She's a beautiful long haired Shih Tzu. She knows exactly what's going on and she can read me perfectly. I'd like to swap places with her so I could silence the critics."

Andi knew she should have extended the question and asked which critics Elizabeth was referring to, but she tapped her pen on the question sheet and decided to stick to the more upbeat of question, instead. "Right, okay, what is your favourite quote?"

"Good things happen to good people."

"I like that one," smiled Andi.

Elizabeth nodded and waited for the next cue.

"Who do you admire the most?"

"My father."

Andi left a gap for an expansion on her response but when there wasn't any, she continued. "When is it okay to lie?"

Elizabeth shook her head. "Never."

Andi noticed another wiry orange hair ping out of place. "Never?"

"Never." Elizabeth tightened her feet at the ankles.

"Okay. Next question. Does life fascinate you?"

Elizabeth straightened in her seat. "Immensely and I challenge anyone who says otherwise."

Andi was impressed with the confidence. "Such as?"

"Well, these youngsters who have no regard for the world, or the wondrous opportunities they've been given."

"Are all children fortunate?"

"Of course."

"What about those whose parents disown them because of their sexuality."

Elizabeth coughed and glanced at the huge Proud Unity poster behind Andi's desk. "They're fortunate to have you."

"Nice recovery," smiled Andi.

"What I meant to say is that good can be found in every situation. You just have to look hard enough."

Andi felt responsible for Elizabeth's flushed cheeks. "It's okay. There are no right or wrong answers. It's the way you handle the questions that I'm interested in." She smiled. "And on that note I was wondering if you'd be able to entertain me for the next five minutes. I'm not going to talk." She lifted her hands in presentation. "Just entertain me."

Elizabeth nodded. "Ah, ha. I see. You're putting me on the spot and seeing if I panic."

Andi shrugged and raised her eyebrows.

Elizabeth stood up. "Well I won't. I'm actually thrilled to have a chance to talk to you about my vision as your PA." She started to pace. "I believe you could take Proud Unity in a whole new direction, with me at your side."

Andi almost broke her self-enforced silence.

"Instead of focusing solely on LGBT issues, you could look to gain the moral vote. You could clean up this country and tackle other problems such as drug abuse or prostitution. Both of which actually affect a disproportionately high percentage of LGBT people. Government figures may appear to show that drug abuse is on the decline, but it's not. Figures are being manipulated, especially figures amongst the youth of this country."

Andi wasn't sure if it was the off kilter subject matter or uninspiring tone of voice, but she stopped listening and found herself instead thinking of Pippa and wondering how she'd respond to the same task.

Elizabeth sat herself back down. "I think that's been five minutes."

Andi checked the clock. It had been more like ten. "Yes, great." She paused. "Thank you very much for answering my questions, I have just one last request before you leave me for your written assessment."

"Yes?"

"Could you turn your chair around so that it's facing the door?"

Elizabeth frowned in confusion, but did as instructed.

"Right, now if you could sit down please, and without looking over your shoulder, could you describe to me what I'm wearing?"

Elizabeth sat down and straightened her back in her seat. She thought for a moment and then spoke. "I'm very sorry, but I don't have the foggiest idea."

****

Andi took a quick sip of water and waited for the knock. Pippa would be sent in straight away and she wished she had requested a minute or so to recover between candidates. That's what it felt like, she decided; a need to recover from Elizabeth's formal, yet intense, persona. She'd probably be a brilliant PA, structured, efficient, loyal; but possibly not a brilliant friend. Andi paused in thought. She'd been spoiled with Stella. It was ridiculous to think she could ever replicate their bond.

The knock was loud and the door opened before Andi had chance to shout come in.

"Hello again. Shall I sit down?" Pippa was smiling widely, deepening the crevice caused by the dimple in her right cheek.

The beam was infectious and Andi found herself smiling in response. "Yes, please, take a seat. Are you ready?"

Pippa nodded. "Born ready."

Andi swept her short blonde fringe across her forehead and glanced at the question sheet. "Good. Okay I'm slightly conscious of the time because you've got your final written assessment after this, so let's start." She smiled. "Right, if someone wrote a book about you, what would the title be and why?"

Pippa leaned forwards in her chair. "How to tame wild hair."

Andi laughed.

"It's taken me years to figure out the best combination of shampoos, conditioners and smoothing creams."

Andi studied the mass of bouncy brown hair with clearly defined ringlets and limited sign of frizz. "Sounds like a bestseller."

"There's a definite market for it."

Andi held Pippa's eyes; aware of the insinuation. It took a great deal of effort not to acknowledge the glint. "I'm sure there is," she said, thinking of Elizabeth and her electric shock treatment. She coughed lightly and returned her eyes to the questions. "Okay, what makes you angry?"

"Frizzy hair."

Andi couldn't help but laugh. "Anything else?"

Pippa paused and thought carefully. "The only people who really make me angry are bigots."

"Okay."

"Just the idea that there are people out there who think they're better than others. People who think they have more right, or more entitlement, or more of a moral high ground than others. I guess it's just people who judge. They make me cross."

"Good answer. I like that."

Pippa smiled. "Better than my frizzy haired one?"

"Miles," laughed Andi, dropping her eyes back down to her questions and trying to hide her enjoyment of the chat. She took a moment and composed herself. She was finding it quite difficult to ask such informal questions so formally, but she nodded and continued. "Okay, if you could trade places with one other person for a week, famous or not, living or dead, who would it be and why?"

"Your wife." Pippa gasped at herself. "Sorry, that was too much! I'm just having too much fun. I love questions like this. Argh! What a faux pas."

Andi felt her cheeks redden.

Pippa was running her fingers through her curly hair. "Please, let me retract that. Sometimes I speak before I think!" She bent her head into her hands. "Cringe! I can't believe I said that. Right, let me focus." She lifted her face back up and tried to look serious. "I would change places with-"

"You're going to say Jesus, right?"

"I wasn't, no. Should I?"

Andi shook her head. "Sorry, I shouldn't have prompted you." She thought for a second, feeling her pulse quicken at her own flirtation. "Let's go back to your original answer. Why would you want to swap places with my wife?"

Pippa stared at Andi. "So I know what it feels like to be an actual success. She's the boss of a FTSE 100 company. What more could anyone with ambition hope for?"

"Oh, okay." Andi straightened the papers on her desk and dropped her eyes. "So you have ambition then?"

"Of course."

"And will this job be a stepping stone to bigger and better things?"

"I hope so."

"Such as?" Andi was aware that her questions should be focusing on personality and compatibility, but she felt thrown by Pippa's honesty.

"Eventually I'd love to become campaigns director here at Proud Unity."

Andi smiled. "Okay. That's okay. Good answer." She studied Pippa sitting confidently on the hardback chair. She looked composed and eager to respond. She wasn't fiddling, or twitching, or glancing around. She was just sitting and waiting with a smile on her face. "What's your favourite quote, Pippa?"

"The early bird gets the worm, but the second mouse gets the cheese."

Andi smiled. "I've never heard that before."

"Well, it was a toss-up between that and *boring women have clean houses*. But I thought the mouse one illustrated the need to sometimes stop for a second and plan your response." She acknowledged her own previous error. "Something I might need to work on." Pippa smiled. "However, if I got this job then I'm sure my housework will also be put on the back burner."

"Do you house share?"

"No. I live alone."

"You're twenty two, right?"

"Yes, but I have my own place in West Hampstead."

Andi unintentionally raised her eyebrows. "Wow. That's impressive. Not a bad commute then? Jubilee and Bakerloo?"

"Yes, it's perfect. Twenty minutes tops."

"I get on at St John's Wood."

"Oh fantastic!" Pippa paused. "It would be handy being so close."

Andi thought about it. Stella was a good forty minutes by tube, but she often found herself making the round trip to collect paperwork, or hold impromptu meetings. Having Pippa so close would indeed be a bonus. She made a mental note to check exactly where Elizabeth lived. She glanced at the clock, conscious of the time. "Right, let's carry on. Who do you admire the most?"

"Strong women."

"Anyone in particular?"

Pippa thought about it for a moment. "Suran Dickson, the ex PE teacher, who started the Diversity Role Models Charity. She's brilliant. She's made it her mission to go into schools and tackle homophobic bullying."

Andi nodded in agreement. "Yes, I admire her too."

"I think it's the grassroots women who make the difference." Pippa paused. "In fact it's anyone who's out and proud in their day to day life."

"Are you?"

Pippa laughed. "With bells on!"

Andi couldn't help but warm to the light-hearted openness of Pippa's endearing manner. "Moving on then, when is it okay to lie?"

"I think it's okay to lie if you're saving someone else's feelings."

"Really?"

"As long as they won't ever find out otherwise, then yes. Why intentionally hurt someone if it can be avoided?" She paused. "You don't agree?"

Andi realised she was frowning. "I'm not sure. I think I believe honesty's always the best policy."

"Even if your partner asks you if she's looking plump? Which *hypothetically*, she is. You'd tell her the truth?"

Andi smiled. "Okay, I see your point."

"I'm not a liar, and in fact I think it's one of the worst traits that a person can have. I just don't like intentional meanness disguised as honesty."

"Right then. I'll try to be as kindly honest as I can, in response to your next task."

Pippa smiled. "Which is?"

"I'd like you to entertain me for the next five minutes. I'm not going to say anything. I'd just like you to entertain me."

Pippa nodded to herself, as if gearing up for her big moment. "No problem." She stood from her seat and straightened her black *Hobbs* skirt, bowing slightly and addressing Andi as if she was an audience of a thousand. "The song that I'm going to sing to you is called *Listen.* It only lasts for three minutes and forty seven seconds, so I'll fill in the time by introducing it and explaining why it means so much to me." She looked to Andi who gave nothing back in response. "So it's called *Listen* and was sung originally by *Beyonce* when she was in the film *Dreamgirls.*" Pippa smiled. "I'm a tortured ballad singer at heart and I have a passion inside me that only ever comes to life when I'm singing. I'm not the best, hence why I'm here looking for a day job, but I hope it's not so dreadful that you stop me mid-flow." She grinned. "Well you won't, will you, because you're sitting there not saying a word!" Pippa moved the hard backed chair to the side of Andi's desk and took a huge breath. "So, this is *Listen*, and I love it because it perfectly describes my life so far. I never seem to do anything for myself and I guess I've never fully believed in my own abilities." She paused and closed her eyes. "Until now."

Andi didn't know where to look. She was desperately trying not to laugh. Not out of amusement for Pippa's choice of entertainment, but out of nerves. Nerves for Pippa and nerves for herself. She held her breath and decided never again to make such a ridiculous request during an interview. Andi finally raised her eyes to Pippa, who immediately opened her own and locked them together as she started to sing.

"*Listen, to the song here in my heart. A melody I start but can't complete.*"

Andi couldn't break the eye contact. The endearing eyes were penetrating and intense, as if Pippa was singing just to her. Andi chastised herself internally. Of course she was singing just to her, there was no one else in the room.

"*Listen, to the sound from deep within. It's only beginning to find release.*"

Pippa had started to sway and Andi could feel herself rocking gently backwards and forwards in her padded chair. Still their eyes remained locked.

"*Oh, the time has come for my dreams to be heard. They will not be pushed aside or turned, into your own, all cause you won't, listen.*"

Andi swallowed. It was absolutely brilliant. Pippa was about to reach the chorus and Andi was unsure whether she would be able to stop herself from standing up, grabbing her pencil holder and bursting into song with her.

Pippa closed her eyes, threw her arms to the side and belted out the chorus. "*Listen, I am alone at a crossroads. I'm not at home in my own home, and I've tried and tried to say what's on my mind. You should have known.*"

Andi slammed her hands onto the desk. "And stop!"

The silence was deafening and Pippa clasped her hands together in front of her skirt. "I'm so sorry. I just tend to get carried away."

Andi signalled to the chair. "Please, sit down." She waited for Pippa to pull the chair back in front of the desk and take a seat. "Pippa, that was brilliant and as much as I love Beyonce, I just wanted to see how you handled the request."

"Too OTT?" quizzed Pippa, nervously.

Andi allowed herself to laugh. "No, but certainly one I'll remember." She smiled, slightly flushed from the onslaught. "Okay, one last thing before your final written assessment, could you please turn your chair around and face the wall."

As with each other question and request, Pippa did as instructed.

"Right, without looking, could you describe what I'm wearing?"

Pippa nodded, giving Andi a view of her bouncing brown curls. "I'll start at the bottom. You have a pair of effortlessly chic faux snakeskin court shoes on. Some tan tights, probably around ten denier. A perfectly fitted grey pencil skirt that drops just below your knee. Tucked neatly into that is your quirky, but stylish dog and polka dot pattern white blouse, which is buttoned right up to the neck. You have a single breasted grey jacket, which matches the skirt, but is not done up. And you also have a beautiful pair of tiger-eye gemstone earrings that complement the unique red-brown colouring of your eyes." She paused. "Amber. Yes, I'd say you had amber eyes. Your hair is naturally blonde and cut into a modern pixie style with a sweeping fringe that accentuates your small, but perfectly formed features and wide intuitive eyes."

Andi bent her head and lifted her pen. She pretended to write. "Thank you, Pippa. Janet will be waiting outside and she'll talk you through the last assessment."

Pippa stood from her chair and lifted it back into position. She walked slowly towards the desk and stood still, forcing Andi to look up. "Thank you for your time."

Andi looked at the outstretched hand. She stood up and shook it, conscious of her fully exposed blushing cheeks. "Great interview, thank you."

Pippa smiled and turned to leave.

Andi counted the seconds that it took for Pippa to exit the room. Her walk across the office and departure into the hall seemed to take forever. She watched as the door handle finally clicked back into place. Andi immediately pushed herself backwards on her chair and opened her mouth in a colossal silent scream. She frantically fanned her face and lifted her phone. She dialled Stella's number and was relieved when she picked up. "Are you in labour, Stella? ... No? ...

Good, I'm coming round after work ... I need your help ...Yes ... Yes, it's about the candidates ... No, not over the phone ... How did you guess? ... Right, see you at six!" She returned the receiver and fanned her face once more, trying to slow her breathing and gain some composure. She took another deep breath, stood up and walked to the coffee machine, making herself a frothy cappuccino with extra sugar. She waited for the whirring to finish and carried it carefully back to her desk, placing it on her question sheet and biting her bottom lip. She shook her head, unsure of quite what it was she was feeling.

Janet's familiar rasp sounded at the door, followed by her predictable first sentence.

"Only me," said Janet walking quickly into the room. She flapped a piece of paper in her hand. "One of the candidates has finished the essay. I've told her we'll contact her by 8.00 p.m. this evening."

"Elizabeth? Wow, that was quick. What's she had? The half hour that I've been in here with Pippa? Forty five minutes at the most? She was allowed all afternoon."

Janet raised her eyebrows and shook her head. "She's still in there. This is Pippa's."

Andi reached out her hand. "Pippa's? What? It can't be."

"It's *Pippa's* essay."

Andi looked at the sheet. Both candidates had been given the same question and had at least two hours to write their responses. She read the title of the essay question: "*What is Bravery?*"

Pippa had written two words: "*This is.*"

CHAPTER EIGHT

Stella shovelled another heaped forkful of curry into her mouth, chewing hungrily and swallowing with gratification. It was her latest attempt at inducing labour. She'd tried the walks, the pineapple, the blowing up of balloons and she'd even tried her mother's slightly embarrassing suggestion of nipple stimulation, all of which had failed. An order of the hottest curry she could handle had been picked up by Andi, en route, and Stella had everything crossed, apart from her legs that was. She paused her eating and looked up at Andi from the carpet of her lounge. "It takes bloody balls to do that!"

Andi was sitting on Stella's sofa, nibbling at the crust of an oversized naan bread. "I guess it takes bravery."

"Exactly!" Stella took a long slug of sprite. "The question you set them said: '*What is bravery?*' and if that's not bravery then I don't know what is!"

"Is it cockiness?"

"No, it's not. It answers the question perfectly. It demonstrates that bravery is about risking everything. Pippa Rose has risked her chance of getting the job she so clearly wants, by writing a two worded answer to an essay that should have taken about two hours to complete."

Andi sighed. "The purpose of the essay was to see how well the candidates could form an argument and articulate themselves. We hoped they would link it to the bravery of the LGBT community and give us an idea of their ability to produce good sound bites for press releases and so on."

"Did you tell them that?"

Andi shook her head. "No, we just set them the question."

"So, she answered the question in a manner that I think is quite frankly genius!" Stella reached for the bag of onion bhajis and tipped four onto her already overflowing plate. "I'm being a pig, I know, but this could be my last ever meal."

"You're not dying."

"No, childbirth is more painful." Stella popped the whole bhaji into her mouth and somehow still managed to talk. It reminded Andi of the scene from the film Junior where Arnold Schwarzenegger was pregnant and binging on all manner of foods. She thought about mentioning it, then realised that no pregnant woman would ever want to be compared to a greedy, pregnant, Arnold Schwarzenegger. Andi opted for: "Pardon?"

"Sorry, mouthful! I said, what did Elizabeth write?"

Andi pulled the three thousand word essay from her work bag. "This."

Stella eyed the wad of paper. "Any good?"

"Yes, it is actually. I read it on the tube over here. Elizabeth is clearly intelligent, articulate and able to form a good argument."

"But..."

Andi smiled. "But I'm not sure how well we'd get on."

"Elizabeth was Janet's front runner."

"Really?"

"Yes, women of a certain age I think."

Andi reached back into her work bag and pulled out Elizabeth's CV. "She's only in her thirties."

"Never!"

"Let me work this out." Andi looked at the date of birth and did a quick bit of mental arithmetic. "Thirty nine next year."

Stella gulped down another mouthful of Sprite. "No! I'd have put her in her fifties, easily! That frizzy orange hair does her no favours."

Andi puzzled. "She must have had something that everyone on the panel liked?"

"I wasn't privy to all of the interviews, but from what I saw, I'm confident that she'll be a hard worker. She'll be reliable. She'll be good at her job." Stella studied Andi. "She'll make you a good PA."

Andi nodded and picked the naan back up. "Yes, you're probably right. Janet and the team said exactly the same thing." Andi reached down to the carpet for her fork. Stella had insisted that the floor was the only place where she could get herself comfortable to eat, surrounded by cushions, with legs spread wide. "Did Elizabeth mention her sexuality in the panel interviews?"

Stella chewed over her words. "The fact she's straight?"

Andi nodded. "Yes."

Stella swallowed and wiped the corner of her mouth with the back of her hand. "She brought it up actually and used it to her advantage, saying that it would give us another insight into how we could bite back at the critics. I think she said she'd represent the '*supportive straights*,' or something like that."

"We have straight people working for us."

"Do we?"

Andi shrugged.

"I know you, Andi Armstrong; you don't want her, do you?"

"I know I *should* choose her."

"Why?"

"She's the safe option. She's been a PA before. She's had experience. She'll do what it says on the tin."

Stella stuck out her tongue. "Boring ... and I always hated that advert."

"I'm just not sure about Pippa."

"Why not?"

Andi laughed. "Because she stood up and belted out a Beyonce classic!"

"That's the first thing you told me!" Stella tipped the remainder of the pink coloured masala onto her plate. "It sounded great! I would've loved to have seen it."

"It *was* great. It was *hilariously* great. She's a real character. Bursting with life. Quick witted. Easy to talk to. Thought provoking."

Stella grinned with freshly pink teeth. "And exactly which thoughts did she provoke in you, Mrs Andi Armstrong?"

"Oh behave."

Stella spooned in another mouthful of masala. "She's gorgeous though, isn't she?"

Andi lifted her eyebrows with nonchalance. "Do you think so?"

"Being married doesn't stop you from appreciating someone else's beauty."

Andi laughed. "And Sandy agrees with this, does she?"

Stella patted her huge bump. "At this very moment in time, my wonderful wife would agree with anything." Stella grinned. "She'd even nod if I claimed cat shit was a delicacy."

Andi laughed again. "Sandy's doing and saying all the right things then?"

Stella placed her plate back down on the carpet. "She pretty much did already, but yes, she knows not to disagree with a heavily pregnant lady! But stop avoiding the question, you!"

Andi tore a small strip off the naan bread. "Whether Pippa Rose is, or isn't, a bouncy haired, buxom beauty, makes no difference to me." She popped the sweet tasting bread into her mouth and nodded in decision. "I think she's too young."

"Look, she passed all of the aptitude tests with flying colours. Her typing and computer skills were off the scale. She shows initiative. She's got ideas. She's got drive. But most of all she's got passion. It was her passion for equality that struck me when we chatted. Yes she's young, but she's young, free and single and you need someone like that who can drop everything the instant that you need them." Stella grinned. "Not everyone's partner is as accepting as mine."

Andi reached down and gently squeezed her friend's rather plump thigh. "Oh Stella, you really have been the best. I'm going to miss you so much."

Stella put her hand on top of Andi's and squeezed back in return. "No you're not. You're going to be far too busy swanning off to the karaoke with Pippa Rose."

"Am I?"

"Yes, and saving the world, like you always do."

Andi put the shredded piece of naan bread back down on her plate. "I'm not sure she's the sensible choice." She bit her bottom lip, embarrassed by the admission. "She seems quite flirty."

Stella laughed. "Go you! That's even better then! Seriously Andi, you need a bit of fun in your life!"

Andi shook her head. "No I don't. My life's full of fun, and anyway, mistakes are made when you see the warning signs, no matter how small, and you choose to ignore them."

"That's just boring," said Stella popping in another chicken ball. She chewed noisily and shook her head, forming her final point.

Andi sighed. "I just think-"

"Wait, wait…" Stella wiped her mouth and cleared her throat. "I was about to say … people who never make mistakes aren't admirable; they're just people who've never tried anything new."

Andi laughed. "Oh how I'll miss your apparent wisdom. Come on then, who should I choose?"

Stella rolled her eyes. "Andi, my darling, you'd made your choice the moment you called me on the phone."

CHAPTER NINE

Nine months later: *Tues 20th November 2012*

Andi was sitting in her lounge at home, slowly dictating a list of questions. "So," she said, trying to be as clear as possible, "if the Church of England votes today, in favour of allowing female bishops, we'll angle our questions to assume they're willing to do the same for equal marriage; i.e. most of society has now changed to accept the fact that women are equal, and likewise, most of society has now changed to accept the fact that all love is equal." She paused. "We must applaud their progression and assume their progression will continue within the field of equal marriage." Andi exhaled, checking that her scribe was keeping up. "But if, on the very unlikely chance, the Church of England votes against allowing the ordination of female bishops, we need to ask how they can possibly claim to represent the people of this country. Women are equal and completely capable of doing the same job as men." She nodded. "All clear on the angles?"

Elizabeth Burns jotted down the final question and lifted her trusty pencil from her well-worn pad, pushing it tip first, into her tight orange bun. She coughed lightly. "Mrs Armstrong, there are *some* jobs where women aren't as good as men, for example fire fighting. I'm not sure you and your petite frame could haul me out of a burning building."

Andi found it very difficult to ignore the quick witted response that popped into her mind, along with the vision of Elizabeth *deliberately* left in the said burning building. "It's been nine months now, could you please call me Andi?"

The door to the spacious lounge swung open and Pippa Rose waltzed in with a tray of tea. "Aren't you glad you chose me to be your PA? Blimey, I'd even shorten your name if I could, but Ann just doesn't sound right. It makes you sound old!" Pippa lowered the steaming tray onto the modern coffee table. "And a fuddy-duddy you are not!"

Andi smiled at the light relief always brought by Pippa. "We've had this chat before. You need to stop teasing. Proud Unity thought that you'd both make wonderful PAs, and it just so happened that Janet's workload increased enough for her to need an assistant and she asked specifically if she could have first dibs on Elizabeth."

Pippa lifted a mug of tea and passed it to Andi, turning her back on Elizabeth. "*Liar*," she mouthed.

Andi tried not to laugh. "Proud Unity's never been so strong, and it's a privilege working with the pair of you."

Elizabeth almost bowed as she stood from her sofa seat. "Thank you, Mrs Armstrong, and thank you Pippa for the tea, but I must go and meet Janet and pass over these questions. The announcement's due soon and we want to be in the hubbub of it all, don't we?"

Pippa stretched out on the sofa. "I'm glad I'm PA to the lady who chooses to watch the results from the comfort of her own home." She turned to Elizabeth and grinned. "Will your PA-ing involve standing outside in the cold with Janet?"

Elizabeth lifted her brown leather handbag and walked to the lounge door, completely ignoring Pippa's banter. "Mrs Armstrong, you can count on us to deliver you some good sound bites," she tapped her brown handbag, indicating to the notepad inside, "obviously tailored to the alternative outcomes that we've just been discussing."

Andi stood up. "I'll see you to the door, and thank you for coming round." She glanced back at Pippa and wagged her finger. "And don't get too comfortable, you. We've got work to do and my wife will be back soon."

****

Zara glanced in her rear view mirror at the policewoman quickly approaching on foot. She checked the time on her dashboard clock and kept her hands firmly on the steering wheel. The busty figure stopped alongside her window, but Zara pretended not to notice. The tap, however, was too loud, and the winding hand signal too exaggerated, to ignore. Zara reached out and pressed the button under the window of her luxury Overfinch Range Rover. The window silently slid down. "Can I help you, officer?"

The female police officer bent down, stretching her black utility vest even wider. "You can't park here, sorry."

Zara noticed the metal handcuffs and black truncheon that were attached to the lady's leather belt. "It's an NCP car park."

The police officer rested her elbows in the window frame and pushed her chest forwards. "This level's out of service. Look, there's no one around."

"There weren't any signs," said Zara looking about and confirming that they were indeed alone.

The police officer reached into her breast pocket and pulled out a small white notepad. "We've had reports of vehicles coming up to this level and engaging in criminal activity." She tapped her finger on the pad. "In fact, it's vehicles like these with large boots and blacked out windows that are causing the problems."

"Shall I move?" asked Zara.

The police officer pushed her notepad back inside her breast pocket. "No. I'm going to have to check inside the vehicle."

"I've got nothing to hide," said Zara, pressing another button and opening the central locking. "I've opened the passenger door for you, officer." Zara buzzed her window back up and watched in her wing mirror as the police officer walked slowly around the car, she was pressing her hands against the back windows and peering inside. She wouldn't see anything, thought Zara, remembering the extortionate price paid for top of the range one-way windows.

The passenger door opened and the female police officer pulled herself inside. There was a real art to entering an Overfinch Range Rover with elegance and this woman had clearly been inside one before. The officer pulled the door closed behind her.

"So," said Zara, "what do you need to see?"

The police officer peeled off her black leather gloves and placed them on the dashboard. "I'll need to check your pockets."

Zara unbuckled her seatbelt and slid out of her linen blazer. She handed it over.

The police officer felt inside the silky lining of each pocket before glancing into the back of the car. "Why are the seats down? Are you picking something up?"

"You could say that," smirked Zara, reaching out and touching the top of the black truncheon.

"Please remove your hand and enter the back of the car. I'd like to see inside those compartments." The police officer signalled to the pull out storage holes in the side panels of the backdoors.

"No problem," said Zara twisting in her seat and climbing through the gap into the huge space where the seats usually were. She crouched down and pulled open one of the compartments. "See, nothing here."

The police officer followed Zara, pulling herself through the gap, in order to take a closer look. "What about these." She indicated to the pull down flaps in the ceiling.

Zara tutted. "If I was going to conceal something, I'd conceal it in the smallest, tightest of places, not in some boring storage hole next to the de-icer."

The police officer reddened. "I'll do the talking from now on."

"That's better," grinned Zara.

"Right. Lie on your stomach and place your arms to the side. I'll need to give you a rub down."

Zara did as instructed.

The police officer stayed kneeling and worked her fingers along Zara's arms, squeezing gently and pausing slightly as she made the re-route down her back and towards her buttocks. "Spread your legs please, Madame."

Zara lifted her head. "Madame?"

"I mean, Mrs." The police officer stopped. "What is it they say?"

Zara rested her head back down on the fresh smelling carpet. "I don't know, but I know their rub downs would be much more searching and not quite as gentle."

"You want it rough do you?"

"You know I do," smiled Zara, enjoy the feeling of her legs being parted and her crotch being rubbed.

"Turn over. I think I feel something. I'll need to take off your trousers." The police officer unzipped the linen suit pants, pulled them off and threw them against the front seat of the car.

Zara sat bolt upright. "Sweetie, they're Dior linen. I have to wear them this afternoon!"

"Sorry." The police officer quickly reached for the trousers and folded them at the knee, draping the over the front seat's headrest. "Sorry, where were we. Oh yes, spread your legs, lady. I'm giving you an internal."

"It sounds like I'm at the doctor's."

"That's it," said the police officer, "you're about to be silenced." She untied her black and white chintz neck scarf and looped it over Zara's head, pulling it between her teeth and tying it tightly at the back. "Is that okay?"

"You're not meant to ask!" came the muffled response.

"No, right, sorry, okay. Silence!" The police officer paused and found her confidence. "You, Madame, have been a very bad lady, loitering around public car parks and disturbing the peace. It's about time you paid the penalty."

"Umm hmm."

The police officer unclipped the handcuffs from her utility belt. "Put your hands together behind your back."

Zara did as instructed, her arousal heightened by the feel of the cold metal against her wrists and the sound of the cuffs being clicked into place. She pretended to resist, thrilled that she couldn't actually get free.

"Now, where was I?" The police officer pulled at Zara's knickers. "You're wet already, you bad, bad woman." She pushed Zara's legs as wide apart as they'd go. "Now, what exactly have you been hiding in this moist, warm cubby hole?"

Zara moaned with desire.

"Let me see," said the police woman, gently sliding a finger between Zara's legs. "I'll have to go deeper." She pushed another finger further inside, pressing forwards and touching the soft mound of Zara's g-spot. "There's definitely something in here. I'm going to have to make you wider."

Zara growled with anticipation.

"My truncheon should do the job." She unclipped the leather buckle around the truncheon and lifted it into her hands, patting it gently in her palm.

Zara twisted her head to the side and looked up with wild eyes, almost begging her assaulter to continue.

"You want this?"

Zara nodded quickly.

"Straight in?"

Zara nodded.

"All the way?"

Zara nodded again and closed her eyes, bracing herself for the onslaught.

The police officer did as instructed, grabbing hold of a buttock and forcing the truncheon deep inside. "You're a bad, bad, lady and I'm going to make you pay."

"Faster," moaned Zara through the damp neck tie.

"Like this?" asked the police woman, almost jerking Zara's whole body forwards and backwards in the boot of the car.

"My clit!" came the muffled cry.

The police woman used her left hand to feel under Zara's hips, plunging her hand down towards the action. She pinched the clitoris between her first two fingers and pulled it roughly.

Zara was moving her body up and down, arousing her own nipples on the smooth carpet and pushing down harder on the truncheon. She felt herself coming and arched her back in spasm.

The cry was deep and drawn out and the police officer held the black truncheon in place, stopping the spasms from forcing it out. She gave it one final shove, causing Zara's body to jolt forwards before flopping in complete limpness. She slowly pulled the offending instrument back out of position. "I think you're clear," she smiled, wiping it on the carpet and clipping it back onto her belt.

Zara still didn't move.

"Don't let me see you hanging around here again, do you hear?"

There was a faint nodding and a wiggle of the handcuffs.

The police officer reached into her top pocket and found the small key. She twisted it in the lock, springing the shackles free.

Zara immediately rolled over and pulled the scarf from her mouth. "Come here, that was brilliant." She pulled the police officer down on top of her and kissed her with urgency and passion. "Let me fuck you."

"Really?"

"Yes, Melody, really. That was wonderful, sweetie."

****

Andi and Pippa were still sitting in Andi's plush front lounge, mesmerised by the television. There were at least three brown-leather three-seater sofas in the large room, not to mention the brown leather ottoman and the matching brown leather recliner; but here they were, huddled closely together, eyes transfixed on the cinema-sized television, anxiously awaiting the result.

Pippa sighed as another banner trailed across the bottom of the screen, announcing a further delay in the results. She wiggled backwards on the sofa and turned to Andi. "I need a cushion to squeeze." She glanced around the huge room, once again admiring the way it managed to look chic and minimalistic given the plethora of sofas, complementing lampshades and coffee tables. "Shame you haven't got any."

Andi grabbed one from the seat to her right and swung it into Pippa's stomach. "Don't make me laugh! All you've done for the past nine months is make me laugh! We've actually bought two new cushions to match the Tal Walton we've got coming on Friday."

Pippa looked around and did a quick mental count, "So that makes twenty four cushions in your lounge, which, by the way, could pass as a hotel concierge area," she frowned, "and what's a Tal Walton?"

Andi gasped, still managing to keep one eye on the television screen. "Don't let Zara hear you saying that, she got Kari Whitman to design this room."

"Who?" shrugged Pippa. "Mr Ike Ear did my house."

Andi ignored the joke, instead reading the new banner that trailed along the bottom of the BBC live news channel: '*Results from the vote due in ten minutes*.' She turned to Pippa and gave her her full attention. "*Tal Walton,* is a wonderful artist who paints in the Tonalist genre, oil on hard surfaces, mostly imagined landscapes. He has a trademark where he divides the image into three sections, which he describes as representing the past, present and future."

Pippa pretended to awaken herself from sleep. "Sorry, what was that?"

"Oh stop it, you tease."

Pippa looked at her boss carefully. "You don't really care about all of this stuff, do you?"

Andi ignored the probe and glanced back at the screen. "They're dragging it out, aren't they? I'll give Zara a quick ring. She thought she might be home in time to watch it."

Pippa took the hint. "Okay, I'll stop teasing you about all of this opulence, but I do hope I've done more as your PA in the last nine months than just make you laugh?" She grinned, "I'll go and make us a cuppa. Shout me if anything happens ... not that I'll hear you in your restaurant sized kitchen. I'll try and remember the way."

Andi shouted after her. "See if the maids want a drink too."

Pippa grinned. Slowly but surely Andi had eased up and let her in. It had taken a while, from a slightly nervous start, with Andi not 'getting' her jokes, or tightening up at her teasing, but their friendship had blossomed and Andi, for the most part, was now actually managing to laugh at herself and the lifestyle she was privy to.

"No, the butler's making theirs," quipped Pippa in response.

****

Zara's second orgasm of the afternoon morphed from a pleasurable scream of, "Ahhhh," to an annoyed groan of, "Arghh." Her phone, sitting on the polished car dashboard, was ringing once again. She caught her breath. "I should have turned it off! Sorry, sweetie."

Melody collapsed next to her, exhausted from their mutual climax. "Don't worry," she sighed, "I know my baby's busy."

Zara sat up and twisted herself around, leaning against the back of the driver's seat. She pulled her knees into her chest. "I'm not your *baby*, Melody."

"You call me sweetie."

"I call everybody *sweetie*."

Melody rolled onto her elbows on the soft grey carpet. "It's been almost ten months. Surely I have the right to give you a pet name?"

Zara pulled her long black hair over her shoulder and started to smooth it back into position. "It's not been ten months."

Melody nodded. "It has," she paused, unsure of how far to take it. "It's actually been the best ten months of my life."

"Oh be quiet!"

"Zara it has." Melody pulled herself up onto her bottom and swivelled round to face her boss. "I sensed something different in you today. You made me feel like you really wanted me."

"You dressed as a police officer and fucked the brains out of me with that big black truncheon of yours. I didn't know what I was saying."

Melody reached out and stroked her boss's face. "I know you. I know you put on a tough act to keep our relationship *professional*. But we're not at work now, Zara. You can tell me how you feel."

Zara coughed. "Do your vest back up. I need to get going."

"Not until you tell me."

"Tell you what?"

Melody sighed. "Fine. I'll say it first." She took Zara's hand and held it tightly. "I know you feel it too, we've been getting closer and closer, so I'll just say it."

Zara rolled her eyes. "Say what?"

"I love you."

"SHUT THE BLOODY FUCK UP!" Zara threw the hand back to its owner and clambered into the front of the car. "Don't be so BLOODY FUCKING RIDICULOUS! Honestly, I've heard it all now!"

Melody quickly followed her into the passenger's seat. "I do, you know I do. We've been meeting more regularly and you've been chatting more at work."

"Stop right there!" Zara turned to Melody with narrow eyes. "Have we ever spent the night together?"

Melody shrugged. "No."

"Have we ever gone on a date?"

Melody bit her bottom lip. "I guess not."

Zara banged her fist on the leather steering wheel. "Have I ever said anything, and I mean ANYTHING, at all about my feelings for you?"

Melody shook her head. "No, but I saw it in your eyes."

"Saw what?" Zara continued to shake her head in disbelief. "Have I ever bought you a gift? Have I ever phoned you for a chat? Have I ever written you a lovey dovey message? Have I ever taken an interest in your life outside of work? Have I ever tried to hold your hand? Have I ever cooked for you? Have I ever held you or even just hugged you?" She paused and stared Melody straight in the eye. "For fuck's sake Melody, it's just sex."

Melody maintained the stare. "But you slag off your wife, Zara."

"Everyone slags off their wife when they're shagging around." She shook her head. "I love Andi. *This* is just sex."

Melody took a deep breath. "I don't believe you. I saw you watching me in the meeting this-"

Zara's ringtone interrupted Melody's protest. "I'm taking this. Be quiet." Zara lifted the mobile and tapped the green button. Speaking to anyone would be better than listening to this nonsense. "*Hello … Oh, Andi ... Yes ... Sorry, sweetie ... I'm on my way ... Which vote? ... Oh, yes ... They've voted against? ... Is that good or bad?*" Zara glanced at Melody who had taken her own mobile out of her vest pocket and switched it into life. Zara shook her head and mouthed the words, '*turn it off.*'

Melody ignored the demand.

Zara twisted her body to the right and looked out of her own window at the top level of the empty car park, continuing her own conversation. "*You'll have to explain this vote thing to me again ... I know I should know ... Yes, I know it's important ... Yes, I'm on my way sweetie ... Yes, yes I-*"

A sexy, *Santa Baby,* ringtone suddenly blasted out from Melody's mobile phone.

Zara frantically waved her left hand in Melody's direction and pressed her own phone further into her ear, trying to silence the noise.

Melody let it ring.

Zara kept waving, but increased her own volume. "*Yes, it's someone outside ... Their phone's got some crappy Christmas tune ... Yes, I know it's only November ... My window's open ... No, I'm not cold ... Look, I'll see you in a bit.*" She hung up quickly, throwing the phone back onto the dashboard and glaring at Melody. "You idiot."

Melody shrugged and silenced the sexy singing. "It's my voicemail. It rings when I've got a message."

"You could have turned it off!"

"Oops."

Zara dismissed Melody with her fingers. "Right, your fun and games are over. Out you get."

Melody looked down at her ripped fishnet tights and fake police vest that was now torn at the shoulder. "I can't get out like this! I'm down on level two. I got the lift up to make it look more authentic."

"I've seen women at hen parties that make more authentic police officer's than you do." Zara reached for her trousers. "Fine, I'll drive you. I need to pay for my ticket anyway."

****

Andi hung up the phone and placed it back on the coffee table. "Sometimes I wonder if I'm actually married to a man!"

Pippa laughed. "Why?"

"She hasn't got the foggiest idea about the vote today, even though I spent all morning talking about it." Andi shrugged, "And she's certainly not a lesbian aware of current issues."

"How can Andi Armstrong's wife not be aware of lesbian issues?"

"Exactly!" laughed Andi reaching for her mug of tea.

Pippa paused for a moment. "That's the first time in nine months that I've ever heard you say anything negative about your wife."

Andi swallowed the hot tea quickly. "Was that negative? Oh no, I didn't mean to be negative, I just meant she can be a bit forgetful at times." Andi laughed. "Oh no, that's negative too! I don't mean that-"

"I'm teasing. It's nice to think that the golden couple have their moments just like the rest of us. Not that I'm actually an *us*, still just a *me*."

Andi raised her eyebrows. "Oh, we certainly have our moments."

"Really?" Pippa was intrigued.

Andi reached onto the coffee table for her laptop. "Come on, let's write this article and get it out to the Pink Press before Zara gets back. If she reads it and understands it then it's a good piece."

Pippa nudged Andi's arm. "Ooo, that's another dig!"

"No, no, I didn't mean it like that! I meant we need to carefully explain how this vote will affect our campaign for equal marriage."

Pippa smiled, displaying her dimple in its full glory.

"You were teasing, right?"

"Right," grinned Pippa, taking the laptop from her boss's lap and starting to type.

****

Zara zipped her trousers back up and slung her seatbelt over her shoulder. She twisted the key in the ignition and revved the engine, flooring the accelerator and speeding across the concrete car park. She stared straight ahead and turned the steering wheel with force, screeching the tyres down the first of many exit ramps.

Zara didn't notice the person hiding in the shadows of the stairwell.

But Melody did.

CHAPTER TEN

Andi returned from her home office and proudly placed the print outs on the coffee table in the lounge. They had worked on the article for over an hour, with Andi dictating and Pippa typing. Pippa had also chosen to add her own variation on words or phrases, most of which Andi eventually sanctioned. In fact, Andi did admit that her PA always seemed to give their articles an added edge with her well thought out turn of phrase and thought provoking analogies. Both women picked up a copy of the article and settled back onto the sofa, giving it a final read through before its upload to the Proud Unity website, aware that it would be seized, almost immediately, by all major LGBT news sites, and quoted for further articles, some of which would undoubtedly make the national press.

Andi was the first one to finish the proof read and nod her head in satisfaction. She placed the article back on the table. "We're a good team you and I!"

Pippa trailed her finger across the final line, bobbing her mass of curly brown hair in agreement. "It's a cracker! A controversial cracker."

Andi frowned. "It's not too controversial though, is it?"

"Anything that dares to criticise the Church of England will be seen as controversial. But it's great. It needs to be said."

"Agreed. Let's upload." Andi pulled the laptop back onto her knee and logged into the Proud Unity admin page. She dragged the article from her saved documents file and dropped it into the upload box, clicking the link and watching the blue bar race across the screen. "And it's up!" She copied the link from the address bar and opened up her Twitter and Facebook accounts, quickly writing the title: *'Has the Church of England just consigned itself to extinction?'* Andi pasted the link to their article and hit the tweet button. "I know I say it all the time, but social media is such a revolution." She repeated the process on Facebook and clicked the post button. "Now watch this." She opened a third tab and signed into her Google analytics site. "Twenty three hits, twenty four, twenty five-"

Pippa leaned closer into the laptop. "On the article, already?"

"Yes look. It shows how many hits the article gets, how long the reader stays on the Proud Unity website for and whereabouts in the world the person is accessing the site from."

"Forty four hits! In less than a minute!" Pippa tapped the other tabs on the screen. "Look, twelve interactions on Twitter and fifteen notifications on Facebook."

Andi switched to the Twitter feed. "It's a hot topic. Look the hashtag #CofE is trending." She clicked on the link, scanning the most recent tweets. "And it looks like most people share our viewpoint."

Pippa took Andi's hand and squeezed it lightly. "That's because we're right. You're right. Proud Unity's right. You're a courageous lady, Andi Armstrong, and I'm in total awe!"

"Cosy," said Zara, with her hand on her hip in the doorway.

"Hey, darling, I didn't hear you come in." Andi moved her hand and beckoned her wife to sit down next to them. "Come and take a look at our article."

"Sweetie, I've just had the drive from hell. People are parked in the street without permits, and I've had to leave the Range Rover miles away."

Andi looked at her wife's crumpled linen trousers. "Come and sit down, I'll make you a cup of tea."

"Make it a G and T please, sweetie," said Zara, entering the room and collapsing onto her large brown recliner.

Andi got up from her seated position and walked over to her wife, bending down to kiss her on the cheek. "Of course." She looked back at Pippa. "Shall we have a cheeky Pimms, to celebrate?"

"I didn't think anyone actually drank Pimms!" laughed Pippa.

Zara lifted her nose at Andi. "Exactly. Get the girl a G and T like me. No one wants to be offered Pimms."

"I rather like it," said Andi, reaching up on tiptoes to pull open their slightly stubborn spirit cabinet door. "It's Pimms o'clock."

Zara straightened her long black hair. "No one likes that advert."

"I do," smiled Andi reaching for the almost empty, green bottle of gin.

Zara pressed the recliner button on the arm of her chair, closing her eyes as her body was shifted into a horizontal position. "And what exactly is it that you're celebrating?" She opened one eye and looked from Pippa to Andi. "The fact that PA Pippa's still putting up with you?"

Andi poured a tiny amount of tonic into the tumbler of gin and took the drink over to her wife, picking up a print out of the article on the way. "Very funny. No, we're celebrating this." She handed both items over to her wife and was thanked with an immediate tut.

"Buzz me back up then. I can't drink and read lying down like this."

Andi pressed the button on the arm of the recliner, sending her wife slowly back into the seated position. She turned to Pippa, clapping her hands together. "So, what will it be?"

Pippa smiled kindly. "I think I'll join you in a Pimms."

Zara snorted. "So you're a suck up too!"

"Oh Zara, stop it." Andi paused as she walked past Pippa, squeezing her gently on the shoulder. "Pippa's not used to your sense of humour yet."

"I wasn't joking," whispered Zara, taking a slug of gin.

Andi gave Pippa a reassuring smile. "Yes she was, and the way Stella handled it was to give as good as she got."

Pippa nodded in thought. "I'll remember that."

Zara peered over the rim of her tumbler. "Stella also wore shorter skirts than you, and lower tops." She winked. "That always helped my mood."

"Behave," shouted Andi, making the final preparations to the two tall glasses of Pimms which chinked together as she lifted them from the cabinet. Andi carried them carefully back to the sofas and passed one to Pippa. She sat back in her own seat and took a tentative sip, enjoying the minty fruit taste. She glanced at her wife. "So, come on. What do you think?" She lifted her glass to Pippa and winked in a silent toast. "You can always be sure you'll get an honest critique from my wife."

"*You don't say*," mouthed Pippa, aware that Zara's eyes were transfixed on the article.

Zara let out an elongated sigh, as if chastising a young child. "The title alone will bring you a whole heap of shit, sweetie."

Andi swallowed quickly. "What do you mean?"

"*Has the Church of England consigned itself to extinction?* It's as if you're asking a rhetorical question. You're saying the Church of England's about to become extinct."

Andi shook her head. "No, if you read on, the article examines how their vote today affects their long term future."

Zara shrugged. "Suggesting the Church won't have a future will bring many more bigots out of the woodwork and you'll be lucky if it's only a box of offal they send."

Andi placed her drink back down on the coffee table. "Zara, today the Church of England voted against allowing female bishops. They've shown themselves to be so far removed from twenty first century Britain that it's beyond a joke. Their opposition to equal marriage will now be called into question because they've lost credibility."

"I *can* read."

"I mean, who'll listen to an institution that doesn't believe females are capable, or worthy, of becoming bishops. It's a joke. It really is."

Zara rolled her eyes. "Calm down."

"No, I won't calm down. Today's monumental. Today will go down as a day in history that saw the main opponents to equal marriage wounded beyond repair. They've shown themselves to be totally and utterly archaic."

"Oh no, I can feel a speech coming on." Zara pointed in the direction of the CD player. "Pippa, go and put the National Anthem on."

Pippa held Zara's eyes. "Actually I agree with Andi. The Church of England, by disallowing female bishops, has shown its complete lack of relevance to the modern world. Any objection they have to equal marriage will now be taken with a pinch of salt. They don't even rate females, so of course they won't like equal marriage. They'll no longer be taken seriously."

Zara tutted. "I can see why you two get on so well." She leaned forwards and thrust the article back towards the coffee table, watching it floating forwards and backwards before landing with a skid. "You'll get some shit from it."

Pippa turned to Andi. "Good. That's why I wanted this job in the first place. To have the privilege of working with someone who's not afraid of shit."

"To shit," smiled Andi, raising her glass and chinking it naughtily against Pippa's.

"Oh grow up, girls," sighed Zara pressing the recliner button on her chair and returning to her horizontal state.

"*Never*," mouthed Pippa to Andi, with a cheeky wink.

CHAPTER ELEVEN

Pippa emerged from the Baker Street Tube Station to a crowd of tourists queuing around the curved green dome of Madame Tussauds. She checked her watch. It was almost eight pm, well past the final admission time. Possibly the unveiling of a new waxwork, or a celebrity appearance, she decided, crossing the busy road and heading towards the dark green Starbucks on the corner of Porter Street. Pippa took a deep breath and swung open the door, greeted by a familiar warmth and new enticing cinnamon smell. It was only November but the coffee shop had already started to promote their seasonal favourites range. She didn't bother to scan the seating area, confident that Jayney would be late. Instead she walked straight to the front counter and weighed up the options. A tall Americano would sober her up and help ensure she didn't do, or say, anything irrational; but the Christmas Toffee Nut Latte, described as a rich buttery flavour of sweet toffee, combined with the warmth of toasted nuts, was screaming out at her from the overcrowded chalk board.

Opting for the inappropriate choice, Pippa clutched her tall red mug of frothy whipped cream and navigated through the clusters of tables and chairs to a tall bench seat by the window. She deliberately avoided one of the cosy, more private booths, opting for a spot in full view of the other customers, where she would have to remain calm and level headed. She placed the fragrant mug of nutty cream onto the table top and pulled herself up onto the tall stool, suddenly aware of just how squiffy she was. Andi had poured them both a further three Pimms which they had consumed, amongst quiet giggles, as Zara actually slept on the brown leather recliner. Pippa was about to ponder the dynamics of her boss's marriage when she felt an apprehensive tap on the shoulder.

"Pippa, hi. How are you?" The voice was timid. "Thanks for meeting me."

Pippa turned to see the redhead stood behind her. "Oh Jayney, lose that silly voice."

The voice disappeared. "You're still pissed? Ten months on and you're still pissed?"

"Of course I'm still pissed. I'll always be pissed." She looked into the defiant eyes. "But you said it was really, really important. In fact, your message concerned me so much that I left what was a very pleasant evening with a very pleasant woman."

"So you've got someone new then?"

"Maybe," replied Pippa with a nonchalant shrug of the shoulder.

Jayney shifted her weight from side to side. "Oh, right. Well I still want to talk to you. What did you think of the vote today?"

Pippa frowned. "You haven't called me here to talk about a vote! Get yourself a drink, sit down and tell me what you really want." She used her forefinger to scoop a heap of nut sprinkled cream, into her mouth. "This latte's lovely."

"Fine, but can we sit somewhere more private?"

Pippa shook her mass of brown curls. "This is fine."

"No, I'll get a coffee and meet you in that booth at the back."

Pippa watched as her gorgeous ex-girlfriend strolled to the front counter, cursing her own inability to hold her ground as she slid from the tall chair and dutifully carried her mug to the booth at the back. She settled into the much comfier seat and couldn't help but admire Jayney's slender figure and pert behind, suddenly overcome by a vision of remembrance, made worse by the hungry pang of a ten month celibacy. Jayney turned around, so Pippa dropped her gaze, missing the exaggerated hip swing that was making its way back to the booth.

Jayney placed her frothy mug on the table and smiled. "Yours looked so appealing that I thought I'd give it a go."

Pippa frowned, daring to look up once again. "I thought you only drank black coffee?"

"I've changed."

"Oh right. Is this how it starts?"

Jayney pulled her sleek red hair behind her ears and slid into the booth. "I have."

"Is that what this is then? Ten months on and it didn't work out with lover girl, so you've come back to try your luck?"

Jayney picked up her mug and tried to sip some of the sweet latte, instantly overwhelmed by the whipped cream. She picked up a napkin and wiped her nose. "I knew I should have gone for the coffee."

"That'll teach you to try and impress me," laughed Pippa, using her finger to sweep around the rim of her own mug for the last bit of froth. She lifted her latte and drank with ease.

"I'm not here to impress you," said Jayney, trying to blow some of her cream to the side of her mug. "I just wanted to catch up."

"Why today? Why now?"

Jayney gave up on her drink and looked across the table. "I saw something today that made me realise what a fool I've been."

"What did you see?"

"It doesn't matter. What matters is that it made me realise how badly I treated you and I just wanted to make amends."

Pippa folded her arms. "You saw your girlfriend with someone else?"

"I haven't got a girlfriend."

"So who did you leave me for then?"

Jayney sighed. "A woman, who I now realise I meant nothing to."

"Oh, so you've asked me here to wallow with you in our loss of lovers?"

"No! This is coming out wrong." Jayney paused. "I just wanted to catch up. It's been so long. How's your auntie?"

"Dead," said Pippa, lifting her mug and draining the last of her drink.

****

Zara woke herself with a loud snort, visibly twitching in the brown leather recliner, shaking her head from left to right in an attempt to orientate herself and figure out if anyone had heard.

Andi was sitting in the far corner of the lounge under the soft glow of an overhead lampshade. She quietly lifted her head from her reading and whispered. "You were sleeping."

Zara buzzed herself back into the seated position and wiped the corner of her mouth with the back of her hand. "No I wasn't. Just dozing. Where's Pippa?"

"She left a while ago."

"Good, she was annoying me."

Andi returned her eyes to her pamphlet. "Stop being irritable. There's no one here to impress anymore."

Zara stretched her arms up and yawned, feeling a blanket slide to the floor. She peered over the side of her chair. "What's that?"

Andi kept her eyes on her work. "I covered you."

"I'm not eighty! I hope you didn't do it while Pippa was here."

Andi circled an important quote and continued reading. "Of course not. It wouldn't have mattered though."

Zara rolled her eyes. "Yes it would. I think she likes me."

"I'm sure she does," said Andi without looking up.

****

"Dead?"

Pippa nodded. "A week after you dumped me."

Jayney tucked her long red hair firmly behind her ears. "Make me feel worse why don't you?" She shook her head. "I'm so sorry, Pippa. You should have called."

"Yeah right. '*Hello, you've just ended our year long relationship, having spent half of that year cheating on me with some woman at work, not that it mattered because you were planning on ending it anyway as I was far too boring, with no work or housing prospects ... but please come and comfort me, my great auntie, who I've spent the last year of my life nursing, is dead.*' I don't think so, do you?"

Jayney continued to look aghast. "But Gee-Gee, she meant so much to you."

Pippa looked away. "We were expecting it."

"It's still a shock though."

Pippa shrugged.

Jayney reached out across the table and took Pippa's hand. "What you did for her was incredible."

"I didn't have a job. I got free board and lodgings." Pippa pulled her hand away and chose to sit on it instead. "It was no big deal."

"Stop it. You wouldn't have let anyone else look after her and you know it."

Pippa used her other hand to prop up her cheek. "She didn't quite know what was going on at the end, bless her."

"Did Gee-Gee ever know what was going on?"

Pippa laughed. "Remember that time when you arrived and she thought you were that '*nice actress off the telly*.' I never did figure out who she meant."

"Then there was that time I came over and she thought I was there to curl her hair."

"Which you did, and which I loved you for." Pippa shook her head. "It's fine. It was expected. Dad's okay, and so is Mum. In fact, I probably learnt more in that one year than I've ever done."

Jayney tried once again to sip her latte, a feat made slightly easier by the sinking of the cream. "The old are wise, as they say."

"No, I meant looking after myself and someone else." She paused. "I think it proved a point to my parents."

"You're their youngest daughter, they're meant to mollycoddle."

Pippa laughed. "They still send up a weekly food hamper."

"From Devon?"

"Yes, they're still there, still loving retirement."

Jayney swallowed and tried not to grimace at the sweetness of the drink. "That figures! So where are you now?"

"Still in West Hamstead."

"In Gee-Gee's house?"

Pippa nodded. "It's my house now. She left it to me."

"You're joking?" Jayney failed to hide her surprise. "It must be worth a fortune!"

Pippa shrugged. "Maybe. I'm just pleased she wanted me to have it."

"And your family? Were they okay with that?"

"Of course." Pippa smiled to herself. "Old Gee-Gee made sure everyone got a fair share. She even managed to put aside half of her old age pension every week for the past twenty five years."

"And where did that go?"

"To the cats."

Jayney laughed. "No need to worry about work then."

"I've actually got a job and have been very happily employed for the past nine months."

Jayney frowned. She had only ever known Pippa as a glorified carer, with no real money or possessions to her name. "Doing what?"

"Making use of my degree in *Politics and International Relations.*"

"Oh wow, Pippa. That's brilliant." She raised her eyebrows. "You're doing really well for yourself then."

Pippa shrugged. "Well I'm actually only a PA, but it's for someone who's incredibly political and focused on improving international LGBT relations."

Jayney took a sip of her latte. "Who's that then?"

Pippa's smile was wide and her dimple was deep. "Andi Armstrong."

Jayney coughed up some froth and reached for a napkin, hastily wiping the drips from her chin. "Andi Armstrong?"

Pippa nodded with pride. "She's the most inspirational awe inspiring woman I think I've ever met."

Jayney pushed her mug to the side and stared at her ex-girlfriend in disbelief. "You work for Andi, *frigging,* Armstrong?!"

****

"Andi, *fucking*, Armstrong!" shouted Zara, squeezing her legs together and intensifying the final few pulses of her orgasm. It was her forth of the day and second of the night. "You're incredible!"

Andi slowly emerged from under the covers and placed a gentle kiss on her wife's rosy cheek. "My pleasure."

Zara caught her breath and wrapped an arm around Andi's waist, pulling her close. "No, you really are incredible."

Andi rested her head on Zara's shoulder, nuzzling gently into her neck. "And so are you."

"No I'm not. I'm a miserable old trout who falls asleep in the middle of the afternoon while you have a giggle with your young, fit and very hot PA."

Andi smiled. "You work hard. It's fine." She paused. "Pippa's my PA and you're my wife … And anyway, I like watching you sleep."

Zara started to stroke the short thick tufts of Andi's blonde hair. "Really?"

Andi nodded. "It reminds me that you're all mine."

"I am."

"Forever and a day?" asked Andi, lifting her head and looking at her wife with sincerity.

"Forever and a day," whispered Zara, planting a gentle kiss on the soft, smiling lips.

CHAPTER TWELVE

Pippa burst into Andi's office, out of breath and slightly dishevelled. "I'm so sorry I'm late, Andi!"

Andi looked up at the large clock. It was still only ten to nine. "It's fine. You don't officially start work until nine."

Pippa tried to tame her wild hair. "Why do we all get in at eight then? And I'm sure Elizabeth gets in at seven thirty!"

Andi smiled and patted the chair. "Sit down. I'll make you a coffee. You're not late."

"I'm late for me, so I apologise." Pippa took a seat on the comfy chair next to Andi's. "I look like I've had my fingers in the sockets, don't I?"

Andi burst out laughing. She had, in fact, noticed Pippa's slightly wilder than usual bouncy brown hair. "I don't know about fingers in the sockets, but you do look more, '*on the go*,' as they say!"

"Do they say that?"

"No, possibly not," smiled Andi. "So what were you doing putting your fingers in the sockets?"

Pippa laughed, resting her head back onto the firm fabric and stretching out her neck. "My ex-girlfriend got in touch."

Andi had started to rise from her seat to make the coffees, but quickly sat back down again. "Ooo, Pippa. You've never spoken about an ex."

Pippa grinned, turning her body towards her boss. "I have had *some* experience with women, Andi."

"No, no, I wasn't suggesting-"

"I'm teasing! It's fine. We were together for about a year and we split up just before I got this job."

"Oh, I'm sorry."

Pippa smiled. "Don't be. She was a cheat."

Andi glanced at the clock; there was always time for a quick gossip. "You finished it?"

"No, she did. I had no idea." Pippa shrugged. "She had an affair with someone at work."

Andi rose once again and headed towards the coffee machine. "I just don't understand people's inability to stay faithful. Did you know the person she had an affair with?"

Pippa continued to stretch her neck. "No, Jayney was a temp, always moving around and I never really got to know any of her work colleagues." She shrugged. "It's no big deal. It was never particularly serious with us."

Andi added an extra sugar to Pippa's coffee. She looked like she needed it. "Together for a year and it's not serious?"

Pippa nodded. "If lesbians have been together for more than six months and they're not living under the same roof, then no, it's not serious."

Andi laughed, passing the steaming mug to Pippa and sitting back down with her own. "Why did she get in touch?" She paused. "I hope you don't mind me prying, but I've often wondered why you're not with someone."

Pippa looked at her boss. "Have you? I didn't know that."

Andi's warm amber eyes were smiling. "Yes, I have actually."

Pippa felt her cheeks redden, but managed to maintain the eye contact. "I'm my own worst enemy. I want perfection."

Andi blew some of the steam from her coffee. "No one's perfect."

"Some are pretty close."

Andi looked back up, aware of Pippa's embarrassment, but unsure of its cause. "Does she want you back?"

Pippa shook her mass of brown hair. "No. I think she wanted to ease her own conscience. I think she got a taste of her own medicine and wanted to apologise."

"And did she?"

Pippa thought back to the previous evening that had begun in the coffee shop and ended in a shot bar at three am. She sat up in her seat. "You know what? I don't actually think she did."

Andi smiled. "So what were you doing that gave you the finger in the socket hair?"

Pippa laughed. "Not what you think."

Andi rolled her eyes. "Hmmm."

Pippa frowned. "No, I promise!"

"It's fine, you don't have to tell me what you get up to."

Pippa angled her body closer to Andi's. "No, I promise. She was actually far more interested in you."

Andi frowned. "In me?"

"Yes. As soon as she heard that I worked for you she came to life. One of the companies she used to work for was G-Sterling. Her claim to fame used to be that she'd once worked for Andi Armstrong's wife, but now, since last night, she says her claim to fame's going to be that she's slept with a woman who now works for the actual Andi Armstrong!"

Andi batted away the compliment. "Aren't people silly."

"Anyway, she wanted to know all about you, asking me to carry on to a bar and quizzing me non-stop." Pippa ruffled her hair. "Hence the, *on the go*, look! I drank far too much and woke up far too late." She smiled. "I bet you get it all the time, but she was infatuated with you, your work, our relationship."

"Our relationship?"

"You know, how we get on. Whether we spend time together outside of work." Pippa smiled. "I think you improve my date-ability!"

"Oh Pippa, she sounds like a rogue."

"Ha! A rogue. She probably is. But she's a gorgeous red-headed rogue."

"Are you seeing her again?"

Pippa leaned forwards in her chair and tapped her teeth together. "Ah! I hate admitting this, but I did, in the haze of an alcohol fuelled evening, consider asking her to be my plus one to your party on Saturday."

"Really?"

Pippa shrugged. "What's worse? Coming alone, or coming with a cheating ex?"

Andi placed her mug back on the coffee table. "You'll be fine. And anyway, I'll need someone to talk to."

"It's your thirtieth! You'll be swamped with people."

Andi laughed. "Exactly. I hate all of the fuss. Zara knows I do, but every year she insists on organising a big party and inviting all and sundry, for her to then spend the whole evening schmoozing the celebs."

"They'll be celebs there?"

Andi brushed off the interest. "Well, the ones who like a good photo op will be there."

"It's your thirtieth; they'll be coming to celebrate your birthday with you."

Andi raised her eyebrows. "I've been in this game a lot longer than you. I know how it works. Yes, Andi Armstrong from Proud Unity is ever so popular, and big faces will show up to celebrate. But not many of them actually know Andi from Wimbledon. The girl with the fang teeth and stick legs."

Pippa tried not to laugh.

Andi tapped her incisors. "I got my teeth fixed, and now, approaching thirty, I'm pretty proud of my stick legs."

Pippa let out a small laugh. "I'm sorry. I can't imagine you with fangs."

Andi smiled with beautifully straight teeth. "I'm being serious. With Stella drowning in new motherhood, you're fast becoming my closest friend."

Pippa tried desperately hard not to blush and in consequence felt her cheeks burst into immediate colour. The past nine months had indeed seen them spending more time together both in and out of work, but Pippa had never dared entertain the notion that Andi Armstrong might actually regard her as a close friend. "Really? I'm touched." She grinned. "But I only call someone a friend if they've held my hair back on a night out."

Andi pulled a sicky face. "Eugh. Okay. That's our plan for Saturday night then!"

"You're on!" laughed Pippa, lifting her mug with renewed energy and sipping her coffee. "So, what's first on the agenda this morning then, boss?"

"Well either I stick my fingers in the sockets or you brush your hair. We've got photos at ten and we need to look harmonious."

Pippa laughed and pointed at the skirting board. "Andi Fang Sticks ... the plug socket's over there."

****

"Come," shouted Zara impatiently. She looked up from her desk on the top floor of the huge G-Sterling building. "Oh, it's you," she said with disappointment. "You don't have an appointment."

Melody Fickler stepped into the office and shut the weighty door. "Anne said you weren't to be disturbed."

"So you chose to ride the lift up here and disturb me." Zara pulled her poker straight hair over her left shoulder and narrowed her eyes. "This had better be work related."

Melody approached the wide desk and shrugged her shoulders, glancing at the chairs in the corner and admiring the London skyline that was perfectly framed by the large office window.

"Don't even think about sitting down. It's barely ten a.m. You of all people know how important the morning trading is." Zara looked at her sparkling Cartier watch. "Really Melody, what is it?"

"Can we talk about us?"

Zara made a flicking gesture with her long fingers. "Oh, stop it! You sound about twelve."

Melody stuck out her chest and tried a different tack. "Fine. Let's meet after work ... Let off some steam."

Zara looked her employee up and down, lifted her nose and scrunched her mouth in bitterness. "Been there. Done that. Move along now, please."

Melody flared up with embarrassment and turned to leave the office, pausing at the door and flicking her head over her shoulders. She spoke with force, "Fine. But it'll be your loss in the end."

"I never lose," said Zara shaking her head. "Seriously Melody, you need to learn some office etiquette. You're showing yourself up. We're all in high profile positions. We all work in this stressful environment. A little light relief here and there is to be expected." She scowled. "But acting like a silly school girl is not."

Melody rolled her eyes. "Has anyone ever stood up to you?"

Zara raised an eyebrow. "No one's been that stupid, and I don't advise you try it."

Melody shrugged and pulled open the door. "I like trying new things."

Zara watched her employee strut out into the corridor and was about to yell a final warning, but the heavy office door swung closed too quickly, leaving her cursing under her own breath instead.

****

The funky female photographer stepped away from the camera and surveyed the background, consisting of Andi's desk, a flow chart on a flip board, and a newly erected Proud Unity banner. "I'll need you ladies closer together." She placed her hand on her hip, chinking the mass of bangles on her wrist, and tilting her head. "Closer. Yep, closer still." She smiled. "It has to be intimate."

Andi and Pippa shuffled sideways, both stopping at the touch of their shoulders. Pippa kept her eyes on the female photographer but whispered under her breath. "Why does it have to be intimate?"

"She means natural," smiled Andi.

"Oh," nodded Pippa.

The photographer returned to the camera, bending into the lens. "Andi, turn to the side. You're instructing, you're empowering, you're divulging." She looked back up at Pippa. "PA, you're absorbing, you're grasping, you're enthralled."

Pippa turned to face Andi, who was literally inches away. She whispered through closed teeth. "Do we ever stand this close when I'm absorbing?"

Andi stifled a laugh. "Do I ever enthral?"

"No, but I'm close enough to grasp."

Andi and Pippa laughed just as the photographer started to click.

"Perfect, perfect. A couple more." The flashes continued, as did the natural flushing of their cheeks.

"Brilliant." The funky photographer stepped backwards and unlocked the camera from its tripod, lifting it to her eye line and scanning the pictures on the small screen. "Got it. That was perfect. So natural. So intimate. So empowering."

Andi immediately stepped backwards and leaned against her desk. It suddenly felt rather hot in the office. She ran her fingers through her short blonde hair and looked at the clock. "Are these for the brochure or the website?"

The photographer placed her camera back into the padded bag that was resting on the comfy chairs. She picked up the briefing sheet and scanned the information quickly. "The ones in here were for ... let me see ... the *Out Magazine* promo."

Pippa looked over her shoulder at her boss and pulled a face. "Why did I need to be in them?"

The female photographer answered the question. "It's their piece on Andi Armstrong, the empowerer. I wanted to show her divulging and enthusing, with an aura of magnetism."

Pippa laughed. "And me stood there like a doughnut showed that, did it?"

The photographer signalled them over, once again jangling the array of bangles on her wrist. "Yes, and you were far from doughnut-like." She lifted the camera back out of its bag and pressed the replay button. "Look."

Andi and Pippa made their way over to the camera and tilted their heads together at the outstretched screen. Snapshots of an intense, but pleasurable connection trailed across the display. The photographer pressed the pause button. "This is my favourite." She passed the camera to Andi. "Look at the way she's listening to you, absorbing your comment and lighting up in response."

Andi grinned teasingly. "Oh she is, isn't she!"

Pippa angled her head to get a closer look. "You just made me laugh, that's all."

The photographer took the camera back. "She had an effect on you. That's what the article's about. There's a real chemistry between you."

Andi didn't want to see Pippa's reaction, so she ignored the observation and turned to the photographer instead. "I thought all the shots were for the website?"

The photographer zipped up the camera bag and began to fold down her tripod. "No, a whole host of places. You've got them going off here there and everywhere. I just followed the briefs."

"All done though?" asked Andi, hopeful for a reprieve of the staged scenarios.

"Yes, you two are done. I'm off to take photos of the rest of the staff now." She stretched out her hand. "It's been a pleasure to meet you, Andi, and I do hope Proud Unity use me again."

"Of course." Andi shook the hand with warmth. "Great meeting you too." Andi had in fact lost count of the number of photographers used by Proud Unity. To her they all seemed much of a muchness, but to Maggie in Media, the use of a range of well-known photographers was essential to maintain the image and status of the organisation as a current and relevant force to be reckoned with. Or so she had been told. Andi smiled to herself, making a mental note to Google the name of this latest one.

Pippa waited for the photographer to collect her belongings and leave the room, before turning to Andi and smiling. "I think she's right. You do have an effect on me."

Andi walked to the drinks machine and reached for a mug. She placed it under the two silver spouts. "Really?"

"Yes, you make me happy."

Andi fumbled with the buttons and adjusted the position of the mug.

Pippa walked up to her side, forcing Andi to turn back around and give her her full attention. "You do. You make me happy. And this job makes me happy. My whole life at the moment is brilliant and I just wanted to say thank you for employing me, Andi."

Andi smiled. "Oh Pippa, that's such a sweet thing to say."

"I mean it. You're a brilliant boss to work for and that photo does capture a level of awe in my eyes." She grinned. "I'll have to work on disguising my feelings from now on though!"

"There's nothing wrong with a bit of mutual admiration," said Andi with a nod.

"It's my hair. I know. You admire my hair and its bouncy fabulousness."

Andi lifted her cup. "I admire your ability to make me so nervous that I end up asking this machine for an oxtail soup."

Pippa sniffed the steam rising from Andi's mug and laughed. "I don't know what I'm more impressed with. The fact that I can make you nervous, or the fact that this machine does oxtail soup."

"Okay, maybe not nervous, just embarrassed," smiled Andi, daring to sip the hot drink and immediately wincing at the taste. "You're so open and honest. I would never dare tell Janet that she makes me happy."

Pippa tilted her mass of brown hair. "Janet makes you happy? I thought Elizabeth was more your type?"

Andi slapped her playfully on the arm. "Stop it! You know what I mean. Your openness makes me nervous. I never know what you're going to say."

Pippa grinned. "This is me on my best behaviour! I've been holding it all in for nine months! You wait until Saturday night when I'm allowed to let loose!"

Andi placed the mug of soup back on the counter and folded her arms. "Oh no! Prepare me! What can I expect?"

Pippa stepped in closer. "Have I ever told you I like your eyes?"

"Right, I get it, you're one of those!" Andi laughed. "Come on, I'm sure there must be some work for us to do."

Pippa lifted her hand. "And your hair. It's so blonde and funky and it frames your face and your beautiful little features perfectly."

Andi rolled her eyes and started to walk back towards her desk, but Pippa trotted teasingly behind her.

"Not to mention that figure. You're so dainty, yet in proportion, and very, very se-"

The office door crashed open. "LADIES!!! WE HAVE A SITUATION!"

Andi jumped and Pippa immediately dropped her loyal puppy impersonation.

Janet was standing in the doorway with her hands on her hips. "WE'RE ON THE SIX SHOW!" She flustered into the office, followed quickly by Elizabeth and her infamous brown handbag, and took a seat on the comfy chairs. "Well, you are Andi. That gives us about three hours to prepare. They want us there at four thirty." Janet looked up over the rims of her rectangular glasses. "Well, they want *you* there at four thirty, Andi."

Andi joined Janet and Elizabeth at the chairs, sitting down and paying full attention. "Today?"

Janet nodded. "Yes. The Six Show want us to discuss our take on the bishop thing." She pushed her drooping glasses higher onto her nose. "Well, they want your take, Andi."

Pippa sat down opposite them. "Okay, Andi's up front, but it'll be a team effort. Right, let's start. Have they given us any questions?"

Elizabeth shook her head as another wiry orange hair sprang free from her bun. "It's an audience and phone in segment. Andi will be on a panel, along with one of the bishops who is anti-women-bishops."

"Which one?" asked Andi.

Janet cut in. "They don't know yet. But whoever they get will certainly be anti-gay marriage too. And that's definitely the route the segment will take."

Andi lifted a pen and pad of paper from the centre of the coffee table. "If only they were all as sensible as the Bishop of Buckingham."

"Yes, let's quote him," said Pippa reaching across the table for the laptop. "He's the only one who seems to talk any sense." She tapped in a quick Google search. "Here we go." She tilted the laptop so Andi, Janet and Elizabeth could see the screen. "Look, he's just recorded an Out4Marriage video saying that the Church of England risks squandering a precious opportunity to *get real* by backing same-sex marriage."

Andi started to make notes on her pad. "That's just it. The Church does need to get real. Let's focus on the bishop question first. Can you find me a list of those high up in the clergy who were against allowing female bishops and a few of the ridiculous things they've said about it?"

Pippa tapped the keyboard quickly. "I'll also get you a list of the countries who already allow female bishops." She clicked the mouse and scrolled down the screen. "We've got Australia, New Zealand, Canada, Cuba, obviously the US." She paused and shook her head. "Wow. They've even got a female Bishop of Swaziland in South Africa."

Andi continued to scribble. "Exactly. I mean, what the bloody hell is our country playing at? We're meant to be a world leader. A trend setter. A pinnacle for equality and democracy."

Janet stood up and made her way towards the small clothes closet in the corner of Andi's office. "They'll say it was a democratic vote within their own institution." She pulled at the small round handles and nodded at the contents of the cupboard. "Great. Your Hobbs Marion jacket and skirt are back from the dry cleaners. You always look the business in these."

Pippa looked up and nodded. "I take pride in every part of my job description, even the dry cleaning pick-ups."

Andi smiled. "Thank you."

Janet reached for a suit bag, hanging the camel coloured jacket and skirt inside, and adding Andi's favourite tight-fit black polo neck to a hanger. She bent down and lifted up Andi's size four black suede ankle boots and placed them in a bag along with a new pair of ten denier tan-coloured tights. Janet walked to the office door and hung the bags on the back of the handle. "We'll get a car to take you. Pippa, you can help her change when you get there."

"Now that's a part of my job description I have yet to relish," smiled Pippa with a fully exposed cheek dimple.

Andi noticed the twinkle in Pippa's eye and raised her eyebrows. "The teasing stops now. This is business. Janet, sit down, please." She ripped a piece of paper from her pad and placed it on the coffee table, pushing it in Janet's direction. "I need these facts from you please." She then did the same for Elizabeth and Pippa. "And these from you two, please." She took a deep breath. "I'm going to make a list of potential questions and possible answers. We could really get the upper hand if today goes well. I just need to be prepared."

"When are you not?" said Janet, Pippa and Elizabeth, almost in unison.

CHAPTER THIRTEEN

Andi had enjoyed the afternoon thrill of last minute preparations. It was always the same when it came to unplanned, live, appearances. There was a feeling of nervous apprehension at the questions that could be asked, and a sense of anxiety at the host and audience hostility levels. But today, both had seemed to add to her excitement. Possibly because she knew the argument to disallow female bishops was so weak, and, in fact, supported by so few. The Six Show was unlikely to be biased one way or the other and Andi had met the hosts at various other formal occasions. They were a male and female team who liked to play good cop bad cop; deliberately being provocative for the sake of good ratings. But still, she felt positive. Janet, Pippa, and Elizabeth had quizzed her over and over from the mundane to the ridiculous. She felt prepared.

Around ninety percent of Andi's appearances for Proud Unity were planned. They would receive a list of possible questions that would be asked and a rough guide about how the interview would flow. This evening's show, however, which included questions from the audience and a telephone call in, meant that anything could happen. Andi closed her dressing room door, pleased to be out of hair and make-up. The run-through with the hosts, Rita and Mike, had been easy enough and the bishop did indeed look, and sound, like he had been dragged out of the dark ages.

Andi settled on the small seat in the private dressing room and turned to Pippa. "Oh bugger, I've got the black polo neck. I should have put it on before I let them slap all of this foundation on me!"

"Are they trying to make you look more tough with that spike?"

Andi twisted in her seat and looked at herself in the small mirror above the dressing table. She laughed. "I've got a hairbrush in my bag." She started to flatten her hair with her fingers. "Any chance you could reach it out?"

Pippa crouched down next to Andi's red work bag and started to finger through its contents. She lifted a number of files and flicked away the stray tampons, lip balms and body sprays until she felt the soft bristles of Andi's hairbrush. She lifted it out, noticing a small photo-booth picture stuck to its handle. She pulled it off and wiped it clean, handing the hairbrush to Andi and studying the picture. "How old is this? You two look so young."

Andi glanced over her shoulder, immediately recognising the photo. "It was from our first date. I don't know why, but I transfer it from bag to bag each time I get a new one."

"I do that with my picture of Gee-Gee."

"Your auntie?"

Pippa smiled. "Yes. But she's not half as good looking as you two. Zara looks so different."

Andi used the brush to gently coax her hair back into its usual position. "That's Zara pre-work."

Pippa opened her mouth in shock. "No way! You'll be telling me that nose isn't hers next!"

"It's not. She wanted to have a slight ski jump effect. Look closely, you can see her original nose was hooked."

Pippa laughed. "Andi Armstrong! What's going on? Giving away the family secrets! Next you'll be telling me the pair of you row like the rest of us!"

Andi spun around on her swivel chair, displaying her perfectly styled hair. "Those are the two biggest lies that people tell."

"What are?"

Andi stuck out two fingers, grabbing one at a time. "One, when people say their children sleep through the night, and two when people say they don't argue."

Pippa laughed. "And you have lots of friends with children, do you?"

"Yes, and they're all *Moasters*."

"Moasters?"

Andi stood up and started to unzip her suit bag. "Yes, Moasters. They spend the whole time moaning about their partners and boasting about their children. Claiming they sleep through the night and eat all of their vegetables. They're Moasters."

Pippa laughed. "I hope I'm a Moaster one day."

"Really?"

"Oh yeah, I love children. I just need to find myself a partner to moan about!"

Andi laughed. "Be careful what you wish for." She nodded towards the black polo neck jumper that was folded over the back of the chair. "You're going to have to help me with that, sorry."

"Okay," said Pippa, disappointed that her planned smart remark was halted by a loud knock on the door.

The producer popped his head into the small but adequate dressing room. "If you could be up on stage in ten minutes, Andi, that would be great."

"No problem," smiled Andi feeling a sudden rush of adrenaline. She waited for the door to close and unbuttoned her white work blouse, passing it to Pippa who fastened it onto one of the spare hangers and placed it back inside the suit carrier. Andi unbuttoned her black pencil skirt and slid it to the floor, stepping over it and lifting it to her PA. "I think these tights will be fine." She looked over her shoulder and kicked out her legs at the back. "I haven't got any ladders, have I?"

Pippa swallowed involuntarily. Andi was twisting and turning in front of her in just a pair of see-thru tan tights and a black g-string and bra set. "Bend over, I think you've got one there." Pippa laughed as her cheeks flushed. "Sorry, no I didn't mean it like that. I meant," she paused, "look, I think you've got one there." Pippa pointed to a tiny hole just above the back of Andi's right knee.

"Oh bugger. Okay, don't worry. I'll take them off." Andi sat back down on her swivel chair and started to roll down the tights, pulling them over her small feet and dropping them into the metal bin underneath her dressing table. She turned back to Pippa and took the outstretched box of ten denier. "Are you warm? It's warm in here, isn't it?"

Pippa laughed. "Why? Are my cheeks red?"

Andi looked up at Pippa's flushed appearance. "You're not embarrassed are you? I'm so sorry, we've never done this before have we? Stella used to have to hoist me into some of my outfits. I should have checked if you were comfortable with this."

Pippa started to dust off the black polo neck jumper that she had lifted up in preparation for Andi. "Of course I'm fine! Don't be silly. It's not like I've not seen a super fit, scantily clad body before." She coughed. "Admittedly it's been a while."

Andi stood up and pulled the tights neatly around her waist. "I'm nearly thirty. There's nothing to look at here. We need to fix you up with someone. My friend Ruth will be there on Saturday. She's lovely. I'll introduce you."

Pippa continued to flatten the black jumper. "No, no it's fi-" She stopped as her chunky ring snagged a piece of the fabric. She quickly glanced up at Andi who was too busy pulling on her skirt to notice. Pippa quickly unattached the piece of black cotton and hung the jumper on the back of Andi's chair. "It's fine. I'll probably bring Jayney."

"Don't you dare," said Andi, reaching for the jumper and working her arms into the sleeves.

Pippa couldn't help but notice the way Andi's defined stomach muscles rippled with the action. "Do you need a hand getting it over your head?"

"Please," said Andi, glancing at the clock above the door.

Pippa stepped forwards and took hold of the neck of the jumper, easing it open with two hands. She made the hole as wide as possible before lifting it above Andi's head. "Okay, it's coming over."

Andi kept her head still as Pippa eased on the jumper. Andi pulled it into position and looked at her PA. "Very delicately done. Thank you."

"No problem," smiled Pippa, stepping backwards and feeling herself flush once again.

Andi reached for the suit jacket and slid it over her shoulders, turning around to check herself in the mirror. "All done. Perfect, thank you." She paused and leaned in closer. "Hang on, there's a loose thread." Andi looked down at her chest and wrapped the piece of black cotton around her index finger. She gave a sharp tug, aghast at the sudden hole that appeared just above her cleavage. "Bugger, bugger, bugger! Look what I've done!" She checked the clock once again and eyed the hole in the mirror. "Is it noticeable?"

Pippa couldn't lie. "Yes. You can see your skin." She reached into the suit bag for Andi's old shirt. "You'll have to wear this white one."

"Not with this camel suit, I'll look completely washed out. Plus I've got some pen on the pocket." Andi looked at Pippa's black blouse. "Is there *any* chance I can wear yours?" She nodded in earnest. "Please? I'm so sorry."

"My what?"

"Your blouse. It's black. I always wear black with this camel suit. Please, Pippa. I can't go out looking like this."

Pippa looked down at her own black blouse, quickly trying to remember the state of the bra she had chosen to put on this morning. She breathed out, relieved, but slightly embarrassed. It was her new red bravissimo with added uplift. Bought for the upcoming December party season and on its first outing today. It had been such a rush getting ready for work this morning, after her late night with Jayney, that she had grabbed the first piece of lingerie to hand. The boxed red underwear set lying on top of her bedside cabinet was the most convenient. Pippa started to undo the buttons. "I'll expect a pay rise for this."

"Done," smiled Andi, pulling the ruined black polo neck back over her head. No longer did it matter if she got orange foundation on the fabric. She flung it onto the chair behind Pippa and noticed her fumbling with the buttons. Andi glanced at the clock again. "Are the buttons stuck? Let me try." She stood still in front of Pippa and relieved her fingers. "I hate it when they make the button holes too small." She looked up at Pippa, who was literally millimetres away. "But apparently that's the sign of a good shirt." Andi felt the button spring from the hole. "There, done! I'll do the rest."

Pippa threw her head backwards and spoke to the ceiling. "I have to say it! I can't hold it in!" She looked back at her boss. "Andi Armstrong, standing half naked in her bra, unbuttoning my shirt. No other job will *ever* beat this!"

Andi laughed. "Hmmm, Andi Armstrong, unbuttoning your shirt, and revealing a very sexy piece of red lingerie!" Andi stepped backwards and smiled, allowing Pippa to pull the blouse from her arms. "Pippa Rose! Do you always wear such spicy underwear to work?"

Pippa threw the black blouse at her boss and grabbed Andi's white work shirt. "Says you with the sexy black thong!"

Andi laughed, leaning forwards once again. She wrapped an arm around Pippa's shoulder. "Thank you. This means a lot."

Pippa kept her arms by her side, but still felt the sensation of Andi's breasts against her own. She closed her eyes and dropped the white shirt.

Andi pulled away and looked at the clock. "I've only got about a minute. Right. Here goes." She pulled on the black shirt and buttoned it quickly. "It's fine. It fits."

Pippa quickly bent down to retrieve the white work shirt and pushed her arms into the sleeves, struggling even more with these buttons. "It's a bit tight," she grinned, looking down at the gaping holes around her cleavage.

"It's that lacy red maximiser bra that you're wearing," laughed Andi, pulling on her suit jacket and reaching for her shoes.

Pippa fingered her mass of brown curls. "I'm the one who's meant to do the teasing. Stop making me nervous." She grinned. "And anyway, they're all natural."

Andi pulled up the zips on her black ankle boots and smiled. "Pleased to hear it," she said with a wink.

CHAPTER FOURTEEN

Andi glanced at the replay monitor to the left of the stage. Her image filled half of the screen, and Bishop Bob, in his full regalia, filled the other half. Andi was pleased with the way the borrowed black shirt complemented her suit jacket, but noticed that her skirt looked like it had ridden up slightly, so she wiggled discreetly in her seat and pulled it back into position. She swept her blonde fringe across her forehead and did a final cursory scan of the small audience; all still chatting quietly. She took a deep breath, feeling the nerves of anticipation flutter across her chest.

Hosts, Rita and Mike, were standing directly in front of the large studio camera and a runner was offering them a final sip of bottled water. They shooed the young lad away, and continued their in-depth discussion. The popular pairing were constantly subjected to tabloid, *are they aren't they*, speculation, and from Andi's position it looked like they quite possibly were. There was an intensity about their chat and a rolling of eyes from Rita which indicated to Andi a silent scolding, saved for someone more than just a work colleague. Mike shrugged his broad shoulders and turned his back on his co-presenter, signalling for the runner to bring back the drink.

The floor manager took to the stage and addressed the audience. Calling for silence as the countdown began. Andi shifted once more in her seat and looked back down at the monitor. The camera had switched focus and Rita and Mike were now full screen, standing side by side with blazing smiles and eager eyes. Andi laughed to herself. Janet had been right. Rita did indeed look like a well coiffured Princess Di and Mike did seem to resemble a slightly older and chunkier, Enrique Iglesias.

The overhead lights suddenly intensified and Rita's familiar northern voice filled the studio. "Hello, and welcome to the Six Show." She paused as more of the show's introductory jingle played. "On tonight's show we're discussing yesterday's vote by the Church of England which disallowed the ordination female bishops." She paused for the chuntering to subside. "We're going to have an audience discussion and phone in debate."

Mike cut in. "We also have the pleasure of hearing from eighties pop sensation Sonia on her latest venture." He turned to his co-presenter. "Did you know that she's from Skelmersdale in Lancashire like you, Rita?"

Rita maintained her broad smile. "I did actually, Mike, and I also know that *it's better the devil you know.*" She winked.

"One of my favourites!" smiled Mike.

"We can look forward to a sing-a-long then folks!"

"Only if you're dancing!" smiled Mike.

Rita acknowledged the whirring of her producer's hand and glanced back down at her clipboard. "We'll also follow our intrepid reporter, Dusty, on his latest adventure in the great Australian outback."

Both presenters did their trademark salute to the camera and chimed in unison. "*It's the Six Show, folks.*" The grand finale of the show's jingle sounded in the studio as the hosts took their seats on the red sofa opposite Andi and Bishop Bob. Rita stayed seated, but lunged her upper body towards the fast approaching camera, speaking in a serious, newsreader-esque voice. "Yesterday, the Church of England voted against allowing the ordination of female bishops, sparking outcry from all sections of society."

Mike took over in an equally serious tone. "The Church's legislative body, known as the General Synod, made the decision late yesterday afternoon, with the two-thirds majority vote that was needed, falling short by just six votes." He turned to face Bishop Bob and the red light on top of camera two started to flash. "Can I welcome the Bishop of Bognor, Bob Downings."

There was a rapturous burst of applause from a lady sitting on the front row and a muted shuffling from other members of the audience.

Rita pursed her lips and made a frown as if she didn't quite understand her own question. "Bishop, I gather from the televised statement you made this morning, that you're pleased with the outcome of yesterday's vote?"

Bishop Bob nodded solemnly and spoke in a slow voice. "The Bible teaches that men and women are required to play complementary roles within the Church." He paused, bringing his hands together under his chin and closing his eyes.

Rita and Mike shared a nervous glance, they hadn't accounted for impromptu praying. Rita was about to cut in when the monotone voice erupted back into life.

"The apostle Paul says in Timothy, '*I do not permit a woman to teach or to exercise authority over a man.*'"

Rita nodded and opened her mouth to speak, stopped again by an eruption similar to the climatic section of a sermon.

"And it's not just Paul." Bishop Bob was wagging his finger. "The apostle Peter also makes it clear that wives *must* submit to their husbands."

Andi couldn't help herself. "Sorry, but I have to cut in."

Rita nodded, thrilled. "Do, do." She addressed the audience. "This is Andi Armstrong, the CEO of Proud Unity and a prolific campaigner for equal rights."

Andi nodded. "Thank you." She looked at the bishop sitting on the chair next to her own and noticed the red light on top of camera three starting to flash. "I'm terribly sorry, Bishop, but this is 2012, and I hate to inform you, but women are already equal." She paused as the audience started to clap. "Quoting out of date passages from the Bible to illustrate a misogynistic view of a woman's role is simply not acceptable. Nor is the fact that the Church of this country has allowed a few members of its Synod to disrupt its slow, but applaudable, quest for equality." Andi could feel the adrenaline flowing and continued her spiel. She looked at the bishop directly. "What is it that you're so afraid of?"

The bishop's silence only lasted for a split second, but for Andi it seemed prolonged, so she did something completely off the cuff. She jerked her head and shoulders forwards towards the bishop and said: "Boo."

Some in the audience gasped while a few tittered.

It had, in-fact, come out rather more loudly than she had expected, and she had certainly not anticipated the overly dramatic shriek from Bishop Bob.

Mike turned to face the close up camera. "Andi Armstrong has just booed a bishop. Live on the Six Show."

Andi felt herself flush. "I was just trying to illustrate that there's nothing to be afraid of. I wasn't expecting you to jump!"

Bishop Bob continued to fan himself, swallowing profusely and signalling for some water.

The runner bent under the camera and offered the bishop a small bottle of Evian, which he dramatically opened, spinning the lid onto his lap, and gulping with gusto.

Andi didn't know where to look. She glanced from host to host. Both were watching the spectacle, aware of what great ratings this would make. Andi chose to lean across to the bishop and place a hand on his knee. She spoke with sincerity. "I do apologise. That was probably the worst point I have ever made."

The bishop fluttered his eyelids and returned the bottle to the outstretched runner's hand. He nodded solemnly. "It's a good job I'm in the business of forgiveness."

Andi reddened and removed her hand. "Thank you. I was just trying to illustrate that equality is nothing to be afraid of. Women are equal to men, just as homosexuals are equal to heterosexuals. People should not be afraid of people, because underneath it all, we're all exactly the same."

There was a loud applause from the audience, but a lady on the front row was frantically shaking her head. Mike spotted the disagreement and grabbed the foam-headed microphone from the table. "I'd like to take this into the audience, if I may." He stretched the mic out towards the lady. "Hi, what's your name, and what do you think about this debate? Are women equal? Should they be allowed to become bishops?"

The lady spoke with an incredibly high pitch. "Doris. And no, and no." She took the microphone from Mike. "And can somebody please tell Andi Armstrong that she is the most disrespectful woman I have ever seen. Booing a bishop." She narrowed her eyes and stared at Andi. "You will not be allowed to get away with this, young lady. You and your team of *homosexuals* forcing sin and disrepute on the rest of us."

Mike tried to take the microphone, but the lady kept a tight hold.

"It's disgusting. You should be ashamed of yourself. Peddling such filth."

Mike yanked it away with force and stepped back onto the stage. "We do like to offer a rounded view of opinion here on the Six Show, but such comments are not endorsed in any way by the channel." He looked at Andi. "I do apologise."

The lady started to tut, but silenced herself at the threat of the floor manager pointing towards the exit.

Andi swallowed, thrown by the course of events. "People are entitled to their opinions, but there is a difference between opinion and hatred."

The woman couldn't control herself, standing up and shouting in her high pitched voice. "You're a sinner. You're bringing out God's hatred. Don't you realise what he did to Sodom and Gomorrah? The same will happen to you!"

Andi tried to focus on Rita who was creating a distraction by talking into the camera and detailing exactly how the vote had been lost, but everyone was still aware of the kerfuffle in the audience.

The shouting lady was finally escorted by the arm to the exit, and ejected from the studio. Rita carried on. "I want to go to the phone lines. We've got a caller here from London, called Lizzie." She tilted her head to the side, as if actually listening to the phone. "Lizzie, give us your thoughts."

The line was crackly and the voice muffled. "Andi Armstrong needs to shut up before she gets shut up." The line went dead.

"Oh dear, Andi. This isn't your day. I do apologise, that's not what we thought the caller was going to say."

Mike looked into the close-up camera. "Where's Sonia when you need her? We need some of her loving in the studio, folks!"

Rita nodded. "I know." She started to sing. "*Cos you'll never stop me from loving you.*"

Mike looked at his co-presenter. "Shall we go to a break?"

"I think we should," smiled Rita.

"OFF AIR," came the shout as the producer stepped onto the stage. "Andi, I'm so sorry. It's just one of those days." He hesitated. "But I think we should leave it there."

Andi nodded. "Fine," she stammered, getting up from her chair and walking towards the corridor. She paused and made her way back onto the stage, towards the bishop. "I really am sorry about the boo."

The bishop nodded. "No harm done. Not to me anyway."

Andi walked away, shaking her head at her own stupidity. *What a complete and utter disaster.* She pushed open the doors to the green room and the sight of Sonia practicing her latest dance routine failed to produce a smile. Walking along the studio's corridors towards her dressing room, she turned at the sound of running feet.

Pippa raced up to her and threw her arms around her shoulders, enveloping her in a huge hug. "It's okay. Don't worry. It's okay."

Andi clung on for dear life, unaware of how emotional she actually felt. Yes, she had been called names in the past and been accused of things like devil worship and the downfall of the human race; but never on such a public scale. She inhaled Pippa's brown curls, comforted by their familiar smell. "I'm fine."

"No you're not." Pippa ushered her, under her arm, back into the dressing room, quickly pulling her boss back into their comforting hug. "Squeeze as tight as you like."

Andi actually managed to smile. "I am."

"You can squeeze tighter than that!" said Pippa squeezing even harder herself.

Andi started to laugh. "I'm squeezing!"

"Squeeze it out," said Pippa, moulding her body around Andi's. "Feels better, doesn't it."

Andi leaned backwards and looked at Pippa. "It does. You're right." She shrugged. "Was it a complete disaster?"

Pippa grinned. "Far from it. The hashtag #BooABishop is trending! It's trending globally!"

Andi frowned. "You're kidding?"

"I'm not." She broke free from the hug and unlocked her phone, scrolling quickly to the Twitter app. "Look."

Andi stared open mouthed at the YouTube clip of her saying, '*Boo,*' to Bishop Bob and his subsequent shriek.

"If people didn't know who you were before, they certainly will do now!"

Andi exhaled heavily and flopped onto the swivel chair. "I never meant to scare him or show him up. I was expecting him to sit still and shrug, proving my point that women and equality are nothing to be afraid of."

Pippa crouched down next to her. "Andi, stop worrying. This is quite possibly the best bit of PR you've ever given us. You haven't shown him up. You were making a point ... and guess what ... the World Wide Web gets it! They're on your side! You've highlighted our cause and brought massive amounts of traffic to our site in the last ten minutes alone. It's going global, Andi."

Andi shook her head. "It's not exactly the publicity we want, is it?"

"Hey, all publicity's good publicity. You taught me that." Pippa paused and looked up at her boss. "It'll be fine." She took Andi's hand and squeezed it gently. "I promise."

Andi bit her bottom lip. "I'm not sure." She stroked the hand with her thumb in response and managed a smile. "You're always so positive."

"You taught me that too," laughed Pippa, leaning into the chair and whispering into Andi's ear. "You're one incredible lady, Ms Armstrong."

Andi felt the soft brush of Pippa's cheek and smiled. "Thank you." She pulled back and looked into Pippa's kind eyes. "You're not so bad yourself." She paused and broke the connection. "But I'm a Mrs, not a Ms."

CHAPTER FIFTEEN

Zara was in her office at the top of the G-Sterling building, banging her fist on her huge office desk and shouting into her mobile phone. "WHAT THE HELL DID YOU THINK YOU WERE DOING? ... It's on the news! You booing a bishop! ... Yes right now, Andi! ... I'm still at work ... Yes I watched it! ... How did it seem to me? ... It seemed offensive. Juvenile. Cheap. Ill judged ... You looked foolish!" Zara inhaled sharply and tried to lower her tone. "I'm really ashamed of you ... YES I CAN SAY THAT!" She shouted again. "That's my opinion, and it's also the opinion of that lady in the audience and that caller on the phone ... NO I HAVEN'T LOOKED AT THE PISSING TWITTER FEED! ... No. No. You're wrong. It's gone viral because it's so offensive! ... It's on the FUCKING NEWS, ANDI! ... I don't care how they're reporting it. The FACT that they're reporting it, is an issue! ... Sorry, WHAT?? ... Good PR? I bet I know who's been feeding you that bullshit ... Little Miss fucking sunshine! ... Yes, I am pissed off ... Yes, with you! ... SUPPORT? ... You want my SUPPORT? ... Get real, Andi. Seriously, you've made a right tit of yourself this time!" Zara hung up.

****

Andi looked at the screen to see if she had lost connection. Four bars. She always got great connection at her home in St John's Wood. She sighed and pressed the re-dial button, fully aware that Zara had hung up. It rang through to the answer phone. She glanced at the rainbow clock hanging on the wall in her home office. Zara had not allowed the brightly coloured clock in any other room, saying it was cheap and garish, even though she knew it had been a 'coming out' gift from her parents. Andi looked at the rainbow clock with fond memories. 8.00 p.m. If Zara left work now, she may well be back within the hour. Andi swivelled around in her padded chair and looked at the computer screen. It had been non-stop since leaving the studio, with numerous congratulatory calls from Janet and Stella, and a whole host of media enquiries passed on from Pippa. Andi clicked through some more tweets. It wasn't congratulations that she sought, just understanding. The fact that the hashtag #BooABishop was still trending, was a bi-product of a rather dead end debate, cut short by the station in favour of a sing-a-long with Sonia. Andi leaned back in her chair and exhaled heavily. She knew Zara would have an opinion on the matter, but she had no idea it would be this harsh. She checked the clock again. If she could get everything wrapped up within half an hour, she could greet her wife at the door with the offer of a takeaway and night of television.

Andi clicked on her Twitter connections, pleased with the plan. She scrolled through the list of interactions, smiling at the fact that nearly every third one was an alert to show her that she had a new follower. Pippa had been right. It *had* brought them more attention; and lots of it. She stopped at a mention from the host of the popular *Morning Time* programme.

Phil @iPhilScoff Watch @iAndiArmstrong on @iMorningTime tomo at 10am. The hero of the hour. Summing up our dismay with the CofE in 1 word #Boo

She paused and clicked on her email inbox. It was the first she'd heard of it. A new message from Pippa was flashing, informing her of the array of offers they had received and the invites already confirmed. The 10.00 a.m. slot on Morning Time being one of them. The message ended with a smile and a vow to call no later than 9.00 p.m. with the final itinerary for the day. Andi checked the clock and contemplated making the call now. The last thing she needed was an interruption to her planned evening of grovelling. She continued to scroll through the connections. Most tweets seemed positive, most included a link to the YouTube clip, and most saw the funny side of the whole debacle. *Most.* Andi stopped scrolling at a message from Bethy.

Bethy @iWatchThemFall2 U have done it now. No going back. This is the end for you @iAndiArmstrong Trust me. I will make sure of it. #NastyPayback

Andi reached into the top drawer of her desk for her notebook. She scanned down the list of blocked Twitter accounts, uneasy at the familiarity. She tapped her finger on a name. ***Beth @iWatchThemFall.*** She read her hand scrawled note. **Blocked on Feb 28th.** Andi glanced back at the screen. The user had clearly set up another account. She wrote down Bethy's details and pressed the block button. The message disappeared.

****

Zara walked quickly through the two tall pillars of number six Wellington Place. She clipped up the short path in her noisy high heels and glanced over her shoulder. Nothing. She reached into her bag and removed her keys, twisting them quickly in the lock, frustrated that the door wasn't opening fast enough. She paused and scanned the empty street once more, pleased that the only shadows seemed to be the ones coming from the street lamps. She took a deep breath and used her shoulder to push open the door. She turned into the house, jumping at the sight of Andi in her dressing gown. "Shit, you scared me!" Zara thrust a large bunch of flowers forwards. "These are for you." She shrugged her shoulders. "Sorry."

Andi took the expensive bunch of pink and red roses, and stroked one of the soft petals. "You don't have to be sorry. I deserved it. You were right. I made a fool out of myself. The interview was cut short and I didn't have any opportunity to actually discuss the issues."

Zara quickly pushed the door closed and slid over the security chain. "I should have watched the whole thing before I called you. I only saw the section on the news and I freaked out." Zara shook her coat off and walked over to the antique coat stand. "I actually thought you handled the whole incident pretty well." She smiled. "I've just watched it on my laptop. Am I forgiven?"

"And forgotten," smiled Andi.

"Thank fuck you're not one of those women who like to analyse everything." Zara sat down on the chaise longue and flicked off her high heels.

"Life's too short," shrugged Andi, "plus I know how you work."

"Do you now? And how's that then, sweetie?"

"Blow off first and think about it later."

Zara collapsed backwards onto the soft velvet. "I'm a shit wife, aren't I?"

Andi gently placed the flowers on the floor and squashed in next to Zara, straightening her dressing gown as she got comfortable. "You're not a shit wife. You're just a stressed wife, with an incompetent doctor who's not quite got your medication right." She paused. "And I know you think my job's rather silly compared to yours, but it's important to me and I enjoy it." Andi squeezed her wife's thigh. "And I *am* trying to make more time for us." She smiled. "I'd love it if we could just snuggle up tonight with a takeaway and a spot of trashy television."

Zara raised her eyebrows. "Really?"

"Really," nodded Andi, "even though I *am* booked in for three television appearances tomorrow."

Zara sat up. "You had to drop that in, didn't you?"

"I'm just teasing."

Zara swung her legs off the chaise longue. "So you're not on TV tomorrow?"

"Well, I am, but it's fine. There's no prep. They just want to chat to me about today's debate and the work of Pride Unity."

"Ooo, look at you."

"Oh Zara, stop being such a grouch."

Zara stood up. "Why don't you stop-"

The sound of the doorbell stopped them both.

"Is Pippa coming round?" asked Zara, anxiously glancing at the front door.

Andi shook her head and stood up, walking towards the door. "I really think you should go back to the doctor." She peeped through the spy glass and slid the chain free, reaching for the handle and opening the door with a smile. "Hello."

"Hi, Zara asked me around."

Andi pulled the door wide and stepped to the side. "Please excuse the dressing gown, Zara didn't tell me she had a meeting."

Melody pulled the brown file closer into her chest and stepped into the warm house, pleased to be out of the cold. "There's a lot your wife doesn't tell you." She winked. "I hear it's your birthday on Saturday."

Andi closed the front door and pulled her dressing gown even tighter around her chest. "Oh no, please tell me this isn't some last minute bit of surprise planning?"

Melody grinned at Zara who had moved in front of the old fashioned hall radiator. "You might be in for a surprise, or two," she said.

Andi frowned. "Sorry, I thought Zara said you weren't able to come to the party?"

Melody slapped herself on the back of the wrist. "Oops, I keep forgetting what I'm allowed to say and what I'm not. But yes, don't worry, Andi, I'll be there." She smiled at Zara. "Come on then, we need to finalise our plans."

"Right, I'll leave you ladies to it," nodded Andi heading towards her office. "Are you okay with the drinks in the lounge or shall I put the kettle on?"

Zara turned and faced her wife apologetically. "We'll be fine with the whiskey." She paused. "And I promise we won't be long."

"Take as long as you need," said Andi, pleased with the opportunity to see if the final itinerary had come through.

Zara waited for Andi's office door to close, then spun back around to Melody. She grabbed her by the arm and hissed under her breath. "Don't say another word."

Melody allowed herself to be pulled along the corridor and into the plush lounge, quite enjoying the excitement of it all. "You've never shown me this room before."

"My fucking wife doesn't even know you've been to my fucking house before!" Zara continued to speak through gritted teeth. "What the hell are you doing here?" She shut the door and squeezed Melody's arm even harder.

"Stop it. You're hurting me."

Zara flung the arm back to its owner and headed to the spirit cabinet, reaching for the bottle of amber liquid and pouring a hearty amount into a crystal tumbler. "Start talking," she hissed.

Melody straightened herself out and placed the brown file onto the coffee table. "I just popped round to let you know that I can make Saturday."

"I didn't even invite you!" sneered Zara, between glugs.

"You were meant to though, weren't you?" Melody raised an eyebrow. "How naughty of you. What *must* Andi think when none of your *closest* friends from G-Sterling are able to make her party? What excuses did you come up with this time?"

"It was you following me on the way home, wasn't it?"

Melody frowned. "No. I waited at my desk for ages. I told you earlier that I wanted to talk, but Anne said you'd already left. So I got a taxi over."

Zara re-filled her glass. "For fuck's sake, Melody, there's nothing to talk about, and what the fuck is my secretary doing telling you my day to day movements?"

Melody shrugged. "She was the only one left in the office. I didn't think she was allowed to go home until you did?"

"I don't have to explain my whereabouts to you." Zara took the bottle of whiskey and the topped up tumbler to the sofa and sat down, placing both items onto the coffee table next to the brown file. "Fine. Let's sort this out." She looked up at Melody. "What do you want?"

Melody walked slowly around the low table and placed her bottom provocatively on the seat next to Zara's, rubbing her boss's thigh as she sat. "I want you."

"Not happening, sweetie. What's next on your list of demands? Pay rise? New position? Extended holiday?"

Melody was undeterred. She gently rubbed her hand up the inside of Zara's thigh. "I want what we had." She started to caress between Zara's legs. "I'd rather share you than not have you at all."

Zara exhaled heavily. "Stop it."

Melody lifted her hand and rubbed the hard nipples that were visible through Zara's work shirt. "No. At work you always tell us to go with our instincts."

Zara moaned. "We're not at work."

Melody gently bit the side of Zara's neck. "Good, that means I can do this." She squeezed a nipple through the fabric and pressed harder in between Zara's legs.

"Stop it," whispered Zara half-heartedly.

"No. I know you want me."

"No, I just want sex," growled Zara, unable to resist, pressing her lips hard against Melody's and reaching out for her breasts. She kissed her with fire. "Touch me," she gasped.

Melody immediately shoved her hand down the waist of Zara's trousers and plunged her fingers deep inside, drawing out the wetness and rubbing with force.

"Faster," moaned Zara, spreading her legs and enjoying the pressure.

Melody edged herself forwards, angling her arm so she could work more freely. "Like this?"

"Yes, yes, keep going, sweetie, keep going." Zara closed her eyes and threw her head back against the sofa. She tilted her pelvis upwards and moaned at the perfect rhythm of Melody's fingers.

****

Andi glanced at the rainbow clock. She really ought to go in and be social, but this was too good an opportunity to miss. If she could get hold of Pippa now, then there would be no interruption to their evening and no need for Zara to get grouchy. She dialled Pippa's number once again, hoping that she'd pick up.

****

Zara grabbed a cushion and pressed it against her own face, feeling the dryness of its material on her tongue as her mouth opened in a silent scream of pleasure.

Melody felt Zara's hand clasp on top of hers. It was always the same, like she wanted to suck the last drip of pleasure from the pressure.

Zara whispered. "Fuck, sweetie. That was good."

Melody used her other hand to peep under the cushion. "Look at what you'd be missing." She pulled the barrier away and looked into Zara's eyes. "I'm wet if you want me?"

"You know I fucking want you, sweetie, now pull up your skirt."

Melody did as instructed and watched as her boss swivelled off the sofa and onto her knees on the floor. There was a desire in her eyes; a desire mismatched with detachment. Melody had noticed it before. It was like Zara was taken over by a sexual rage of wanting, where nothing else seemed to matter.

"I love it when you wear suspenders." Zara inhaled deeply. "It means I can just pull your thong to one side and take you in my mouth." She gasped and did just that.

Melody felt a surge of adrenaline course through her body. She leaned backwards on the sofa, pushing her bottom towards the edge of the seat. She tilted her head towards the door, watching the handle and praying it moved.

****

Andi counted the rings. "Nine ... and ten." Pippa's phone went to voicemail once again. Andi tapped the red button and placed the mobile back down on her desk. "Bugger." The last thing she needed was a phone call from Pippa interrupting their evening. She checked the rainbow clock. Melody's impromptu arrival had in fact given her a much needed excuse to send on the details of the vicious tweet to the human resources department at Proud Unity. They usually handled things well, assessing the threat, informing the police when necessary, and offering advice when needed. Andi nodded and spun around on her chair. It would be fine, she reasoned, standing up and opening the door to the hall. She pulled her dressing gown tighter into her body, still slightly embarrassed about her level of undress. It was so unlike Zara to invite a work colleague round. She smiled as she reached for the lounge door handle, aware that it *must* be something to do with her party.

****

Melody saw the door handle move and almost came on the spot. The power rushing through her body was like nothing she had ever felt before. She ripped at her shirt, sending a button flying across the coffee table and causing her tits to spill out on display.

****

Andi pressed on the handle, stopping suddenly at the sound of her phone. She pulled the handle gently back into position and scampered back across the hall, skidding into her office. She reached for her mobile and swiped the screen. "Pippa! Phew, I was hoping it would be you. So, what's on the agenda for tomorrow then?"

****

Zara looked up. "What the fuck are you doing?"

Melody quickly pulled her shirt back into position. "Nothing."

"Why the fuck are your tits out?" Zara looked towards the door. "Oh no you don't!" She wiped the corner of her mouth with her thumb and forefinger. "Do yourself back up. *This* is finished."

Melody felt herself redden. "I just got carried away."

Zara stood up and dusted her knees. "Yeah? And so did I." She shook her head. "*Fuck*. What am I doing?"

Melody pulled her shirt back together and did up the top button, but the gape at the chest was still obvious. "I lost my button."

Zara grabbed her tumbler of whiskey and necked its contents. "Well get on your hands and knees and find it then!"

Melody spotted it teetering on the edge of the coffee table. "Got it."

"Good, now get your crappy brown file and get the hell out of here."

Melody lifted the file to her chest and started to walk towards the door, only to have it opened by Andi before she could reach for the handle.

"All finished?" said Andi with a smile.

Melody looked back at Zara. "Zara's satisfied, but I'm not."

Andi laughed. "Oh no. I dread to think what she's planning this year. Did she tell you about last year when she got me a stripper-gram?"

Melody raised an eyebrow. "No! Female I hope?"

Andi walked towards the drinks cabinet. "Yes, and very inappropriate for the type of do that it was!" She paused. "That's right, you and the other girls from G-Sterling were away on a hen do."

Melody glanced at Zara with scolding eyes. "Were we? I can't remember." She turned back to Andi and smiled. "Well, I'll definitely be there on Saturday. Just make sure you're prepared for some surprises."

"Oh crikey!" Andi reached for the bottle of cherry brandy and clocked Zara's empty tumbler, unable to spot any signs that Melody had had a drink. "Can't I get you a drink, Melody?" She started to pour the purple liquid into her glass.

"No, no, I must-" Melody's excuse was interrupted by a ringtone from her blazer pocket.

Santa Baby started to blast out.

Andi cursed herself as a slosh of brandy spilled over the glass.

Melody pulled the phone from her pocket and looked at the display. "Sorry, I need to take this." She nodded in apology and stepped into the hall, closing the lounge door and starting to speak. *"Hello? … Who, sorry? … Oh right, yes I remember you … Yes, I saw you too … You want to meet? … Well isn't that interesting, I'm with her right now ... Fine, if you insist … I'll see you there."*

Melody hung up the phone and dropped it back into her blazer pocket. She lifted the brown file to her chest to cover the gape, and popped her head back into the lounge, speaking with a renewed level of confidence. "Sorry, I need to dash ... I'm sure we can finish this another time, Zara." She smiled. "I'll see myself out."

Andi wiggled her eyes at her wife.

Zara got the message and pulled herself up from the sofa, following Melody into the hall. "I'll see you out."

"And no more plotting," shouted Andi after them both.

"BOO!" shouted Melody in return. "You've *everything* to be scared of." She giggled and shouted once more. "Sorry, Andi, the BOO couldn't be helped!"

Andi tutted and took a swing of cherry brandy, realising that the BOO jokes would just keep on coming. She took another sip, calmed by the sweet hit of alcohol. *What the hell were they planning?* she thought, breaking her self-imposed rule of never second guessing, and always trusting implicitly. She heard the front door bang closed and the soft padding of feet.

"Don't ask!" gasped Zara, re-entering the room.

"I never do," smiled Andi, dropping onto the sofa and lifting her glass. "To Saturday," she cheered, with deliberate dismay.

"To Saturday," nodded Zara, with equal disdain.

CHAPTER SIXTEEN

Melody trotted gleefully down the path from number six Wellington Place. The whole evening had gone better than expected. Not only was she still able to manipulate Zara and her insatiable appetite for sex; now, following the phone call, it appeared there would be a whole other dimension to the game. She checked her watch and pulled her phone from her blazer pocket. She swiped to the last caller and clicked on the green redial button. Melody spoke with adrenaline. "I'll be there in ten minutes."

The walk was quick and easy, and she strode with pace, past the St John's Wood library, right onto St Anne's Terrace and left onto Allitsen Road. It was getting late, but she felt the way that many Londoners did when walking alone at night; safe. The streets were always well lit, and the cosmopolitan nature of the city meant that people were out and about at all hours, commuting, jogging, cycling, or walking their dogs. She passed one such woman walking a little Shih Tzu, noticing the way its long hair was tied in a neat bow with a pretty pink ribbon. She would usually have stopped and fawned over the creature, but tonight she had a more pressing engagement; plus the lady looked slightly strange.

Melody rounded the bend and looked up at the old red bricked building on the corner of St John's Wood high street. Café Rouge, open till eleven, and a perfect location for a meeting like this. She noticed the logo as she pushed through the red door - *Restaurant - Bar - Café* - and knew which area to try first. Just as expected, the lady with the long red hair, who used to temp in the IT department at G-Sterling, was perched on a stool, away from the chatter of diners, nervously nursing a drink. Melody raised her eyebrows in greeting and waltzed confidently to the high topped table near the bar.

Jayney slid off the stool and stretched out her hand in greeting. "Hello, thanks for coming."

Melody spoke firmly. "Pleasure." Jayney might have called the meeting, but she was the one who had the agenda.

"Can I get you a drink?"

Melody looked at the hand that was still outstretched and chose to leave it where it was, instead, she dropped her brown file onto the high topped table and lifted herself onto a stool. "No. I won't be staying long." She raised an eyebrow and reached out her hand, tapping a red painted nail on the side of Jayney's discarded glass. "So, how long have you been spying on me?"

"What?" said Jayney dropping her hand and pulling herself back up onto the chair.

"You know that feeling you get when you're being followed? I've had it for a while. I guess I can safely say it was you?"

Jayney got comfortable and reclaimed her glass, taking a final sip of the vodka cocktail. She composed her response. "I haven't been spying on you."

"Yes you have. I saw you in the stairwell, in the car park."

Jayney met her eyes. "I know you did. That's why I called. But I've not been spying on you."

Melody folded her arms and sighed. "So why the fuck were you skulking around some dark car park? And by the way, I want the name of the person who gave you my number." Melody paused. "Or did you get it off the system at work? No, I've not seen you at G-Sterling for ages." She frowned and curled her lip. "Urgh, have you been stalking me for all this time?"

Jayney leaned forwards and tried to connect. "I'm going to be totally honest and upfront with you, and I'd like it if you could just listen to me."

Melody sniffed and tilted her head to the side. "Fine. I'm listening."

"I've not been stalking you, but I've come here to warn you."

Melody looked around the pleasant restaurant and bar and tittered. "Oh shut up, Jayney. I'm all for dramatics, but please, just tell me what you want. I assume you're going to try and bribe us. You're going to lay out your demand to me, which I have to pass on to Zara, because you obviously know from temping at our company that she's loaded. So come on. How much do you want?"

Jayney frowned. "I don't want your money. I want to warn you."

"What about? That you're about to expose us?" Melody laughed. "Well I'm one step ahead of you, honey."

"Please, just listen."

Melody re-folded her arms. "Fine, but make it quick." She tapped the brown file. "I have another entry to make."

Jayney took a deep breath and began. "You know I used to temp at G-Sterling, right?"

"Yes. I may not have paid you much attention, but..." Melody pretended to glance under the table, "...I did happen to notice your figure, once or twice."

Jayney carried on. She didn't want to play games. "I was in the IT department for about ten months, on and off."

"So?"

"So, I had an affair with Zara."

"What?" Melody scrunched up her nose in bitterness.

"I had an affair with Zara."

"As if! Zara doesn't venture down to IT! Plus, she'd never give a temp the time of day!"

"I bumped into her in her corridor on my first day. I'd taken the lift to the wrong floor and we started talking."

Melody shook her head. "And then started an affair? Yeah right!"

Jayney straightened in her seat. "Look, you can believe what you want. I'm just telling you what happened."

Melody shrugged. "Go on then. Let's hear it."

"We started seeing each other. Secret meetings." Jayney twisted the empty glass between her fingers. "Lots of sex."

"She wouldn't do that with a temp!"

Jayney snapped back. "Well she did. She liked me."

"She said that, did she?"

"Of course she liked me! She shagged me enough times!"

Melody recited Zara's words. "Did she ever take you on a date? Phone you for a chat? Did you ever sleep over somewhere? Did you ever go to her house?"

"No, but-"

Melody knew she had the upper hand. "Well I've just come from her house." She smirked triumphantly. "She got down on her knees and sucked me dry."

Jayney closed her eyes and shuddered.

Melody continued. "And her wife ... Do you know who her wife is?"

"Of course I do," said Jayney.

"Her wife was in the other room." She nodded in self-congratulations. "Andi Armstrong was in the house the whole time her wife was kissing me and licking me-"

"Stop it!" Jayney shook her head in disgust. "Let's not turn this into a competition. Fine, you're still seeing her, I'm not."

"I've been seeing her for ten months." Melody didn't want to give too much away, but the temptation to out-do was too great.

Jayney coughed. "So there's an overlap. She was seeing both of us at the same time. I guessed as much."

"You're still seeing her?!" Melody was aghast.

"No. That's what I came to warn you about." Jayney's cheeks started to redden, but she carried on all the same. "I did have a girlfriend, but I ended it when I realised I was falling for Zara. I told Zara I loved her. I told her I wanted more." She paused and lifted the empty glass further away from her distracted fingers. She looked up at Melody. "I think it's a power thing. Zara's so direct. I'd never seen that in a woman before. I was taken by it. She told me that if I left G-Sterling she would '*see what she could do.*' I'm not stupid. I knew about her wife. I wasn't demanding anything; I just wanted us to spend a bit more time together. You know, doing regular stuff." She paused. "So I left G-Sterling. It wasn't a big deal. My agency sorted me out with another firm. We kept up the relationship, but it was just the same. We would meet up, have sex, and then she'd disappear." Jayney sighed to herself. “I don’t know, maybe I did start to get a bit demanding?”

“When was this?”

“A couple of months ago.”

Melody pursed her lips, trying to stay in control. “Go on.”

“She cut all ties. I mean *all* ties. She blocked my number, hung up each time I called from another line.” Jayney looked up. “I don’t like admitting this, but I popped back into G-Sterling and demanded a meeting. Obviously I was ignored, but she called me later that evening and told me that she’d blacklist me from all of the major London firms if I ever tried to contact her again.” Jayney shrugged. “I don’t know if she could actually do that, but I got the message. I’m not a psycho, I know when things are over.” She exhaled heavily. “But then I guess when I saw you two together in the car park I realised I’d been played. I realised there was definitely never any going back.”

“What were you doing in the car park?”

Jayney shrugged. “I was walking to meet a friend for coffee and I saw her Range Rover pull into the multi-storey. We used to meet there too and I figured she must be meeting someone else.” She raised her eyebrows and looked directly at Melody. “Morbid curiosity. I wanted to know who she was with.”

“So now you know. Can I go?” Melody started to slide off her stool.

“She’s playing you.”

Melody walked around the high-topped table and whispered into Jayney’s ear. “Now that’s where you’re wrong, honey. I’m the one who’s doing the playing.”

Jayney grabbed Melody’s arm. “I hope you’re right, for your sake. She’ll hurt you in the end.”

“We’ll see about that,” smirked Melody, reaching for her brown file and turning to leave. She suddenly paused and looked mischievously over her shoulder. “Saturday night, what are you doing?”

Jayney shrugged. “Why?”

Melody sidled back over to the table and whispered, once again, into her ear. "I've got a plus one to Andi Armstrong's birthday party. I think you'll be the perfect accompaniment to the night."

CHAPTER SEVENTEEN

Andi Armstrong walked into her office, bright and breezy on Friday morning. It had been a busy, yet exciting week and she was looking forward to the day's relatively easy workload.

The long draping curtains suddenly twitched.

"Surprise!" shouted Pippa, Janet and Elizabeth, almost in unison. Pippa's spring out from their hiding place was the best, Janet made a fair effort, but Elizabeth seemed to become tangled in the curtain pulls and only managed a slight tumble out of position. The static from the charged velvet had also intensified her shocked, frizzy appearance.

"Ha! What are you lot doing?!" laughed Andi.

Pippa was the first one to walk over. She wrapped her arms around Andi and gave her a squeeze. "Happy birthday, for tomorrow."

Andi was still clutching her workbag in one hand and morning paper in the other. "Strange, but thank you."

Janet came over next and repeated the celebration. "Your parties, lovely as they are, can be rather formal, and you're always gracing each and every one of your guests with your presence, which leaves little time for us work ladies, so we thought we'd celebrate today!" Janet stepped aside to make way for Elizabeth.

"Happy early birthday, day," nodded Elizabeth, reaching out to touch Andi with a slight stroke on the arm.

Andi smiled and walked to the coffee area, dropping her bag to the floor and her paper to the table. She turned back around to them all. "Thank you. That was very sweet."

"Ooo, we're just beginning," grinned Janet. "This week has been a sensation. You've surpassed yourself in every single television and radio appearance. You're the nation's LGBT hero. You've managed to summarise the country's confusion and disappointment in the established church with one single word-"

Pippa cut in. "Hence why we chose to shout surprise instead of boo! It's become an old joke already."

Janet continued. "So today is a day off. We've planned a trip out for us girlies. Obviously the rest of the crew have to stay here and work, but this is our little treat to you."

Andi couldn't help but smile. The idea that the four of them would go out socialising on a work day seemed rather strange. Pippa and Janet yes, but Elizabeth as well? She wondered what they had planned that would suit all four of them. Andi thought about it for a moment; a lunch out, no doubt, or possibly a day at a spa?

"We're going to Waterworldz!" shouted Pippa.

Andi laughed.

"Seriously, we are," said Janet with a smile. "It was Pippa's idea, and we all thought it would be perfect!"

Elizabeth coughed lightly.

Andi turned to Pippa. "We're going where?"

"Waterworldz!" she shouted again.

Andi frowned. "The place with the water slides and wave machines?"

Pippa nodded energetically. "And it's got an aqua disco! I thought we could all do with letting off a bit of steam."

Janet took Andi's hand and guided her to the soft chairs. "Sit down. It will be fun! Pippa's convinced me!"

"I can't believe you guys haven't been before!" Pippa grinned. "It will be the perfect place to let our hair down and have some fun! All of the kids are at school so it should be fairly empty."

Andi laughed. "Hang on, I have to ring Stella and tell her I'm off to Waterworldz with Janet and Elizabeth, she will find it hilarious!"

Elizabeth pulled her brown handbag tighter into her side.

Andi readdressed her comment. "I don't mean that in a bad way. I just think it's funny. I've never been anywhere like that before."

Janet sat down next to her. "No need to ring Stella, she's coming!"

"I'm not," said Stella, noisily entering the office and catching the tail end of the conversation.

Andi jumped up and rushed to the door, careful not to hug too hard and squash the baby in the papoose. "You're here, how brilliant!"

Stella shook her head. "No, Jack's been sick all night. I haven't slept since March. Sandy's away on a business trip. The house looks like it's been hit by a hurricane. I've just stopped breastfeeding and my boobs are like watermelons, about to burst, before they deflate and come to their new resting position around my waist. My periods have come back, and I've got piles."

Andi, Pippa and Janet couldn't help laughing. "Oh, poor you," said Andi, putting her arm around her friend's shoulder and guiding her to the coffee area. "Sit down and I'll get you a drink."

"I'll do it," said Janet, standing up and reaching for the mugs. "Coffees everyone?"

"Please," came the joint response.

"One of my camomiles, if you don't mind," whispered Elizabeth.

Stella carefully lowered herself and her papoose backwards into the seat. "I'm so sorry, Andi. I had childcare sorted for Jack and I was all up for riding the chutes with you." She grinned at Pippa. "I knew she'd make the perfect PA."

Andi widened her eyes at Stella.

"And Elizabeth ... I had a sneaking suspicion they'd snap you up too."

Elizabeth nodded politely.

"But I just can't leave Jack. He's too poorly. But I'll be there tomorrow, even if it means Sandy has to stay at home and look after him. I'll be there. I promise."

"I'm dreading it," said Andi. "Zara and Melody have been planning something."

Stella frowned. "It's the same sort of set up though, isn't it? Black tie, canapés, polite conversation and a band?"

Andi nodded.

"But Zara's got another inappropriate trick up her sleeve?" Stella tapped her friend's knee. "I told your wife off for that stunt last year. I'm sure she won't do anything like it again."

Andi agreed. "You'd hope not, especially since we've got John Elton coming *and* the Sapphic Sisters."

"No way!" shouted Stella, startling baby Jack and waking him from his sleep. He started to cry. "Oh sorry, Jack! Shh, shh, shh. It's okay. Shh now." She started to jig in the seat.

Andi nodded. "You know what it's like. They're just there for the photo opportunity."

"Oh stop doing yourself down! You're the hero of the moment. Everyone wants to celebrate with Andi Armstrong."

"Maybe," said Andi without conviction.

Stella frowned. "Is Melody the one with the tits and the teeth?"

Elizabeth shifted in her seat.

"Oops, sorry, Jack. Cover your ears." She paused. "I didn't realise they were that close?"

Andi narrowed her eyes. "Close enough to be plotting something."

"Well let's hope it's something appropriate like a wonderful bunch of flowers, or a sparkling piece of jewellery," said Janet, as she brought over the drinks. "That reminds me." She placed the tray on the table and hopped back behind the curtains. She reached down and pulled out a large pink bag. "Shall we do presents now?"

"Bugger!" shouted Stella. "I was meant to bring mine!" Jack started to cry. "Sorry, Jack, but Mummy's a silly old lady for forgetting auntie Andi's present." The crying got louder so the jigging began again, this time with more force.

"It's fine," smiled Andi.

"I just don't know where my head's at." Stella pulled herself up and out of the chair, regaining her balance and rocking forwards and backwards. "Remind me of this when I say I want another one!"

"You're an earth mother, look at you!" smiled Andi.

"Piss off! Sorry, Jack. Shh, shh, shh. Close your ears, my boy."

Elizabeth crossed her legs and looked away.

"So Liz, how are you enjoying working at Proud Unity then? I bet you and Janet get along like a house on fire!"

Elizabeth turned back around and spoke in a serious tone. "I like to think we complement each other." She paused. "Sorry, but I do prefer Elizabeth."

Stella jigged with more force and pointed down at Jack in the papoose. "He was going to be a Betty if he was a she."

"Bethy?" questioned Janet.

"No, Betty, like Betty Boop. Sorry, he's getting louder, isn't he?"

"Lucky escape then, Jack," smiled Andi.

"What?"

"Nothing." Andi spoke over the crying, "Shall I take him?"

"No, we're all strapped in and it's a bugger to undo. Oops, sorry, Jack! Plus, you ladies don't want a crying baby spoiling the present giving. I'm going to make a move, but I'll see you tomorrow and you'd better give me a good amount of your time, Mrs Armstrong! We need a proper catch up."

Andi stood up. "No, stay, it's fine."

Jack's crying had turned into a thunderous scream. "I'm going, I'm going now. He loves the tube. I'm just going to sit and ride the circle line all day."

"Oh Stella."

"No, I'm off!" Stella shouted over the howls. "I'll see you tomorrow. Make sure you do some splashing for me! Good choice, Pippa. What a star!"

Pippa smiled and waved as the bundle of noise headed towards the door.

Andi jumped up and kissed her friend on the cheek. "Are you sure you're okay?"

"I'm fine. Have fun." She whispered into Andi's ear. "When you're at the pool will you do me a favour?"

Andi looked concerned. "Sure, sure, whatever."

"Dunk that Elizabeth woman for me, would you?"

Andi couldn't help but laugh.

****

Andi closed the cubicle door and opened her gym bag, smiling to herself at the neatly folded swimsuit and towel. She'd occasionally nip into the health club next to the Proud Unity offices, for a swim at lunchtime, and Pippa would always spot the gym bag and get its contents clean and dried. In fact, she couldn't remember the last time she'd had to clean it herself. She started to undress and thought about all of the little things that Pippa did which made her day-to-day life easier. She'd been a real blessing, and this, as an idea for a girls' day out, was perfect. She pulled on her costume and nodded to herself. Relax and have fun, she instructed.

Andi stepped out of her cubicle and made her way to the lockers. Pippa had been right. The place was pretty empty. Andi pushed the fifty pence piece, given to her as one of her presents, into the small slot. She lifted her bag onto its side and shoved it forwards. Janet bustled in next to her and opened the locker on the left, doing the same thing with her designated fifty pence piece.

"She really has thought of everything," smiled Janet, struggling to get her large workbag into the small metal container. "Coins for the lockers. Tokens for the hairdryers, and she says, if we're lucky, she'll give us a pound each for the machines."

Andi laughed. "My dad used to do that when we were little. He'd take us swimming every Thursday evening and as a treat we were allowed a packet of crisps from the machines afterwards." She remembered that feeling of slightly tangled clothes, made damp by a lack of proper drying, and the pangs of hunger that followed a session in the pool. "I'd always choose Monster Munch."

Janet laughed and made one final shove, slotting her bag into position. "I'm not sure *Chez Garrét* do Monster Munch."

Andi attached the plastic strap to her wrist and tucked the metal key inside. "It's ever-so expensive there. You really shouldn't have."

Janet put her arm around Andi's shoulder. "It's fine. It's from all of us, and we did have to get a nice sit down meal into the day somewhere, Elizabeth insisted."

"Good on Elizabeth though, for being so game." Andi smiled as she walked with Janet out of the changing rooms. They pushed through the big double doors and gasped as the brick wall of heat and chlorine hit them with force. "Wow, it's hot in here!"

Janet looked up at the array of different coloured chutes, twisting amongst themselves, some ending outside, some dropping down into huge plastic bowls, and some ejecting the rider into the rapids. "Wow! I didn't know it was this big!"

Elizabeth coughed lightly behind them, making her presence known. "Is there any lane swimming?"

Andi turned around and found it hard not to smile at the pale blue bobbled swimming cap. "I don't think so, but it looks like there's a nice lagoon area over there." She pointed at the shallow pool, but stopped and laughed as a number of water sprays suddenly started to shoot up from the ground. "Maybe not." She looked around. "There's a Jacuzzi over there?"

Elizabeth started to undo her plastic wrist strap. "I read an article once on the amount of bacteria floating about in a shared Jacuzzi and it didn't make for pleasant reading. I'll get my towel and book from my locker and just sit over there." She pointed at a beach area with sun loungers, deck chairs and tables.

"Oh that looks nice," said Janet fiddling with her own green wrist strap. "I think I'll join you." She nudged Elizabeth's arm. "And look, it's right next to the café. We can get ourselves a nice cup of tea."

Pippa burst through the double doors with a grin. "How brilliant is this, ladies! Come on, let's hit the chutes!"

Janet and Elizabeth shuffled past her. "We've found our spot. Don't worry about us, we'll be in heaven," smiled Janet.

Pippa watched them return to the changing rooms and turned back to Andi. "Oh, looks like it's just me and you then, boss." She grinned. "Do you like my spotty swim suit?"

Andi looked Pippa up and down, unable to ignore the womanly curves and swell of her breast. "You're gorgeous and you know it. Now stop forcing me to look."

Pippa smiled at the compliment. "Where do you want to start?"

Andi linked her arm and signalled to the yellow floor arrows, appearing to guide the rider to the chutes. "Wherever you want to take me, Pippa," she said with a smile.

****

Andi and Pippa giggled their way back to the beach area. It was their third visit back there so far. “Everything okay?” asked Andi, shaking off some water and perching on the edge of a deck chair.

Janet lowered her book and frowned at them. “Will you two stop it? It’s like you’re a pair of silly children, checking in every half hour with your parents! We’re fine, aren’t we, Elizabeth?”

Elizabeth had chosen to keep her bobbly blue swimming cap on, and having done no actual swimming yet, had started to sweat. “Slightly clammy, but fine.” She nodded. “I’m actually having a very pleasant relax.”

Pippa sat down on the end of Elizabeth’s sun lounger and tapped her on the ankle. “We’re doing the Double Trouble next, can we tempt you?”

Elizabeth moved her leg and reached down to wipe away the drips. “No.”

“Girls, stop pestering us!” Janet tried to swat Andi with her novel. “Go away! We don’t want to see you until it’s time to go for the meal.”

“Ooo, yes mum!” teased Andi.

“That’s an order! Go on, scram!”

Andi stood up and linked Pippa’s arm, giggling as she pulled them back towards the chutes. “I feel about twelve!” she whispered.

Pippa squeezed the arm in return. “Be brave, little girl. This is the big one!”

Andi giggled. “This is so much fun. It really is! I can’t believe I’ve never been here before.”

“Neither can I. What *have* you been doing for fun, Mrs Armstrong?”

Andi started to climb the steps towards the biggest chute in the complex. “During time off?”

Pippa nodded. “Yes. What do you do when you’ve got a day off and you want to have a bit of fun?”

"I read, I go for walks." She thought about it. "I might go and watch a film at the cinema."

Pippa walked them through an underground cavern. Usually swimmers would be queuing at this point, but today had been blissfully quiet. "What was the last film you saw?"

Andi thought for a moment. "Men in Black."

"Three?"

Andi frowned. "No, I didn't even know there was a two?"

"Yes! And a three! Men in Black one, was out years ago! You've not been to the cinema since then?"

"I'm busy."

"Andi, you're twenty nine."

Andi exhaled. "Thirty tomorrow."

"You're right, that's it, onto the scrap heap."

"I feel like I should be put on the scrap heap sometimes."

"Don't be daft! It's me who's having to keep up with you today."

Andi smiled and released Pippa's arm. "I know! This is brilliant fun!" She pointed at the stack of bright orange inflatables as they walked out of the cavern. "They're double. It looks like we have to go on together. Do you want top or bottom?"

"You tease!" winked Pippa, lifting the inflatable and hauling it up the final few steps. "I'll take control at the top, seeing as this is your first time."

Andi followed her up the steps. "Fine, but I'm a fast learner and I'd like to vary the position if that's okay with you?"

Pippa laughed. "Andi Armstrong! You're getting flirty!"

Andi stared at Pippa's bottom. "I can't help it. I've been following this wiggling, polka dot bottom, up these steps all morning. It's becoming too hard to ignore."

"You wait until we take a hot shower afterwards."

Andi hopped up the final step and giggled. "I feel like a naughty kid ... I'm acting like a teenager ... What *have* you done to me, Miss Rose?"

"I'm showing you a good time," grinned Pippa, lining the double inflatable ring at the entrance to the chute. "This one's fast, so make sure you hold on."

Andi watched as Pippa sat her bottom in the first ring, hanging her legs over the edge and clinging onto the handles at the side. "Are you ready for me?" asked Andi.

"Ready, waiting and eager to thrill," laughed Pippa, looking over her shoulder and enjoying the view.

Andi climbed into the back ring and looped her legs around Pippa's waist, clinging onto her handles and shoving them both forwards with her bottom. The double ring started to shift in the water. "Ahhh!" shouted Andi.

"Here we go!" screamed Pippa as their inflatable caught the gust of water and headed into the dark tube.

Andi squeezed her legs even tighter. Their ring was gaining speed as it hit the first corner, climbing the side of the tube and swinging them from right to left as the chute curved and twisted. The thrill was incredible and she couldn't help but wail with excitement.

"Hang on!" shouted Pippa. "There's a bumpy bit next!"

Andi leaned her head to the right, glancing over Pippa's shoulder, spotting the white frothy water. The ring hit the rapids, bouncing up and down with force, nudging Andi even further forwards.

"Is that your tuppy on my back?!" screamed Pippa.

Andi shouted in laughter. "Stop it! I have to concentrate on hanging on." She peered back over Pippa's shoulder and spotted more white water.

"Stop rubbing yourself on me!" squealed Pippa.

Andi couldn't control her giggling. "I can't. I can't hang on!"

The double ring performed one final twist and dropped out of the chute, skimming them across the landing pool. "We've landed!"

Andi couldn't hear. She was too busy falling backwards out of her ring and splashing into the water. She emerged with a coughing fit of giggles and clambered to the shallow steps. She sat down, waist deep in water and laughed. "That was sensational!"

Pippa floated towards her in the ring, still holding on and still in control. She looked at Andi, leaning back on the steps, flushed with fun. "And so is that breast sticking out from your swimming costume!"

Andi looked down and screamed. She pulled her costume back into position and leaped back into the water. "I knew you had an ulterior motive for bringing me here!" She said, lunging for the ring and tipping Pippa out.

Pippa splashed into the water and grabbed hold of Andi's legs, pulling them forwards and plunging her under too.

They both opened their eyes underwater and saw the other giggling out bubbles of water; a vision they'd both remember for a very long time.

CHAPTER EIGHTEEN

Andi glanced at the large gold clock hanging above the entrance to the elegant reception room in which she was standing. The Grandez Hotel. Booked for almost a year. It was 8.10 p.m. and Andi had been waiting at the end of the red runway carpet for over half an hour, greeting her guests with a kiss, and posing for snaps with the photographer. Zara had been in her element, fawning over the more famous of guests, promising to come and schmooze them later on at the bar. Her treatment of the Proud Unity regulars, however, was quite the opposite. She deliberately ushered them along the red carpet, only allowing them to pose for one, very quick, photograph. Yet when guests like John Elton arrived, she'd insist on a fifteen minute photo-shoot. Andi was starting to get cross.

She looked at Zara, now standing between the Sapphic Sisters, holding both of their waists and smiling compulsively for the camera. Any onlooker would think it was Zara's party, not hers. Andi took a deep breath and reluctantly joined the group. The bright camera flashes started again.

"Hang on, Andi. Can I just have a couple more of just me and the Sisters?" Zara was peering forwards with her eyebrows raised.

Andi stepped to the left, lifting her long silver gown, careful not to catch it on her narrow heels. "No problem."

"Get back in there!" shouted Stella, grabbing Andi's waist from behind.

Andi turned around. "You're here, brilliant!" She gave her friend a big hug. "Where's Sandy?"

"Jack's babysitter's ill. We couldn't get anyone to take him. You look dazzling, by the way. Happy birthday!"

Andi pulled a face. "Oh no. That's such a shame. You should have brought him. And thank you for the compliment. I was given it by the designer."

"Check you out, you celeb!" Stella looked around the beautifully decorated room, admiring the twinkling lights above the stage where the five piece band were now playing a Wet Wet Wet classic. "I don't think Jack would quite fit in, do you?"

"Andi! Phoenix is here!! We need a photo." Zara was waving frantically, and pointing to the buzz going on at the door.

Andi took Stella's hand and walked towards the photographer. "I'd like a photo with Stella first, please."

Zara tutted. "For goodness sake be quick. It's Phoenix!"

"I'm having some photos with my friend." Andi was firm.

Zara chose to focus on Stella instead. "Please be quick, Stella. You know who Phoenix is, don't you?" She smiled in earnest. "One quick photo and then if you'd move on to the Champagne and canapés area. We have so many VIPs still to come and we don't want this area getting cluttered up."

Andi shook her head. "Don't listen to her, Stella. You're my VIP. You can do as much cluttering as you like."

Stella watched as Zara shimmied up the red carpet with open arms, encasing Phoenix like a long lost friend. She shook her head and turned to Andi, posing for the camera and speaking in between flashes and smiles. "So I'm your VIP, am I? I've not been ditched in favour of Pippa?"

Andi laughed. "She's giving you a good run for your money, I'll tell you that!"

"Ooo, I want to hear more. Is she here yet? I'll go and join her."

Andi shook her head. "No, but Janet and Elizabeth are."

"Alone?"

"Yes, Janet's still single, and Elizabeth thought it best not to bring her husband. She worried he wouldn't feel comfortable."

Stella frowned. "Because of the lesbians?"

Andi laughed. "No! Because of the clientele ... I think." She paused for a moment. "I hope."

"Andi, please hurry up!" Zara was hissing from the other end of the red carpet, straining her eyes, completely unable to move her brow after her latest bout of Botox. "A photo with Phoenix is the *absolute* priority right now!"

Andi gave Stella a kiss on the cheek and whispered into her ear. "You'd forget it's my thirtieth, wouldn't you?"

Stella hugged her again. "Oh bless you, Andi. You really are a Saint."

Andi smiled. "I don't know about that. You haven't heard what went on in the chutes yesterday."

"Andi Armstrong!" teased Stella, "I knew I saw a spar-"

"ANDI!" Zara waltzed over and grabbed her by the arm. "Excuse me, Stella. I need my wife. We have some very important VIP celebrities here tonight, please move along."

Stella made a saluting gesture and winked at Andi. "Good for you. Tell me *all* about it later."

Andi hadn't heard; she was too busy being manoeuvred into position and blinded by the continuous lights of the flash.

****

Melody leaned forwards and spoke through the small round holes in the clear screen that was separating the front and back section of the taxi. "Can't you find another route?" She glanced around at the stationary traffic, exasperated by the delay. "We CANNOT be late!"

"Love…" the voice was gruff and unconcerned, "The *Grandez* is on *this* road."

Melody tried again. "Isn't there a back way in?"

The overweight driver shrugged his shoulders and scratched his overgrown stubble. "Isn't it fashionable to be late?"

Melody shouted back. "No, not when it's Andi Armstrong's thirtieth birthday party, it isn't!"

The taxi driver shifted in his seat and looked properly into his rear view mirror for the first time that journey. "That pretty blonde lesbian lady who's always on the television?"

"Yes, but she's not just a lesbian lady, she's a political activist who's making a huge amount of difference to society!"

"I'm just interested in the lesbian bit, love."

"Just drive would you?" Melody sat back in her seat, next to Jayney, her selected partner in crime.

The driver stared through his mirror, admiring their posh frocks and cleavage. "So, how long have you two lovely ladies been together?" He scratched his stubble once more. "I must say, I've noticed lesbians getting sexier over the years."

Melody shook her head. "Just drive, or I'll report you."

"Sexier, but still *bloody* feisty!" He returned his eyes to the road and the red brake lights ahead. "Moody bloody lesbians," he muttered under his breath.

Melody leaned forwards, about to erupt, but Jayney grabbed her arm and urged her to stop.

"Calm down. It's not worth it. I'm nervous enough as it is," said Jayney, looking out of the window, just able to see the impressive lights of The Grandez in the distance. "I'm still not sure about this whole thing."

Melody frowned at her. "What whole thing? You're my plus one to a party. That's all."

"Won't you feel sorry for Andi?"

Melody twisted her body and took Jayney's hand. "Hey, this isn't about Andi. I admire Andi for what she does," she paused, "and from what I've seen she's a truly lovely lady."

"You're shagging her wife," whispered Jayney under her breath.

"And so were you," came the muted reply. Melody exhaled. "Look, I just want to see Zara get what's coming to her. We're going to put the frighteners on her, that's all."

"And the file?"

Melody reached for the brown file sitting on the seat next to her. She picked it up and held it close to her chest. "You leave the file to me."

****

Zara pulled her poker straight hair over her left shoulder and glanced at the bustling room. "I'll go and tell the band to pause after this song. If we get the speeches out of the way then we can start to mingle."

Andi took her eyes away from the doors and looked at her wife. "Relax, this is meant to be a party. My party."

"It's important to network. We've got a better haul of celebs this year than we've ever had."

"Oh Zara, I just want to have a few drinks with my friends." She glanced back down the red runway carpet.

Zara curled her lip. "Who are you waiting for?"

"No one," she said. "Fine, go and tell the band."

Zara nodded and strolled through the crowd, towards the front of the stage, pausing every so often to place her hand on someone's shoulder and bow in admiration. Andi watched her and shook her head. She had known what to expect, she just had to take a deep breath and get through the evening. With that thought in mind, she turned, one final time, to the entrance; what she saw sent excited flutters of delight bouncing across her chest. Pippa Rose was striding down the red carpet in a sensational emerald green evening gown, embellished with sequins on the bodice and taffeta ripples on the skirt. She looked incredible.

"Happy birthday, Andi. I'm sorry I'm late."

Andi didn't look at the clock. Her eyes were fixed on Pippa. "I can't take my eyes off you. You look incredible!" She reached out and touched a brown ringlet that was deliberately hanging loose from the up-do. "Your hair's gorgeous."

Pippa grinned. "You'll make me blush!" She glanced down at her own chest. "Not too much? I always worry about going strapless with these boobs."

Andi looked down and smiled. "All appears fine to me."

"It's true what they say then," grinned Pippa.

"What?"

"Flirty thirty!" She smiled. "I noticed it yesterday at the pool."

Andi laughed. "Yes, I think I'll embrace flirting now that I'm too old for it to be taken seriously."

"Stop it! You're only just beginning!"

Andi took Pippa's hand. "Seriously, yesterday was amazing. I had so much fun. We should do something like that again."

"Already booked," smiled Pippa. "We're going to '*Go Ape*' on the second Sunday in December."

"Are we?" Andi liked the authority. "What's '*Go Ape*'?"

"You said you wanted to broaden your horizons on the fun level, so I took you seriously. Each month I'm going to take you on a fun expedition."

Andi laughed. "Oh Pippa, you're brilliant."

"We'll be swinging from the tree tops and zip wiring to the ground in Trent Park."

"Ha! That's so funny!" She paused. "Can you really see Elizabeth doing that though?"

Pippa reddened. "Oh, I just booked it for me and you."

The pause in response was significant enough for them both to feel uncomfortable.

"It's fine," they said at the same time.

"I'll book them in," continued Pippa.

"No, I was going to say it's fine. It will be nice for us to go alone."

Pippa looked at Andi, sensing a connection; a shared buzz of excitement. "If you're sure?"

"Positive," smiled Andi, continuing to look into Pippa's eyes. "Thank you for coming."

"I wouldn't have missed this for the world. Traffic's a nightmare, so I guess I'm the last one to tell you how truly beautiful you look this evening."

Andi smiled with slight sadness. "In fact, Pippa, you're the first." She paused. "Well the first who's actually meant it anyway. You know what this lot are like, lots of air kisses and false praise."

Pippa grinned. "I know you said you weren't looking forward to tonight, but there's being a cynic and there's *being a cynic*! I'm sure Janet and Elizabeth must have complimented your aura of beauty?"

"Elizabeth said she liked my shoes."

Pippa's eyes followed the flow of Andi's sparkling silver dress. "You can't even see your shoes!"

Andi laughed. "Listen to me, being all dramatic. No, everyone's been lovely. Janet and Stella in particular. They're at the bar. Let me take you over. Stella would love to get to know you better. Plus my friend Ruth is here." She smiled. "Ruth Allen, the one I told you about. Smart, single, sexy. Very, very, funny."

"What will she want to talk to me for then?" laughed Pippa.

Andi heard the loud tap on the microphone and stared towards the stage. "Oh bugger. It's that time already." She caught the eye of a waiter doing the rounds with the glasses of Champagne. "Tell me if I'm a cynic *after* the speeches," she said, reaching for a tall flute and quickly sipping the bubbles.

Pippa took a chilled flute and stretched it out towards Andi. "To you." She chinked the glasses together. "Thank you for everything you do, for everyone like me. Happy birthday, Andi."

Andi stared at her intently. "Oh Pippa, if only my wife could make a speech like that."

Pippa looked at the stage and smiled. Zara was in her element. Shushing the crowd and acting coy at the whistles. "She's a bit '*stop it, stop it … no, don't stop it*,' isn't she?"

Andi was about to reply when the photographer tapped her on the shoulder. "I don't have one of the two of you," he said, stepping backwards with his camera and signalling them together.

Andi swapped the tall glass into her left hand and reached around Pippa's waist with her right. Pippa put her left arm across Andi's shoulder, feeling her warm skin and pulling her closer.

"Smile."

They both squeezed.

"And there she is!" came Zara's booming voice over the microphone. "My wife the superstar. Still being papped!"

The crowd turned to the back of the room and laughed. The champagne had been flowing and there was a general feeling of excitement at being invited to something so prestigious.

Zara put her hand on her hip and pretended to squint. "Or is that her PA trying to get into her knickers?"

The crowd gasped with giggles.

"She won't have me," shouted Andi from the back of the room, condoning the banter.

The crowd relaxed and laughed.

"I would," whispered Pippa, watching Andi stroll away towards the stage.

Zara signalled for her wife to jump up and join her so she could begin the speech. "Dirty thirty!" she joked, watching Andi place her flute down on the table next to the stage. "My wife really is as angelic as she appears." She rubbed her hands together. "Here's hoping that changes!"

The titters turned into rapturous applause as Andi walked up onto the stage and took a gentle bow.

"*Happy birthday to you…*" the impromptu singing was loud and heartfelt and Andi didn't quite know where to look. "*…Happy birthday dear Andi, happy birthday to you!*" The burst of applause and cheers of hip, hip, hooray were thunderous. Andi bowed again.

"When my wife's stopped bowing, I'll begin," shouted Zara above the noise. The room slowly quietened down and Zara took the microphone out of its stand. "Thank you all for coming. I know the pull of free Champagne, food, and top class entertainment is too hard to ignore!"

A few people tittered.

"Seriously, thank you for coming to celebrate my wife's birthday." There was another cheer. "She's one of a kind, and I'm lucky to have her." A general *ahhh* sound cascaded around the room. "I am. I can be a grumpy old woman sometimes, but Andi puts up with me." Zara paused and looked at her wife. "I don't know what I'd do without you, sweetie."

Andi felt a lump building in her throat.

Zara continued. "For those of you who were here last year, you'll remember that the female stripper didn't go down too well."

A shout of: '*She did!*' came from the back of the room.

Zara laughed. "She didn't, and I may not be the most natural of wives, but I do learn from my mistakes, so this year, Andi, I just want to say, I love you. You're great. Happy birthday."

The room erupted into cheers as Zara handed the microphone over to her wife.

"That's it?" laughed Andi, in complete shock.

Zara nodded and made her way off the stage. "Over to you, sweetie."

Andi looked at the crowd in surprise. "My wife never fails to astonish me, but at least it's for the right reasons this time." She smiled. "And I was quite looking forward to seeing that stripper again, now that I'm all dirty at thirty." Andi let the laughter die down. "So, wow, where do I start? What a year! You're here tonight because you've supported me and my work … or, like Zara said, you just came for the free booze and entertainment!"

"*Never*!" came a shout.

"Seriously, I just want to say thank you. The battle for equal rights is almost won…" Andi noticed a slight distraction on the faces in the crowd, "…All of you are playing your part in some form or another…" There were a couple of titters from people at the front and the people at the back were craning their necks. "…Even if it's just holding the hand of your boyfriend or girlfriend, husband or wife, when walking down the street…" Andi scanned the people in the crowd. Most were now laughing. "…It's not meant to be funny. I mean it. We are all equal and we are all-" Andi felt the hands on her waist and spun around. To her horror she recognised the scantily clad body of *Patty the Pudge*. The 60-year-old exotic dancer who had found fame on this year's *Britain's Got Talent* television show for her high tempo shimmying, overly chubby thighs, and lack of appropriate dance gear. *Patty the Pudge* was standing in her union jack bikini, clicking her fingers.

Andi shook her head, returning the microphone to the stand and turning to leave the stage.

"Oh no you don't!" shouted Patty grabbing her hand. "This one's a dance for two!" The Austin Powers theme tune music started to play and Patty began to circle around Andi, walking with a wiggle and making a swimming motion with her arms.

Andi still wasn't smiling.

The music was loud and the famous trumpet section was about to begin. Patty the Pudge dropped into the splits, right on cue, and rolled onto her stomach, bouncing her bottom up and down in time with the trumpets. The crowd burst into applause and laughter.

Andi looked at the wobbling flesh cavorting around on the floor, and was unable to maintain her straight face.

"She's smiling!" shouted Patty, rolling onto her side and hauling herself up in a rather unladylike manner. "She's smiling! Let's hear it for Andi Armstrong!"

The crowd cheered and started to chant Andi's name.

"Follow me," said Patty, talking Andi's hands in her own and pulling her in close. Patty the Pudge let go and immediately shimmied up and down Andi's body, bumping and grinding and spanking her own behind.

"*Andi, Andi, Andi.*" The chants got louder and louder.

Andi didn't know what to do. This was far worse than last year. At least last year she got to sit on a chair. She scanned her memory, quickly trying to think of a basic dance move. She opted for something she'd seen in a Pulp Fiction movie, holding her nose with one hand and using the other to pretend she was submerging into the water. She bent her knees and wiggled up and down.

The laughs got louder.

Andi's embarrassment was mortifying, but she had to carry on. She thought back to the film and made two Vs with her fingers, pulling them in front of her eyes.

Patty the Pudge grabbed Andi's hands and pulled them onto her chubby chest. Smothering them into her tiny bikini top. She held Andi's waist and started to spin.

Andi was so overcome by the crowd's howls of laughter, the feeling of clammy skin, and the dizziness from the spin, that she failed to notice who it was, standing by her discarded glass of Champagne, discreetly dropping in a sachet of Seroquel.

CHAPTER NINETEEN

Andi walked from the stage, trying to maintain her composure. She was sweating, her dress was twisted, and her hair was a mess. *Patty the Pudge* really had done a number on her. She reached for her discarded glass of Champagne and took a huge swig, trying not to choke as another person slapped her on the back and told her what a great sport she was. She drained the flute and looked for a waiter. Her only option now, was to drink away the embarrassment.

"Here, have mine," said Zara with a smirk.

Andi snatched the glass of Champagne and started to drink.

"You can't tell me that wasn't brilliant entertainment?"

Andi looked at her wife with dismay. "Yes, at my expense!"

"Oh chill out, sweetie. Everyone loves *Patty the Pudge*." She looked back at the stage. "We've got those two Greek guys doing that funny dancing later on. The band will be playing all evening. The Champagne's flowing. The celebs are here." She reached out for Andi's waist. "What's not to love?"

"Oh Zara, you really haven't got a clue, have you?"

"I told her it was a bad idea," said Melody, suddenly appearing behind Zara's shoulder.

Zara recognised the voice and spun around. "How long have you been here?"

"Long enough to hear your heartfelt speech," said Melody.

Andi leaned forwards and kissed Zara's work colleague on the cheek. "Thank you for coming."

Melody looked at Andi with sincerity. "I told your wife to book the opera singer."

"No you didn't," spat Zara, suddenly noticing the brown file tucked under Melody's arm. "Don't tell me you've brought work to a party?"

Melody tapped the file and winked. "Oh no, this is *all* play!" She looked over her shoulder at the gorgeous redhead making her way towards them with the drinks. "First I want to introduce you to my friend." She pointed her finger. "Zara, Andi, the sexy redhead approaching is called Jayney." She glanced at her boss. "Zara, you remember her temping at G-Sterling, don't you?"

Zara flared up with rage. "She got fired! What are you doing bringing her as your plus one?"

"Shhh," hushed Andi. "She's almost here." She smiled and signalled the pretty lady over. "Hi, I'm Andi, thanks for coming."

Jayney held the two drinks out to the side of her body and leaned forwards for a kiss. "It's lovely to meet you. I'm Jayney. I hope it's okay that I'm here? I'm actually really nervous. I've never been to anything like this before."

Melody tucked the brown folder back under her arm and took one of the drinks. She wrapped her other arm around Jayney's waist. "Don't be nervous, honey." She tilted her head to the side. "You didn't get fired from G-Sterling, did you?"

Jayney reddened. "No, I left of my own accord."

Andi sensed the tension. "It's fine that you're here, Jayney. Melody can bring whoever she wants." She turned to look at the busty blonde with her signature face-full of makeup. "I did have you down as a man eater though, Melody."

"She's just greedy," sneered Zara, not even trying to hide her disgust. "Are you two together?"

Andi coughed. "It's lovely to meet you, Jayney." She craned her neck. "Please do excuse me. I can see my work colleagues waving at me."

Zara reached for Andi's arm. "Ten minutes max. Then we need to start circling, sweetie."

Andi shook off the hold. "Fine. I'll be over there."

****

Pippa saw Andi approaching the bar and raced to meet her. "That's Jayney! You've just been speaking to Jayney! I thought I saw her come in. I can't believe it? What the hell is she doing here?"

"That's your Jayney? Your ex?"

Pippa nodded furiously, peering over the crowd and staring at the back of Jayney's long red hair. "She must have known I'd be here. What a nerve! Who's that blonde lady she's with? The one with the make-up and big tits?"

"That's Melody, she works with Zara."

Pippa shook her head and exhaled. "Oh my god! At G-Sterling? I guess that's who she left me for then!"

Andi glanced back around. "No, you must be wrong. Melody's a man eater."

Stella joined the two of them and caught the end of Andi's comment. "That Melody would devour anything standing in her way. She's a she-beast."

Andi laughed. "They're all a bit weird, the G-Sterling crowd, but I guess they'd say the same about us." She glanced around. "Where *are* Janet and Elizabeth?"

Stella laughed and pointed to the bar. "Janet's getting the drinks and Elizabeth disappeared ages ago - said she was going to the loo."

"Is she okay?" asked Andi with concern.

"I think she's just a bit overwhelmed."

Andi laughed. "Oh bless her. Splashed in the pool yesterday, lesbian-fest today; she'll be handing in her notice soon."

"How can you be so upbeat after what just happened to you on stage?" Stella stroked her friend's blonde fringe back into position. "Your wife's got a warped sense of humour."

Andi shrugged. "She's great though, isn't she?"

"Who?"

"Patty the Pudge."

Stella laughed. "Yes, if you're sitting in your own home, watching her on your own television, then yes, she's hilarious! But Andi, to have her jumping all over you like that! Eugh, I feel sorry for you."

Andi took another glass of Champagne from a passing waiter. "I'm just going to drink to numb the pain." She lifted the glass in a toast. "Here's to getting through it."

Pippa finally took her eyes away from the group by the stage and raised her glass with gusto. "Here, here!" she said, chinking her tall flute against Andi's. "Now where's this friend of yours?"

Andi laughed. "I didn't know you had such high standards. Jayney's absolutely gorgeous."

"Yes, I do have some pulling power, Andi." Pippa grinned. "What do my standards matter anyway? Is this friend of yours pugly?"

"Pugly?"

"Yes, nice personality, but ugly." She shrugged. "I don't mind pugly."

Andi laughed. "No, Ruth is very, very pretty indeed. I think you're going to hit it off."

Pippa stared at Andi, holding her gaze. "Good, because I'm going to need a distraction."

Andi broke the connection and looked towards the stage at Jayney, who now seemed to be in a rather heated discussion with Zara. "I see what you mean."

"No, I didn't mean from her, I meant from-"

"And here she is now!" giggled Andi, spotting her old friend approaching. She stepped forwards and hugged her tightly. Andi pulled away and presented her friend to the group. "Stella, you know Ruth." Stella nodded and leaned in for a kiss. "Ruth, this is Pippa, my new PA."

Ruth turned to Pippa and smiled. "Nice to meet you. I've heard a lot about you."

Pippa never knew how to respond to such a statement. She opted for: "Don't believe any of it!"

"No, it's all good," smiled Ruth, with warmth. "You were described as wonderfully intelligent, beautifully pretty, and completely fun-loving."

Pippa laughed. "Did you read my CV?"

"It's all true," said Andi, looking at Pippa. "You're a real catch."

Ruth spotted the connection and took a step back. "Can I get anyone a drink?"

Stella grinned. "No, we're all good thanks. The waiters are passing by every two minutes or so with fresh glasses of Champers, and I can see some more canapés coming round." She smiled. "You know what it's like at Andi's 'dos' … you feel like you're at the Oscars!" Stella turned to the stage as the band started playing once again. "And these guys are brilliant!"

Andi unintentionally turned her back on Pippa and Ruth as she looked at the stage, explaining to Stella how they'd come to choose the band.

Ruth immediately used the opportunity to strike up a conversation. "So what's it like working for Andi then?"

Pippa exhaled with a smile. "It's the dream job. She's the perfect boss and I really love the work. You never quite know how each day is going to pan out. It so exciting and Andi is so inspirational, no matter what's thrown at her, she's always smiling."

"And so are you. You light up when you talk about her."

Pippa reddened. "Do I? I guess I'm just lucky to have such a great job and such a great boss." She looked properly at Ruth for the first time, noticing how silky her bobbed brown hair was. "What is it that you do again? Andi did explain it, but it all sounded very technical."

"No, not really. I'm just a psychologist who specialises in emotion and body language."

Pippa opened her mouth in shock. "Oh no! I'm not going to ask what you've spotted in me then!"

Ruth took a sip of Champagne. "Good because I wouldn't tell you."

Pippa laughed. "Oh, I see what you're doing! Reverse psychology. Now I want to know."

Andi heard the laughter and turned back around, steadying herself on Stella's arm. "Ooo, I feel a bit giddy," she giggled, winking at Pippa and Ruth. "You girls seem to be hitting it off." She linked Stella's arm and pretended to whisper. "Did you say you had to go to the bar, Stella? Yes, you did, didn't you? Let's leave them to it!"

"No, no, it's fine." Pippa was too late. Andi and Stella were already tottering towards another gang of Proud Unity colleagues. Pippa rocked backwards on her high heels and turned to face Ruth. "*Sooo…*"

"So, indeed," smiled Ruth. "You don't need a psychology degree to know that this feels kind of set up and somewhat awkward."

Pippa laughed. "I'm sorry. My mind's all over the place this evening."

"I can tell." Ruth took another sip of Champagne. "Do you want to talk about it?"

"Oh god, no!" laughed Pippa. "I'm not that bad a date!"

"So you think this is a date then?"

Pippa laughed again. "Stop it! No, you'll give psychologists a bad name." She studied Ruth's friendly face, spotting the small crevice in her chin and warming to her kind eyes. "Come on, tell me what you do for fun."

"Actually I do have a fun hobby. I write random jokey questions, for an online laughter page."

Pippa raised her eyebrows. "Really? Like what?"

"Like…" Ruth thought about it for a moment. "…Like, what's another name for *thesaurus*?"

Pippa smiled. "I like it. Give me another."

"Okay … How important does a person have to be before they're considered assassinated instead of just murdered?"

Pippa nodded. "I'm getting the gist of it."

Ruth carried on. "Or … if there's an exception to every rule, is there an exception to that rule?"

Pippa nodded. "So, they're more like random ponderings, than rip-roaring jokes."

"Oh I don't know about that. They make me laugh."

Pippa tried to backtrack. "Yes, yes, you're right, they're witty," she paused, "but they're not exactly funny, *funny*, are they? Like…" She thought about it for a moment. "…What do you call a pantry full of lesbians?"

Ruth shrugged.

"A licker cabinet." Pippa couldn't help but laugh at herself. "Or, what do you call a man with no shins?" She didn't wait for a reply. "Tony!"

"Each to their own I guess." Ruth pulled her brown bob behind her ears and looked around the room. "Shall we go and find Andi?"

Pippa stifled her laughter. "No, no, I'm sorry. Come on, give me your funniest random question."

Ruth bit her bottom lip. "Okay then … What do people in China call their good plates?"

"I don't know. What do people in China call their good plates?"

"No, that's just it. It's a question."

Pippa frowned. "Oh, I thought it was a joke?"

"It is."

"Oh, okay, sorry." The silence felt uncomfortable.

Ruth shrugged her shoulders. "It's the same as this: Why is it called a building if it's already built?"

Pippa tried to laugh, but it ended up sounding awkward and false. "Yes, that's a good one."

"No it's not. You think it's crap. I can tell."

"No, it made me laugh."

"Really?"

Pippa couldn't lie. "Umm, no."

Ruth took a deep breath. "Shall we go and find Andi?"

"I think that's best," nodded Pippa.

****

Zara stared over to the area near the bar where Andi had been standing, relieved to see that she had moved further away. The band on the stage were playing a noisy number and Zara knew no one was close enough to hear her conversation. She turned her back to the guests who were partying on the dance floor, and snarled at Melody with full force. "You've had your fun bringing her here," she curled her lip at Jayney, "now piss off, the pair of you."

Melody continued to leisurely sip her Champagne. "I haven't given Andi her birthday present yet." She tapped the brown file with a finger.

"Who gives a shit? Just leave. Now!"

"Here, take a look, let me know if you think she'll like it." Melody handed over the file.

Zara grabbed it and flung it open. She scanned the first page of dates, times and details, immediately looking up at Jayney. "Do you have one too, or are the details of our underwhelming shags in here too?"

Jayney shrugged. "I don't know what that is. Look, I think I should be going. I shouldn't have come."

"Yes, you should," said Melody. "*She* needs to get a taste of her own medicine." She nodded her head towards Zara. "*She* needs to know what it feels like to be shown up."

Zara stared at them both with icy cold eyes. "Do I look like I'm shown up?" She flung the file onto the table by the stage. "Do what you want with your stupid school girl file."

Melody was thrown. "I'll show it to Andi."

"Be my guest."

Melody frowned. "You really don't give a shit do you?"

Zara narrowed her eyes and snarled. "Do you think I'd fuck you, with my wife in the house, if I did?"

Jayney took hold of Melody's arm. "I think we should be going."

"No, she has to be stopped."

"And what are you? The marriage police?" snapped Zara.

Melody shook her head. "Your poor, poor wife."

"ANDI!" The shout was loud, causing Zara, Melody and Jayney to immediately spin around. They peered over the crowd, eyeing the kerfuffle near the bar.

Stella was hauling Andi back up from the floor. "SHE'S FINE, SHE'S FINE," came the giggling shout.

"Pissed already. Perfect," sneered Zara dropping back onto her heels. "Now you pair just do one." She paused and raised her eyebrows. "Unless you think all three of us should just kiss and make up, that is?"

"I'm through with that," spat Melody.

"Me too," shrugged Jayney. "Can we go now?"

Zara puffed up. "Just remember who I am and what I can do." She looked at Jayney. "I meant it when I said I'd blacklist you from every reputable company in the City. I really thought you were smarter than this?" She glared at Melody. "And you … you'd better take your fucking file and thank fuck I don't fucking fire you." She turned to leave. "Now both of you, just fuck off."

Melody watched open mouthed as Zara marched across the dance floor towards her giggling wife. She shook her head. "Zara's right. What *am* I thinking? I've got a good job. I've got great perks. I just *have* to let this go. It's just that I *hate* admitting she's got a hold on me."

Jayney shrugged. "I did try and tell you. That's exactly what I had to do. Let it go and leave it alone. Just be thankful that you still have a job."

Melody sighed. "I guess so." She paused, cursing her own stupidity. "Crikey, what *have* I been thinking? I love my job at G-Sterling. I'm lucky she hasn't tried to work me out of the firm already." She turned back around to the table, ready to take the brown file and dispose of it once and for all. Instead, Melody froze, in instant panic. "Where the fuck is that file?"

Jayney turned around. The table was empty.

CHAPTER TWENTY

Zara weaved her way across the star studded dance floor, stopping every so often to exaggerate a smile and a promise to come back and chat once she had tracked down her elusive wife. The response was always the same, false laughter and lots of air kisses. In fact most of Zara's guest-interactions followed the same format, lots of gushing and mutual back scratching, with one proud of the invite and the other proud of the guest count; but neither actually that interested in the other.

Zara made her exaggerated, over the top excuses, from Rita and Mike, the co-hosts of the ever so popular Six Show, and walked towards the bar, finally squeezing into the group of Proud Unity folk. She wiggled into the centre of the circle and placed her hands on her hips in mock annoyance. "There you are!" She stretched out her hand to her wife. "Come on, sweetie, our guests need us."

Andi swung both arms out in presentation. "*These* are our guests, *sweetie*."

"Someone's been on the Champers," laughed Zara, trying to make eye contact with Andi's work colleagues, most of whom she could barely recognise.

There were a few polite titters.

Andi giggled loudly. "I tripped on the hem of this ever so gorgeous dress, didn't I Stel?!" Andi lifted a high heel and shook her foot, causing the sparkling silver sequins to dance in the light. "Ooo look, I'm shining!"

Zara took a step closer and bent her mouth to Andi's ear. "We can't leave John Elton waiting, sweetie."

Andi stepped backwards, wobbling as she lifted herself onto her tiptoes. "He's fine. I can see him." She giggled to Stella, "It looks like he's singing to old Jerry from the front desk. You never did like his music, did you, Stel?"

Stella linked Andi's arm to stop her from swaying. "He's a bit too eighties for me. I bet you like him don't you, Zara?"

Zara shot Stella an icy look. "I do … and he's here … and my wife and I need to mingle." She took hold of Andi's arm. "Excuse us."

"Ooo, it looks like we're off," giggled Andi, tripping once more, on the sequined hem. She steadied herself on Zara's waist and hauled up the front of the dress, fully exposing her silver high heels and most of her lower leg. "This'll do it," she laughed, striding forwards like a woman on a mission. "Who are we schmoozing first, then?"

Zara rolled her eyes apologetically at the group of Proud Unity folk, most of whom were just pleased to see Andi letting her hair down for once. "Sorry," she mouthed.

"Who are you apologising for?" asked Andi, catching the gesture.

Zara ushered them away from the group, to a relatively quiet spot at the back of the room, and pulled her wife in closely. "You! I'm apologising for you!" She forced a false smile as the Sapphic Sisters stood up from a corner table and passed by. She waited until they were out of ear shot, then hissed through her teeth. "The evening's barely begun and you're pissed as a fart."

"No I'm not," said Andi, rather more loudly than she had intended.

"See," glared Zara. "Now sober up. This evening's important for us."

Andi placed a hand on her hip. "Oh sorry. I thought it was my birthday party? I thought I was meant to enjoy myself."

"You are! But in the company of some great, like-minded people…" she lifted her nose, "…not falling around with that Proud Unity lot."

"They're my friends."

"You haven't got any friends," hissed Zara.

Andi shifted her weight onto her right leg and tried to steady herself. "What's up with you tonight?"

"You haven't. Stella and Pippa are your work colleagues, and you should never trust a psychologist."

"Ruth's lovely," Andi leaned in towards her wife, "and I think her and Pippa like each other!" She exaggerated a wink.

"How old are you?"

"Thirty today," smiled Andi proudly. "Hic!" She giggled and lifted her hand to her mouth. "Ooo, excuse me!"

Zara reached out and took Andi's cheeks in the palm of her hands, tilting her head upwards and staring into her glazed eyes. "You really are pissed!" She dropped the hold. "I can't believe it! You're pissed! Tonight of all nights, my prim and proper wife, decides to get pissed."

"I'm just having a good time!" Andi lifted her hand to her head, suddenly feeling woozy.

"This is so important for us!"

Andi furrowed her brow, trying to get rid of the pain. "Why?"

"To up our status even more," whispered Zara, aware of the odd glance coming in their direction. "Do you have any idea of the type of people John Elton invites to his Oscars parties?"

"Why would we want to go to an Oscars party?"

Zara pulled her long black hair over her left shoulder and took a deep breath. "Pull yourself together, Andi, we're mingling."

"I don't think I can," managed Andi, feeling her legs start to wobble.

Zara caught her by the waist just as her knees gave way. "Stand up! For goodness sake! What's wrong with you?"

Andi clung on to Zara's waist. "I don't … I don't feel well."

Loud Greek music suddenly started to blast out from the stage. "Stand up straight!" shouted Zara, relieved of the noisy distraction.

Andi made a determined effort to move her foot, but the action felt clumsy and she couldn't get her toes to lift properly, causing them to drag awkwardly behind her. "I don't feel right. My legs aren't working and I feel ever so giddy."

"That's what umpteen glasses of Champagne does to you!" snapped Zara, starting to sweat. She supported Andi into a more upright position. "Let's get you out the back and sober you up. We can't have people seeing you like this! What will they think?"

Andi tried to nod her head, but it felt too heavy. "Sorry," she managed.

"You will be," muttered Zara, taking more of Andi's weight and shuffling towards the private door.

****

Pippa continued to watch the altercation at the back of the room. Most of the guests were now cheering the bare-chested Greek guys on the stage, laughing at their funny dancing and wonky blonde wigs. Pippa wasn't interested. She kept her eyes on her boss.

"You like her, don't you," shouted Stella above the din.

Pippa dropped her gaze. "No … Not like that." She nodded in their direction. "I think she might be a bit drunk. It looks like Zara's having to hold her up. Do you think we should go over?"

Stella swigged from her bubbling flute, not tall enough to see the action. "You've got to be kidding! We'll get the blame!"

"Is Zara always that moody?"

Stella raised her eyebrows. "Hasn't Andi told you?" She stepped in closer. "Zara *apparently* has problems with her hormones."

"And that makes it okay for her to be a moody bitch who manhandles her wife?"

Stella opened her mouth. "Oh my god! You do like her!"

"No," she narrowed her eyes and started to walk, "but I'm not having that!" Pippa shook her head as she watched Zara shake Andi's arm once again. "I'm going over."

"Your funeral," laughed Stella, turning back towards the stage.

Pippa weaved through the scattering of people at the back of the hall, dodging the dancing and ignoring the laughter. She stopped next to Zara and tried to stand tall. Pippa took a deep breath. "What's going on?" she said with more confidence than she actually felt.

"She's pissed! That's what's going on! Help me get her out of here."

"Andi, are you okay?" Pippa bent down and tried to look at her eyes.

"No she's not bloody, okay! Take her other arm. Let's get her out the back."

Pippa did as instructed and wrapped her arm around Andi's waist, lifting her slightly, but trying not to draw too much attention. "Are you okay?" she whispered into Andi's ear.

"I am now," muttered Andi with a smile.

CHAPTER TWENTY ONE

Pippa looked down at Andi's head resting across her knees in the back of the taxi. Her short blonde hair was sticking up and her black eyeliner had smudged across her cheek. The plan had been to sober her up and send her back out to the guests, but it had quickly become apparent that she was too far gone, slurring her words and barely able to stand. Zara had completely lost it with Andi, accusing her of deliberately trying to sabotage the evening and their chances of making a good impression with the, 'people of influence,' as she had called them. Andi had responded with a giggle, sending Zara into a complete frenzy, ordering Pippa to take her home to stop her from making a complete fool out of herself, and more importantly, them as a couple. Pippa had requested assistance from Stella, but Zara had stopped her from going back out to the party; accusing her of trying to turn it into more of a drama than it already was, insisting that no one else needed to know about her drunken excuse for a wife.

It was obvious to Pippa that Zara was not in the least bit concerned with Andi's state of confusion or strange inability to properly control her legs. Instead she just wanted to get her out of there, so she could carry on her indiscreet schmoozing, without the burden of a slightly tipsy, and potentially embarrassing, wife.

Pippa looked out of the taxi's window, recognising the turning into Wellington Place. She reached over for Andi's sparkling silver clutch bag, opened the clip and looked inside. There was a Dior soft pink lipstick, a Dior eyeliner, and a miniature bottle of Andi's trade mark perfume, Daisy, by Marc Jacobs. But there were no house keys. She gently shook Andi's shoulder. "Andi, where are your house keys? We're nearly home."

Andi's eyelids suddenly opened. "Home. How nice if we were nearly home. Our home. Me and you. Not like that. Like friends. No, maybe the other. But it's nice. I don't think I'm slurring now. Bit woozy, like druggy. But I've never done drugs. I would never. Not even too many paracetamol. Scares me too much. Would you? Too dangerous. I'm feeling okay now."

Pippa shook her shoulder once again. "Andi, try and concentrate. Where are your keys?"

"Zara's got the keys," she giggled. "I think I'll sit up. Ooo no! Back down. Too spacey!"

Pippa gently stroked the back of the short blonde hair. "Don't worry. We'll go back to mine. Close your eyes." She leaned forwards slightly, careful not to move Andi's head too much. She spoke to the driver. "Sorry, can we go to Goldhurst Terrace in West Hamstead instead, please?"

The driver stopped looking for house numbers and sped up. "She okay?" he grunted.

Pippa nodded, watching Andi's eyes snap shut. She waited for a moment then moved the blonde fringe across the warm forehead, gently tucking it behind Andi's ear. "She'll be fine," she whispered softly.

****

Andi had enjoyed the feeling of the soft fingers moving gently across her forehead and down her cheek. It had reminded her of the way her mother used to stroke her to sleep. The painful feeling of loss and mourning washed over her once again, as it did every time she thought back to her wonderful mother. She opened her eyes, not wanting to remember, suddenly hit with a vision of buzzing colours and wavy surrounding. She could just about make out Pippa's shadow, leaning forwards and paying the driver of the cab. She decided to pull herself upright and reach out for the handle on the inside of the door, attempting to rise into a seated position. The outcome was disastrous. Her fingers lost their grip on the handle and she fell forwards, ending up in the footwell of the taxi.

Pippa immediately fell down onto her knees next to her. "Are you okay? Christ, Andi, what are you doing?! Here, let me help you!"

Andi wasn't sure what was funny about being face down on the dirty floor of a black cab, but she was giggling all the same. "Ooo, you're ever so strong, aren't you?" she mumbled, feeling Pippa lift her from her waist.

"No, there's just nothing to you, that's all."

"Not chubby strong, but leader strong. Maybe like that Roger Rabbit bunny lady with the curly hair. No, not that. I saw your figure at the swimming pool. Womanly figure. Better than being little like me. Where are we? Are we at the party?"

The taxi driver got out of his seat and walked around to the back of the cab, opening their door and grunting his words. "Need a hand, love?"

"Ooo no," giggled Andi, still yapping on, "we don't need men, do we?! She hasn't for ten months. Women, I mean. She says so, but she must. I think ladies must try. She's got a lovely dimple."

"Yes please," said Pippa, struggling to manage Andi's flailing limbs.

"To the door?"

"If that's okay?" smiled Pippa apologetically, thankful for the help.

"This is her house," chatted Andi, floating up the short path as she clung onto their necks, "she owns it all. She's my PA. Five bedrooms. I'm lucky, aren't I, that she's my PA? There's another lady, orange shock hair, she didn't get it, but she's still there." Andi giggled. "With Janet. Janet's old too. Not like my Pippa." She looked up at the taxi driver. "She's my PA. But she's fun and we're doing fun stuff every month. I tried not to look at her bottom in the pool. She's got no mortgage on this house. It's all hers. Are the street light flashing? Some people would sell probably, but she's nice for GinGin. Money doesn't matter to my PA. She's called Pippa."

"What are you wittering on about?" laughed Pippa. "And she was called Gee-Gee not GinGin."

"GinGin sounds nice. I'm feeling a bit better! It's nice and bright tonight. I think we're okay to go back to the party. Have I told you I think your house is nicer than mine? Zara has that interior lady, but she likes wood carvings. Who likes wood carvings?"

Pippa kept her arm around Andi's waist as she pushed her key into the lock, twisting it quickly and jamming her foot in the door. "This is fine, thank you."

"Anytime, Miss. Look after her."

"Ooo she does," giggled Andi, stepping clumsily into the hallway.

"I will," said Pippa relieved to be home. She shuffled Andi inside the hall and shut the door behind her, quickly locking the latch. "Right, let's get you lying down."

"Ooo, can I go upstairs. I've not been upstairs. I didn't want to ask. I should have really. We're close, aren't we? But I do have friends. I'm nosey, I like looking. But I'm feeling better, just a bit spacy. It's a nice warm house. Feels like you. Did you decorate since GinGin? My head feels all light. I've been here loads. Not giggly like this. It's exciting. Let's play a game."

Pippa put her arm back around Andi's waist and helped her into the lounge. "Lie down on the sofa and I'll get you a drink."

"Ooo a Babycham, please."

Pippa couldn't help but laugh. "Andi! What are you doing? You've got verbal diarrhoea!" She lowered her onto the soft cushions and knelt on the floor, taking hold of Andi's cheeks and looking at her eyes.

"Are you going to kiss me? You shouldn't. I don't know what I'd do if you did. I've thought about it. Have I thought about it? Yes, I think I have thought about it once. No, maybe twice. I've not obsessed about it though. But Jayney is so beautiful. More beautiful than me. I think you have a type. Are you going to kiss me?"

"No!" laughed Pippa! "Oh my god, Andi, you had me worried! Falling around one minute, comatosed the next, now you're acting like you're on a clubbers high!"

"No, I've not been clubbing for years. My legs still feel funny."

"Are you always like this when you're drunk?" asked Pippa, rising to her feet and reaching for the brown throw from the other sofa.

"Don't put a blanket on me! I do that to Zara, but she's older. We've been married for seven years. Is she here?"

"No!" laughed Pippa again, dropping the throw back into position. "Look, I hate to ask this, but have you taken something?"

"I'm not a thief. What's missing? Something of GinGin's?"

"Seriously, Andi, try and think. How many glasses of Champagne did you have?"

"No, they were free. We didn't need to pay the bill. Four I think."

Pippa sat down next to her. "And how much do you weigh."

"Ooo, you guess."

"Nine stone?"

"Eight and a half. You weigh about ten, don't you? But you're not chubby. That dimple would just be there whatever. I like the way you look. I like you. But the problem is that I'm married and if you're married then that's it. But you make me laugh. I love this house. It feels warm. Another time, another place. She can be moody, but she's my wife. I don't think about it. Well maybe I have. But Jayney is so beautiful."

Pippa reached for her mobile phone and dialled the NHS direct number that was still stored in her contacts from her time with Gee-Gee. She followed the automated instructions and was surprised to hear an actual person on the line so quickly. She coughed and spoke loudly. "Hello, yes, I think my friend's had her drink spiked."

"Ooo," said Andi in shock. "Who's that then?"

****

Andi's head was fuzzy, but she managed to slowly open an eyelid and peep out at her surroundings, recognising the beautiful floral curtains immediately. She closed her eyelid again and pressed her head deeper into the soft cushion. *Pippa's lounge*, she thought. I'm horizontal on the sofa in Pippa's lounge. What am I doing in Pippa's lounge? She sprung both eyes open and sat bolt upright. "Shit!" she said out loud.

Pippa jumped in the armchair. "You're awake!" She peered at the old grandfather clock, cross that she had fallen asleep herself. "4.00 a.m. Phew, you've had a few hours' sleep. How are you feeling?"

Andi scrunched up her eyes and rubbed her arm. "Ouch. My head hurts a bit, and so does my arm, but I'm feeling okay." She felt the tape and cotton wool and studied the dressing. "What on earth has gone on?"

"What can you remember?" asked Pippa, standing up and passing over the water.

Andi rubbed her eyes. "I remember Patty the Pudge pumping and grinding. I remember Zara being cross at me." She put her hand to her mouth. "Oh no, what did I do? Did I show her up?"

"No, you're fine." Pippa sat down next to her on the sofa and took her hand. The lights were dim, but both could see clearly. "You're fine. Don't worry. You slipped out of your party slightly early, but your dignity was intact."

Andi looked down at the hand rubbing her own. "Did something happen?" she asked nervously.

"Like what?"

Andi bit her bottom lip and looked at the caressing hand once again. "With us?"

Pippa paused for a moment. "Would that be a good thing or a bad thing?"

"Oh shit, Pippa, I'm married. Yes I like you, but I'm married. I'm so sorry, please, it has to mean nothing. A vow is a vow and I'm so cross at myself-"

Pippa cut in. "Sorry, no, Andi, I didn't mean to worry you. Nothing happened. Please don't start that verbal diarrhoea again! I shouldn't have asked the question."

"Why did you? Did I try something? I'm so sorry if I did. I just don't understand why I'm here. I just have no idea what's going on. I feel like I'm in that film, what's it called? The one with the tiger and the face tattoo."

Pippa released the hand and smiled. "The hangover."

"Well I'm not sure if that's kicked in yet," said Andi, managing a half smile and rubbing her temples. "I remember being in the taxi."

"Face down in the footwell?"

Andi laughed. "Yep."

"Do you remember the nurse?"

Andi shook her head.

"The one you said smelt nice?"

"Oh god, no! How embarrassing. Yes I do. I remember now, she smelt of peaches. Crikey, I must have been off my head!" Andi frowned. "She took my blood, didn't she?"

Pippa lifted the glass of water from the table and encouraged Andi to take another sip. "I called the NHS Direct number and told them your symptoms."

"Which were? This is so embarrassing! I can't believe I was bad enough for you to call the NHS Direct."

"I was contemplating taking you to A and E."

"No? What was I doing?"

"You had the giggles. Then there was non-stop chatter. Giddiness. You were unable to support yourself properly."

"I was pissed as a fart then?" Andi reddened. "I haven't been like that since Uni. It's strange, I feel quite normal now."

Pippa shook her head. "No, your pupils were tiny one minute and huge the next. I think you may have taken something by mistake."

"How? I wouldn't take something by mistake."

"The doctor on the phone said they had an outreach nurse in the area who could pop in and see you. She was here within fifteen minutes and she really was fantastic."

"Okay."

"You said it was fine for her to take your blood, but you did make quite a drama out of the pain."

"I'm so ashamed of myself." Andi was open mouthed. "I must find out who she was and apologise. This is just so strange."

Pippa lifted the small card from the table and read the name. "She was called, Sarah Farley. She told me to rouse you every fifteen minutes and keep you lying on your side. If you asked for water then I was allowed to give you just one sip at a time."

"You've been awake the whole time?"

"Mostly."

Andi lifted Pippa's hand. "I'm so sorry. I know I didn't take anything, I never would. I get scared taking more than one-"

"Paracetamol, I know. You told me."

Andi stretched out her legs and wiggled her toes, relieved that the feeling was all there. "I dread to think what else I said."

"You were the perfect drunk. Funny, amiable, and slightly flirty."

"I wasn't?"

Pippa nodded. "You were. But I'm not ten stone. I'm nine and three quarters."

"Ahh! Please forgive me … for everything." She paused. "Seriously, was I inappropriate?"

Pippa pursed her lips and looked at Andi with a twinkle in her eye. "You were a bit too appropriate for my liking."

Andi felt a flutter of pleasant nerves dance across her chest. "You've gone above and beyond, so thank you … and I know it seems dramatic, and probably everyone who has had one too many, questions whether they've had their drink spiked, or picked up the wrong glass," she exhaled, "you never know with some of the celebs … but I honestly didn't think I had too much." She smiled. "Thank you for looking after me though."

Pippa shrugged. "Anyone would do it."

"If that were true, then it wouldn't be you sitting here, would it?"

"You mean Zara?"

Andi sighed. "Has she called?"

"Zara did the right thing by staying at the party. You couldn't both leave. That really would have raised a few eyebrows. It was a great party and she did what she had to do."

"Maybe." Andi looked at the tall clock ticking quietly in the corner. "Blimey, it's 4.00 a.m. The party must be over by now? Is she on her way?"

Pippa stood up and walked back to the armchair, lifting the phone from the small nest of tables. "I left a message on her mobile and explained where we were and what had happened. I said I was more than happy to watch you until the morning, as long as she picked you up by 10.00 a.m."

"What did she say?"

Pippa checked the blank screen once again. "She's not replied yet. But you know what it's like, cleaning up after parties."

"My party was in *The Grandez*. You don't have to collect the glasses when you're done. She's probably wheedled her way into John Elton's hotel room, begging for friendship and favours."

"Ooo, was that a dig?"

Andi sighed and leaned her head back onto the upright cushion. "Maybe." She bit her bottom lip. "Did I talk about her?"

Pippa sat back down in the armchair and shook her head. "No, not really."

"Good, because she works very hard and she has a very stressful job." She nodded. "I'm really grateful for everything that she does."

"You don't need to convince me."

"Good," said Andi.

"Good," laughed Pippa.

"What's so funny?" Andi frowned. "I said something, didn't I?" She shuffled her bottom to the edge of the sofa seat and leaned in Pippa's direction. "Whatever I said, please just ignore me. I'm a perfectly contented, happily married woman. My wife is wonderful and I cannot wait for the next seven years, and the seven after that."

"You don't need to convince me," said Pippa once again.

"Good."

"Good!" laughed Pippa.

"Good," nodded Andi. "Can we go to bed now? I'm exhausted."

"That's the most sensible thing you've said all evening," smiled Pippa, pausing suddenly. "But we'll have to sleep in the same room as I need to rouse you every fifteen minutes."

Andi giggled. "Stop it!"

"I do! Nurse Sarah told me to."

"Okay, I look forward to being roused by you every fifteen minutes!" Andi smiled. "But I'm not sure you're up to it?"

"I could rouse you every ten if I tried."

"Now who's being flirty!" laughed Andi.

"You started it." Pippa smiled. "It's good to see you getting back to your normal self." She stood from the armchair and walked to the sofa, reaching for Andi's hands and gently pulling her into a standing position. "And anyway, I think you'll find that *you* started it when you asked me to kiss you."

Andi opened her mouth in shock. "I did not!"

"Well, not in so many words, but the invitation was there." Pippa linked Andi's arm and walked her slowly out of the room, towards the staircase. "So no funny business in bed please, boss."

"I wouldn't dream of it," smiled Andi, slowly climbing the stairs. "Well, maybe I have, just once or twice."

Pippa laughed, following her carefully, ready to catch her if necessary. "Oh how I love it when you flirt!"

"Can I borrow a nightie?"

"If you must," grinned Pippa

Andi reached out for the large wooden ball on the end of the bannister and pulled herself up the final step. "You'll have to unzip this dress too, because it's far too awkward for me. I'll be all fingers and thumbs." She smiled. "You may have to help with my bra as well."

Pippa laughed. "Stop it. You know I don't like being teased. You're making me panic."

Andi stood on the top of the landing and studied all of the doors. "I must admit something seems to be making me more confident. Who knows what I've got in my system! Right, which way are we going?"

Pippa climbed the final step and took Andi by the hand, guiding her slowly to the third door on the left. "This way, if you will."

Andi felt the same nervous flutter. "I have to stop teasing now. I'm getting far too giggly."

"Good, because this is awkward enough."

"Really?"

"Yes, really." Pippa released the hand and opened the door to her bedroom. She pressed on the lights and twisted the dimmer. "I'll get you a nightie."

Andi stayed by the door and took in the full beauty of the room, admiring its warmth and comfy appeal. "It's huge, but it looks so cosy, and I just love this bed spread. Zara would never let me have anything like this. She'd say it was too busy. Have I started to ramble again? I think the walk up those stairs has made me light headed."

Pippa reached into her chest of drawers and pulled out a black silk nightie, dropping it onto the edge of the bed. "No, I think you're probably still a bit drunk."

"I thought it was drugs?" Andi paused. "Seriously though, I'm not drunk."

"Who knows what's gone on!" laughed Pippa, stepping behind Andi's back and finding the zip at the top of her dress. She slid it down gently and pulled the arms over Andi's shoulders, watching the sequined silver fabric slip down her body to the floor.

Andi kicked the dress from her feet. "Well I'm glad to be out of that," she nodded. "How come you're still in your dress?"

"I didn't want to leave you." Pippa paused. "Shall I undo your bra?"

Andi nodded, shivering at the gentle touch.

"There you go," whispered Pippa, "all done."

Andi tilted her shoulders and let the straps slide down her arms, watching as the bra fell to the floor. "Thank you," she said, slowly turning around and taking Pippa's hands in her own. She looked up into Pippa's eyes and watched them closely. "You've been incredible."

Pippa looked away. "No, no, it's fine."

Andi waited for the eyes to return, holding the gaze and studying them intently. The silence was energised and she could tell from the small movements of Pippa's nose that she was taking lots of shallow breaths. Andi spoke softly. "*You're* incredible."

Pippa gently shook her head.

"You are." Andi closed her eyes, pausing in her own personal darkness. She willed herself to stay silent; but she couldn't. She opened her eyes and connected with Pippa's once more, finally losing her last bit of control and self-restraint. "I want you," she whispered, overcome by desire. "I want you to want me."

Pippa kept the eye contact, desperately trying not to glance down and absorb the beauty that she knew was just inches away. "I can't," she managed. "Please don't tease me."

Andi's response was quiet. "I'm not teasing." She slowly lifted Pippa's right hand, bringing it into her own body and trailing the fingers up her bare stomach and resting them on her bare breast. "I want you to touch me."

Pippa could hardly breathe. The skin was so warm and so soft and she could feel Andi pressing the hard bud of her nipple against her fingertips. Her breaths were shallow.

Andi lifted Pippa's other hand to her waist and stepped even closer. She whispered in her ear. "Touch me."

Pippa could feel the quivers of instant arousal, desperate to push down onto the bed and succumb to desire. But she didn't. She stayed standing, pleading with her eyes. "You have to stop," she whispered.

Andi shook her head and pulled her body into Pippa's, reaching around to the back of Pippa's dress and pulling at the zip.

Pippa let her hands fall from Andi's body, but was still unable to move. She inhaled deeply and closed her eyes, conscious that her dress was falling from her shoulders. She willed herself to stop … to move away … to hide, but the sensation of Andi's fingers on her back, unhooking her bra, was too intense. She gasped as it was pulled from her shoulders, aware that it had fallen away. Pippa opened her eyes. Andi was staring at her breasts.

Pippa reached for Andi's chin and lifted it with her finger, bringing Andi's eyes to her own. "Not when you're like this," she whispered.

Andi bit her bottom lip and shook her head lightly. "It *has* to be when I'm like this."

"Easily excused?" whispered Pippa.

Andi shrugged. "I know what I'm doing."

Pippa studied the amber eyes, aware of a deep sadness. "And so do I. We can't let this happen."

Andi maintained the eye contact, taking hold of Pippa's hand and pulling it forwards. She pressed it gently against her own knickers. "I want this."

Pippa felt the wetness. "Your denial will kill me."

Andi nodded. "I know."

CHAPTER TWENTY TWO

Andi walked towards Pippa's double bed. She pulled back the soft quilt and slid into the smooth covers.

Pippa stayed still, mesmerised by the vision of Andi Armstrong, lying naked, in her bed. She couldn't move. "I have to do the right thing," she whispered to herself.

"The right thing?" questioned Andi quietly. "Sometimes, doing the wrong thing is the only way to know what's truly right." She pulled the quilt further back, inviting Pippa in, and smiling gently. "I know what I'm doing."

Pippa felt a sudden surge of adrenaline race across her chest, aware of the choice she was about to make. She reached for the dimmer switch next to the bed, twisting the lights into darkness. "Okay," she whispered, climbing gently under the quilt and moving her body next to Andi's. "Maybe I could just hold you?"

Andi nodded and slid under Pippa's arm, resting her head onto her shoulder. "Thank you," she whispered into the darkness.

Pippa closed her eyes. She could hardly breathe. Andi's body was pressed against her own, and her lips were gently skimming her neck. She lay still, conscious of every tiny movement. Andi's fingers suddenly touched her side. They were climbing, slowly climbing, onto her stomach. Pippa froze, unable to stop the slow circling. She swallowed deeply, as quivers of arousal started to spark all across her body. Pippa opened her eyes and stared into the darkness, willing herself to say stop.

Andi climbed her fingers higher, reaching the curve of Pippa's breast. She cupped it carefully and continued the gentle caress.

Pippa was in turmoil, desperate to roll over and stop the inevitable, but she couldn't. She chose instead to arch her back and push out her chest, deliberately willing Andi's fingers closer.

Andi sensed the desire and brushed her palm against the hard nipple.

Pippa gasped.

That was all it took. One gasp of wanting, and both of them knew.

They each grabbed the other, rolling in a battle of power, parting their legs, and pressing down hard.

Pippa felt the wetness against her thigh and moaned out in pleasure, pausing as Andi grabbed at her knickers.

Andi pushed the knickers down and told Pippa to kick them off. "I want you naked," she whispered.

Pippa flicked the silk underwear to the bottom of the bed, and spread her legs into Andi's, moaning deeply as their desires merged. She exhaled loudly. They were connected; both arching their backs and pressing down in a blissful rhythm.

Andi moaned loudly, reaching for the breasts that were gently swaying in front of her. She took the erect nipples and teased them forcefully, causing Pippa to gasp and increase the pressure. Andi shuddered. "This is perfect," she whispered. "*You* are perfect."

Pippa lowered her upper body back down onto Andi's, pressing their breasts together and finding her eyes in the shadows. "Let me kiss you."

Andi nodded gently, feeling Pippa's full lips on her own, mesmerised by the softness of the embrace; tender and careful, yet completely fulfilling. She almost started to cry.

"Are you okay?" whispered Pippa sensing the emotion and pulling away.

Andi nodded. "Please. Please kiss me again."

Pippa did as instructed, maintaining the purposeful rocking and bringing her lips back to Andi's.

Andi moaned as she felt Pippa's hands gently teasing her breasts. It had never felt this intense before. This slow. This meaningful. She kissed back with more passion, feeling Pippa's tongue enter her mouth, not in a rough and probing way, but in an electric journey of discovery. She touched the tip with her own, pushing further and harder, reaching for the back of Pippa's head and pulling it in as close as she could. She wanted more. She needed more. She choked back the emotion as she rolled Pippa over, lifting her arms above her head and kissing with force. She was in control and she wanted to please. She kissed down Pippa's soft neck and along her warm chest, shifting her position to continue the descent. Pippa suddenly took hold of her arms, stopping her kisses and pulling her back up.

"I want it like this," whispered Pippa. "I want to look into your eyes."

Andi understood what she meant and kept the eye contact, moving smoothly and starting to moan.

"Yes," whispered Pippa, taking shallow breaths and pulling Andi's bottom in close, "just like that." She groaned in arousal. "Keep going … that's perfect … yes … yes … Andi … that's perfect."

Andi increased her pace, overcome by the look of arousal in Pippa's eyes. She kissed her deeply, moaning into her mouth and gasping as she neared her own mountainous peak. Both bodies were rocking in time; holding out for the moment they wanted to share. Andi pulled away from the embrace first, staring into Pippa's eyes and biting her bottom lip. Her brow starting to furrow.

Pippa watched as Andi's passion took over, finally able to let herself go. She moaned out in pleasure, clinging tightly to Andi's back and pressing forwards with force. "I'm coming," she groaned.

"Me too," shouted Andi, feeling every single spark, pulse, and explosion. "I'm fucking coming!"

Pippa shuddered.

Andi's scream was loud and extended. Andi gasped at her own reaction, breathing quickly and closing her eyes. "I'm fucking coming," she uttered.

Pippa clung-on to the shaking body, holding the moment of passion, waiting for the shakes to become quivers and the breaths to slow down. "I think you've just come," she whispered, gently kissing Andi's neck.

Andi opened her eyes, flushed with exertion. "You might just be right," she said with a smile.

****

Pippa had woken at 9.00 a.m., unable to dismiss the emotion she felt knowing that Andi had been in her arms all night. She looked at the delicate figure, nestled into her neck, and savoured the moment, certain it wouldn't last. She gently moved Andi's blonde fringe across her warm forehead and planted a soft kiss on the side of her cheek.

"Mmmm, that's nice," moaned Andi.

Pippa held her breath, waiting to hear her call out someone else's name.

The instruction was quiet. "Do it again."

She repeated the action.

Andi spoke softly. "I'm so content here." She paused. "And I know that you're worried, but don't be. I know where I am, and I know what I started." She rolled onto her side and opened her eyes. "I've had the perfect evening, Pippa."

Pippa felt her heart swell.

"Apart from the drink, drugs and Patty's dirty dancing," smiled Andi. "It's been perfect. All because of you."

Pippa found the confidence to meet the warm amber eyes. "I thought you'd ignore it, or deny it, or plead that we forget about it."

"So did I," said Andi, "and I have to admit, that might have been the plan. But how can I?" She shrugged. "I've never had those feelings before. I *want* to remember."

Pippa felt a pain in her heart. "Remember, but not repeat?"

Andi shook her head gently. "You know we can't. But please don't think I regret it, or that I'll condemn it, because I won't. It felt so natural and so right and I wanted it. I wanted you." She paused. "For the first time in ages I followed my heart and I don't believe that could ever be the *wrong* thing to do … it just wasn't the *right* thing to do." She looked at Pippa with wide eyes. "It was beautiful, and I think *you* are beautiful … inside and out. But I'm bound by a commitment that I've always tried my best to uphold. Repeating this wouldn't be fair on any of us."

"You mean Zara?"

"Especially Zara. I know I'm going to sound horribly conceited, but I married for life; with the ups and the downs." She twisted the ring on her wedding finger. "I believe in marriage, Pippa. Crikey, I fight for marriage. I could never, ever contemplate divorce. My job is far too important to me."

"What do you mean?"

Andi exhaled heavily. "I couldn't do my job. I couldn't preach about the importance of commitment and marriage for gay people, whilst going through my own divorce. I'd be torn apart." She rubbed her temples. "I'd lose all credibility."

Pippa took Andi's hand. "But what about love?"

Andi squeezed the fingers in response. "I love my job. Proud Unity's my life."

"And Zara?"

"She's my partner. She's the person I promised to spend forever with. I'm bound to her through the promises I made." Andi gently stroked Pippa's arm. "I could never hurt her."

"So why did you do it?"

Andi shrugged. "Because I wanted to. I selfishly wanted to touch you, to hold you," she paused, "to feel you wanting me."

"Do you love her?"

"I love our partnership, our commitment, and our promise to one other. Marriage is so much more than just emotion."

Pippa took a deep breath, prepared for the admission of error. "So what was last night then?"

Andi smiled. "*That*, was emotion."

"Which one?"

Andi closed her eyes. "Last night was joy, surprise, courage, hope, wonder…" She opened her eyes and stared straight at Pippa. "*That* felt a lot like love."

CHAPTER TWENTY THREE

Pippa and Andi were standing in Pippa's hallway, fearfully awaiting the inevitable. The sound of a car pulling into the gravel driveway made their hearts beat faster. Pippa reached out for Andi's hand and held it tightly. "Let's *remember*, but not *repeat*," she said with meaning.

Andi stepped forwards and kissed Pippa lightly on the lips. "Remember, but not repeat," she whispered, feeling a deep pain spread across her chest.

Pippa lifted her hand to the latch, pausing for a moment as if to say one final word. She chose against it. Instead she unlocked the front door and pulled it wide, inviting a cold winter gust of air straight into her home. "It's a taxi?" she said confused.

Andi pulled her mobile phone from the pocket of the baggy hooded top she had borrowed and glanced at the screen. There were no messages. "Zara must have been caught up. I'll just check it's for me."

Pippa watched as Andi padded across the gravel driveway in a pair of trainers that were two sizes too big and a tracksuit that had been her old favourite at Uni. She had offered Andi a selection from her wardrobe, but Andi had insisted on being comfortable and snug, choosing the slightly faded two-piece instead. Pippa smiled at the silver sequined dress slung over Andi's arm, and the heeled silver shoes held by the straps. "Is it for you?" she shouted.

Andi nodded. "It's for me. I'm fine. Stay there."

Pippa ignored the request and dashed across the gravel in her fluffy slippers. "Let me know you get home okay."

Andi stepped forwards for one final hug, inhaling deeply and closing her eyes. "I will." She pulled away and blinked quickly, stung by the cold. "Why do I feel so sad?"

"Because your wife didn't even bother to pick you up?"

Andi shook her head. "No, I don't think that's it," she whispered, stepping into the taxi and closing the door.

Pippa watched the car slowly reverse and pull out into the street. She waited for it to disappear around the corner before she replied. "Well it *bloody well* should be," she said to herself. "What. A. Complete. Bitch."

****

Andi dumped her dress, shoes and glittery bag, onto the backseat of the taxi, exhaling heavily and looking out of the window. "What. A. Complete. Bitch," she said to herself, shaking her head. *Not even arsed to get out of bed to pick me up. Not even concerned about my state of health. Not even bothered to pick up the phone.* There had been one text message at about 9.30 a.m. saying: "I'll get you at 10.00 a.m. Send the address." Well she *hadn't* got her … and it had been *later* than ten. Pippa had graciously cancelled her coffee morning with friends so they could stand by the door and await the inevitable; the end of their moment; the end of their love. Andi almost burst into tears. It sounded so dramatic hearing the voice in her head call it love. But that's what it had been. That's how she felt.

Andi continued to stare out of the window, mesmerised by the traffic, but unaware of its presence. All she could do was think. Ten minutes and she'd be home. Ten minutes and she had to have all of this emotion, this confusion, this uncertainty, boxed off and tidied away. She couldn't, and she wouldn't, dwell. She checked the time on her phone; well maybe she would … for ten minutes. She leaned her head backwards, resting it on the padded headrest and closing her eyes. *Why did you do it?* She asked herself.

Because I wanted to, came the reply.

She shook her head. *Not good enough. What made you do it?* She asked instead.

The emotion of the moment. It felt right. It was too hard to fight.

She exhaled heavily. *So you're a failure. You failed to keep your vow. You fell into bed with the first person who showed you a bit of attention.*

She shook her head again. *Pippa's not just anybody. Pippa's special. I connect with Pippa.*

But you're married.

Not happily. Andi opened her eyes, blinking at the light. Shocked at her own admission. "Fuck," she breathed quietly. "What the fuck am I going to do?" She spotted a couple of girls walking hand in hand down the Finchley Road and smiled. *What's more important?* She asked herself, closing her eyes once more. *The emotion of love or the bond of marriage?*

The bond of marriage, she answered without question.

Okay, so you work on the love in your own marriage. Zara loves you. You know that.

Do I?

Yes. She loves you. She's going through a hard time at the moment. You can't just jump ship because you've started to feel the butterflies again.

I know.

But you don't feel guilty though, do you?

Andi bit her bottom lip. *No.*

Why not?

Because I deserve some happiness too. Andi opened her eyes and wiped away a slow tear. "You *are* happy, Andi," she said quietly to herself.

"You okay, love?" asked the taxi driver loudly.

Andi sniffed noisily and swallowed her tears. "Yes, yes, I'm fine."

"You look upset to me, love."

Andi shook her head and tried to smile. "No, I'm fine."

The taxi driver shrugged and returned his eyes to the road.

No, you're not fine, whispered the quiet voice inside her head.

****

Andi had asked the taxi driver to stop at the end of her street. She needed a moment to compose herself. She walked slowly, hoping the bracing winter air would calm her nerves and bring her strength. She rounded the corner of Wellington Place, watching as her tall and imposing house came into view. A feeling of apprehension washed over her. *Have I always felt like this?* she questioned, conscious of her desire to just turn around and walk away. She stopped, spotting Zara sitting on the front step. She was leaning back against the black glossy front door, holding a yellow dishcloth and some sort of cleaning spray. Andi stood still and watched. Zara was checking her watch. Andi studied her without her knowing, dressed in her tight black skinny jeans, white oversized cricket jumper, padded black gilet, and Ugg boots. Her long black hair was tied in a high pony and she didn't seem to have any make-up on. *She looks tired*, thought Andi, suddenly feeling a pang of regret. *Hold it together*, she instructed herself. *No harm has been done and you love your wife dearly.* And with that, she continued her walk, passing through the tall white pillars and turning up the path towards their house.

Zara spotted Andi approaching and jumped up. She turned to face the door and started to rub the letterbox. "I sent you a taxi!" she snapped over her shoulder. "Why are you walking?"

Andi continued up the path, joining Zara on the front step. "He dropped me at the end of the road. What are you doing?"

"What does it look like I'm doing?" she snapped. "I'm clearing off some graffiti that one of your wackos has left on our letterbox!"

Andi dropped her handful of belongings and grabbed Zara's arm. "Let me see."

"It's almost off," she snapped. "It said: POUR PETROL HERE."

"No!" gasped Andi, just about making out the faint capital letters.

"Yes!" mocked Zara. "That's why I didn't come to pick you up. I've been out here scrubbing all morning."

"Please tell me you took a photo of it."

Zara continued to rub. "No, why?"

Andi shook her head. "For the police file! I have to keep a note of all of these incidents for the police file."

"What police file?" Zara looked shocked. "Just how many incidents have you had?"

"Threats, nasty emails, graffiti. You knew about this, Zara!"

Zara sprayed on some more cleaning fluid. "No I didn't."

Andi reached into the deep pocket of Pippa's hoody and pulled out her phone. "Step to the side and I'll take a photo."

Zara gave one final rub with the yellow dishcloth and the letters disappeared. "I've been letting it soak in the spray. The marker they used must have been water soluble."

Andi crouched down on her knees and studied the shiny gold letter box; there wasn't a single trace of writing left. "Zara!"

"What? We don't want the neighbours reading it and we certainly don't need the police coming round. You just need to sort your priorities out."

"What do you mean?" said Andi, hugging herself from the cold. Her head had started to bang.

"Well look at yourself. Showing yourself up at parties, bringing the weirdos to our door. It has to stop, Andi, all of it. Look at you, crawling home in the morning in someone else's clothes."

Andi bent down and lifted her dress, heels and bag from the step. "Can we just go inside?"

"Fine," shrugged Zara.

****

Andi lifted her knees onto the sofa in their front lounge and hugged her mug of hot chocolate. They had been sitting in silence for the past fifteen minutes. Andi broke first. "Pour petrol here. That's pretty threatening, isn't it?"

Zara was sitting upright, with folded arms, in her brown leather recliner. "Of course it's bloody threatening. It's a threat from one of your weirdo bigots who's found out where you live, and who now wants to burn you alive."

Andi shivered. "And you didn't think to report it?"

"No. If they were going to pour petrol into our letter box then they would have done it there and then, not just written about it."

"Maybe," said Andi quietly. "Can we chat about last night first?"

"What's there to chat about? You got pissed and left over three hundred guests fending for themselves."

"Oh stop it, Zara. No one noticed I was missing."

"Isn't that worse then?"

Andi put her mug of hot chocolate down on the coffee table and lifted her hands to her eyes, conscious of her emotion. "Why are you so mean to me?"

"Oh don't start that again," said Zara with a raised voice. "You're the one that's causing this, not me."

Andi blinked quickly and wiped away a tear. "Don't you love me?"

"Why do you always ask me that?" shouted Zara in frustration.

"Because love isn't meant to feel like this."

"Oh, and what's it meant to feel like?"

"It's meant to be caring, thoughtful, exciting-"

"I don't excite you? I don't care for you? I don't think about you? Cheers!" shouted Zara. "Thanks for that!" She stood up and started to point in Andi's direction. "I've given you everything. This house, my money, my cars-"

"I just want your love," whispered Andi.

"Sorry, what was that?" shouted Zara.

"I just want your love."

Zara rubbed her temples and started to pace. "You'd be nothing without me, you know that don't you? Remember how much money I put into Proud Unity to get you off the ground?" She continued to shout. "Remember that? That was love."

"Love's an emotion, not a thing."

Zara jumped down onto the sofa next to Andi and folded her arms. "Oh sorry, doctor June, enlighten me. What am I doing wrong?" She raised her eyebrows and waited in silence.

Andi sniffed away a tear. "You used to love me."

"Used to? So me organising a huge birthday party with a wonderful array of guests, isn't love? So me making excuses for your whereabouts so you didn't lose face with your guests, isn't love? So me getting up early to prepare the veg for a wonderful roast dinner today, isn't love? Shall I go on?"

Andi wiped her cheeks. "Thank you for doing those things."

"It's okay," shrugged Zara. "I do them because I love you."

"I would rather just be held and hugged and feel like you meant it."

Zara exhaled heavily. "Oh Andi, I do love you!" She reached out and put an arm around Andi's shoulder. "We've been married for seven years, of course it's not going to be all sparks and butterflies, and I know I'm an old grouch, but okay, I'll admit it … I'm scared."

Andi sat up and widened her eyes. Zara had never once admitted to any weakness … ever. "Of what?"

"Of losing you."

Andi reddened. "To who?"

"No, to work!" laughed Zara. "Look at you flattering yourself!" She paused and spoke seriously again. "It's your work that's coming between us and I want you to stop."

Andi frowned. "What? Why?"

"Remember when we first met? We had time for wining and dining, dinner dates and trips out. Andi, we had fun. You were carefree and funny. I'd go off to work and you'd do your odd bits of Proud Unity stuff, but you'd always be home when I got back and we'd always have the evenings and weekends together." She shrugged. "I want that back. I didn't marry a lesbian icon, Andi. I married you, and I think you've forgotten who you really are."

Andi rubbed her eyes. Her head was banging and she felt confused. "Why haven't you said this before?"

"I've dropped hints. But it has to be your decision." Zara exhaled. "But if you're not even willing to give up when your life's under threat, then I guess you never will."

"I'm making a difference, Zara."

"Not to me you're not." She stood from her seat. "But I'll tell you one thing, the fact that you're not even concerned now that *my life's* under threat, speaks volumes."

"Oh Zara, sit down. I hadn't thought-"

"You never do. You never think what it must be like for me, going to bed alone most nights while you tap away on your computer. You never think what it's like for me, seeing other people fawning over you, hailing you as some lesbionic hero. You never think what it's like for me when all anyone ever wants to talk about is you." Zara walked to the doorway and reached for the handle. "I married *you*, Andi, and I want *you* back."

Andi closed her eyes and started to cry.

CHAPTER TWENTY FOUR

Andi was sitting at her work desk, anxious and apprehensive. Not only would she have to get that potentially awkward first meeting with Pippa out of the way, but she'd also have to face the questions from Janet, Elizabeth, and the other Proud Unity folk, about her disappearance from Saturday night's party. She twisted in her black padded swivel chair and looked out of the large office window at the high rise building opposite. No doubt it would be filling up with city workers, all assuming they too, had the most important job in the world; they too, were irreplaceable. Zara had in fact given a very convincing portrayal of what life could be like if she left Proud Unity, full of fun times, frolics, and family. She had actually uttered the words *family.* Zara had said, *'a family for us.'*

The knock on the door snapped her out of the daydream. She swivelled back around and looked at the entrance to her office, watching as Pippa gingerly stepped into the room. "Knock, knock, only me."

Andi stood up and walked towards her. "You never knock!" she said, reaching out and pulling her in for a big hug. "Crikey, you didn't even knock when you were on interview!"

Pippa laughed. "I know!" she said, squeezing in response. "Coffee?"

Andi nodded and let go, leaving Pippa to walk to the machine.

Pippa smiled. "I did do a good interview didn't I? I think we could do with a song now, just to break the ice."

"Go on then," laughed Andi, "Make it a good one."

Pippa placed Andi's mug under the two spouts and pressed a combination of buttons, sending the machine into a grinding and whirring frenzy. She reached for the half empty, small bottle of water, discarded on the worktop, and spun around. She lifted the bottle to her mouth like a microphone and flicked her mass of curly brown hair. "*Close your eyes, make a wish. And blow out the candle light. For tonight is just your night. We're gonna celebrate, all through the night.*"

Andi laughed at the perfect rendition of the Boys II Men classic. "Stop it!"

"No, I'm just getting to the good bit." Pippa lunged forwards and upped the volume. "*I'll make love to you. Like you want me to. And I'll hold you tight. Baby all through the night.*"

"EXCUSE ME!" The shout was loud and neither had noticed Elizabeth entering the office. "Sorry to interrupt. These came for you." She walked over to Andi and placed the huge bouquet of flowers into her arms. "Do continue, Pippa. That was marvellous."

Pippa placed the small bottle of water back on the work top. "I was just messing around," she said, slightly embarrassed. "How did you enjoy the party on Saturday, Elizabeth?"

"Yes, very good, thank you. I haven't got time to stop and chat now, Janet needs me. But I think we're all going to catch up at lunchtime."

"Okay, great," said Andi purposefully. "We've got a lot on today as well."

Elizabeth nodded and turned to leave.

Andi held back the nervous giggles until the office door swung shut. She looked down at the huge bouquet of brightly coloured flowers, then back up at Pippa.

Pippa bit her bottom lip. "They're not from me," she said shaking her head.

Andi felt a strange sensation prickle down her back, unsure if Pippa's admission had left her disappointed or relieved.

"You said to act normal, and that's what I'm doing, and that's what I'll continue to do." Pippa smiled. "Remember what we said? Remember, without regret, but don't repeat … remember?"

Andi laughed. "You lost me at the first remember!" She walked back over to her desk and placed the bouquet down, tuning around and holding onto the lip of the desk with two hands. "Seriously Pippa, I need you to know just that."

"Just what?"

She held the wooden desk tightly. "That I remember, and that I don't regret, and even though I may be very tempted at times, that I'm going to try my very hardest, not to repeat."

Pippa came over and perched next to her. "You don't have to explain." She smiled. "We understand each other. We both wanted it to happen and we're both glad it happened. But we also both value our friendship and our jobs." She gently nudged Andi's arm. "Hey, it'll bring us closer."

Andi turned to look at her and smiled. "I know. I can feel it already."

"This might sound dramatic, but I always remember a story I heard about a mother who lost her son in a traffic accident at the age of nine years old. The mother was in the doctor's surgery, unable to cope with her grief, questioning why this had to happen to her and her son." Pippa paused to check that Andi was following. "Well anyway, the doctor said he was going to ask the woman one question."

"Okay," said Andi slightly perplexed, but definitely intrigued.

"The doctor said to the mother: '*If you knew this was going to happen to your son, nine years after giving birth to him, and you had the choice of going back in time and deciding whether you would give birth to him again or not, what would you choose?*'"

Andi nodded.

"The woman instantly knew that she would choose the nine wonderful years, over no years at all, and her grief suddenly became more manageable. She knew she had to focus on the good times and the memories, rather than the bad." Pippa smiled. "So I guess I kind of think like that."

Andi laughed. "Oh bless you, Pippa. That's such a sweet story," she raised her eyebrows, "if somewhat morbid ... but I understand what you mean."

Pippa walked her fingers along the side of the desk so they were gently brushing Andi's. "If I knew I could share an experience that was so magical, so wonderful, and so precious that it would make every other experience pale in comparison … If I knew I would experience it once, but never again, leaving every other connection, for the rest of my life, completely lacking … would I choose to experience it in the first place?" She bit her bottom lip and held Andi's glistening amber eyes. "I would … one thousand times over."

Andi felt a deep pain in her heart. "Thank you," she whispered, "and so would I."

****

Andi watched as Pippa walked from the office, touched and relieved by the moment they had shared. Both knew that everything would be okay; that everything would continue in the manner that it should. The office door swung shut and Andi immediately turned to the huge fragrant bouquet, puzzled by the envelope. She had noticed it when Elizabeth had passed it over. It wasn't the usual small card, written by the florist, shoved amongst the stems; this was a full sized red envelope with a hand-drawn heart in the corner. She lifted it out from the flowers and walked around to the other side of her desk, sitting in her padded chair and studying the sketched shape.

Flowers were often delivered to the office from researchers who Andi had spent some time with, or radio hosts thankful for her presence during a debate. Or even just individuals who wanted to show their support. But they never usually included large red envelopes like this one.

She stuck her finger under the lip and ripped across the top, carefully pulling out a hand written letter. She opened the notepaper and smoothed out the fold, instantly recognising the writing.

To my darling wife, it read.

Andi closed her eyes, nervous of the words. She swallowed and exhaled slowly, daring herself to read without question.

To my darling wife,

I need to start by saying sorry. I'm sorry for all of the things I have said or done that have made you feel sad. I love you and I never want you to feel sad.

I'm sorry for all of the times I have been mean. I'd like to think that it's not intentional, but sometimes I feel so caught up in myself and my problems, that it probably is.

Maybe I'm jealous? Jealous of you. Your life. Your success. Your fans. Your ability to keep your head up and keep striding forwards, even when I'm holding you back and putting you down.

I've been snappy. I know I have. I can feel myself doing it and I don't know why, but I can't stop. Maybe I should blame my hormones, or the drugs they've made me try. But when I think about it, it's probably just the realisation that this could be an early menopause; that's what may be affecting me the most. I feel like an old woman. I don't want to dry up and lose my passion. I want to keep it alive. I want to know that I've still got it. But if it's not the dreaded M, then they think it could be my thyroid. You might as well just check me into a home now!

Andi had to smile, she could picture the way Zara would have reached for the phone and asked her to ring around all of the local retirement villages. She read on, with intrigue.

Listen to me writing away about all of my ailments. This is probably the last thing you want to hear when you're at work with your fit, young PA, saving the world and doing it in style. Because that's what you've got, Andi. Style. You've always had it. You always will. That's why I fell in love with you.

You're an incredible woman, and I'm proud to call you my wife. But I meant what I said yesterday. I want you back. If that's selfish then so be it. I call a spade a spade … sometimes I even call it a bloody fucking shovel! … but I'm being honest here. I'm pleading for you to stop. If not for me, then for our potentially wonderful, unborn children.

Zara x

Andi gasped. *Our potentially wonderful unborn children?* Zara could barely utter the word *kids*, let alone refer to the little people of this world with any form of endearment. She folded the letter back over, before unfolding it once again, and rereading it twice through.

Pippa popped her head into the office. "Sorry, I've just had a phone call. I need a quick quote for a reporter. Can you do it now?"

Andi nodded and signalled her in. "Can I ask you something first?"

Pippa nodded.

"Do you want kids?"

"Of course! But I hate it when people call them kids, they're children."

"Is there a difference?"

Pippa smiled, making her way to the desk. "Yes, I think there is. Why?"

Andi touched the letter with the tip of her finger, so completely tempted to open up and ask for advice. She had never once bad mouthed Zara, to anyone, not even Stella when she was having digs of her own. The principle of loyalty had always been so important to her, and she had presumed it always would be. "Sorry, no reason," said Andi, "I'm just thinking of doing a piece on LGBT parents."

"Sounds great, I'll help you with it. Let me get this quote first." Pippa looked at her notepad and tapped the end of her pen between her teeth. "A reporter from *The Daily*, wants to know what you think about the lesbian in America who faked her own hate crime to draw attention to the plight of gay people."

Andi sighed. "There are some real nutters out there, I know that for sure!"

Pippa nodded and pretended to scribble. "Great, got it."

CHAPTER TWENTY FIVE

Andi had managed to make it through a lunchtime of jibes and digs from the Proud Unity folk, who were joking about her inability to handle her booze, and suggesting that she'd sloped off with Patty the Pudge or the Sapphic Sisters, or both. Andi had batted away the banter and gained confidence that her party had actually been a roaring success, with all enjoying themselves until the early hours. Andi had then made the most of the relatively light workload and spent a lot of the afternoon searching the internet and printing out pamphlets from all of the local fertility clinics, amazed at the wide range of services offered to lesbians and lesbian couples. Absolutely no distinction seemed to be made between people of opposing sexualities in need of some help in starting a family. Andi had started to get really excited, having forgotten, or possibly dismissed, how deeply she craved children of her own. She tucked the file of print-outs under her arm and slipped her key into the lock of their large front door. "I'm home!" she shouted excitedly.

Zara shuffled out of the lounge, in her work suit and tights. "You're early. I'm not even changed yet."

Andi hurriedly kicked off her shoes and lifted her jacket to the antique coat stand. "I know! I couldn't wait to get home."

"Why?"

Andi pulled the large red envelope from the file and wiggled it with a grin.

"Oh that," shrugged Zara. "I'm not sure where my head was at when I was writing that."

"Don't play it down, Zara. It was wonderful, and so were the flowers." Andi walked over to her wife and smiled at her gently. "I know it must have taken a lot to say sorry, and I'm sorry too. We've both changed from the people we were when we got married and I guess we just have to work together to adjust."

"Or change back to who we were." Zara folded her arms. "And anyway, I haven't changed."

Andi pursed her lips. "Umm, your dry sense of humour might have degenerated slightly into outright insults." Andi watched as Zara pulled her long hair over her shoulder and lifted her nose; realising quickly that she'd have to backtrack. "I'm joking!" she said. "But you know what I mean. You wrote about it in the letter, and I understand it must be difficult not feeling like yourself and wondering why."

Zara shrugged. "They've given me some patches to try."

"Good," smiled Andi with sympathy. "Come on, let's go and sit down. I've got some stuff to show you." She walked through to the lounge, sat down on the large sofa and patted the seat next to her.

"I'll sit in my recliner, sweetie."

"No, come here and look at this." Andi excitedly pulled the wad of print-outs from the file. She leaned forwards and spread them across the coffee table. "I've spent the afternoon doing a spot of research and I think I already know which clinic would be best for us to try."

"Sorry, what?" said Zara, still standing.

"I think you're right. I think starting a family would be such a wonderful thing for us. We've been together for seven years; we're both at the top of our game at work. This feels so right." She smiled. "I'm just so thrilled that you've started to entertain the idea."

Zara coughed and perched down on the sofa next to Andi. "And you'd stop work?"

"Well, even if we started all of the consultations this month, and even if things were fine with our fertility and we ended up going for the IUI-"

"The what?"

Andi laughed. "The IUI. Intrauterine insemination. It's the most natural form of fertility treatment." She was talking quickly but she couldn't help it. The excitement was too much to contain. She laughed again. "So if we had the IUI, where they track your follicles and wait for your egg to be released, before using a catheter to insert the sperm into whichever fallopian tube the egg is travelling down," she took a deep breath, "so if we went for that, and hoped the egg fertilised properly and embedded itself naturally into the wall of the womb … we'd still be looking at a nine month pregnancy, and that's only if everything went to plan." She took another breath. "So I wouldn't have to start my maternity leave until next September. That is, of course, assuming I was the one to carry." She nodded in conclusion. "But Zara, this time next year we could have our own little family!"

Zara put her hand up. "Whoa whoa whoa! Stop right there!"

Andi bit her bottom lip, worried that the talk of catheters and fallopian tubes had been too much too soon.

"What do you mean, *maternity leave*?"

"I'd try and work until the last possible minute, like Stella did." She paused. "But then I think I would like to take the full year off." She waited for Zara to smile.

Zara remained stony faced. "We've had this discussion before. We cannot work and have children. It would be too much."

Andi nodded. "That's why I'd take the full year off."

"Then what?"

"Then we'd do what most other working mothers do, we'd get childcare."

Zara shook her head. "Wouldn't work. You'd have to leave Proud Unity, permanently."

"Why?"

Zara tutted. "We had this chat yesterday. We could get '*us*' back. We could start to have fun again!"

"Oh, Zara, it's tempting, but you know that Proud Unity's my life."

"But you'd have a new life. You'd be a mother and a housewife."

Andi ran her fingers through her short blonde hair. "We're strong women. We can have it all."

Zara's eyes flickered. "No, sweetie. We either go for this properly, or we don't go for it at all. And if we do decide to go for it, then you should stop work as soon as possible so that you can focus all of your attention on getting pregnant."

Andi shifted in her seat. "And you wouldn't want to carry?"

Zara shuddered. "No *fucking* way!"

CHAPTER TWENTY SIX

It was the second Saturday in December, two weeks since her thirtieth birthday party, and Andi was sitting at the back of the cosy presentation room in one of London's top fertility clinics. She glanced at her watch once more. The past fortnight had been strange. Work had been quiet, with everyone nervously awaiting the government's response to the equal marriage consultation, and her home life had also felt slightly muted. Whenever they seemed to chat about their fertility options, Zara would freeze up and get snappy, leaving Andi to remind her that starting a family had, in fact, been her suggestion. The conversation, however, would always end at the same point - Zara insisting that she stopped work to focus her full attention on the pregnancy.

Andi exhaled as a nervous shiver raced down her spine. She glanced at her watch and realised the truth. Zara wasn't coming. The introductory presentation was about to start and she looked around at the other couples in the room, watching them snuggled together at the shoulders, in nervous excitement. A single lady in the corner of the room caught her eye and gave a knowing nod, obviously assuming she too was embarking on this journey alone. Andi slipped her hand into her jacket pocket and checked her phone. Nothing.

****

Zara was sitting in her silver Range Rover, eyes closed, radio on, completely hidden by the dark tinted windows. She had chosen to park next to a large yellow skip on a piece of industrial wasteland in

Upper Walthamstow, waiting until the last possible moment, before texting Andi and crying traffic. Her ringtone startled her and she blinked quickly, rubbing her eyes and looking at the display. She expected to see Andi's name, but the number was blocked. She swiped the screen and tapped the green button, waiting with a smile.

The voice was high pitched and the caller was once again using their unconvincing posh accent. "*This is the end of the second deadline I set you. Have you told her yet?*"

Zara smiled. She had come to enjoy the threatening phone calls, each time gaining more of a clue as to the identity of the caller. She laughed. "Okay, so, I've figured out you're a woman. You were obviously at Andi's party. You clearly stole Melody's *ridiculous* sex file-"

The caller cut in. "*So it's not true? The dates? The times? The explicit details of your liaisons? Is that why you're being so blasé?*"

Zara smirked. "Oh no, it's all true. Every, last, sordid, detail." She listened as the caller tried to stifle a cough. "I have affairs. Big deal."

"*Does your wife know?*"

"Well I haven't succumbed to your ridiculous idea of telling her everything … so no … of course she doesn't." Zara studied her nails, using her thumb to file down any rough sections. "And that, thank you very much, is the way it's going to stay."

"*You really don't care, do you?*"

Zara flicked a piece of dirt from under a fingernail and sighed. "I do care. That's the whole point. Why hurt someone for no reason? It's just sex. Everybody has affairs."

The high pitched voice became even more exacerbated. "*You're making a mockery out of marriage!*"

Zara looked around at the wasteland, trying to decide if it had potential for investment. "Look, as much as I love our little chats I'm starting to get rather bored of all of this. You said last week that you were going to post her the file, and you didn't. You've said this week that you're going to post her the file, and you haven't. So why don't you just take that file and stick it where the sun don't shine, or, in your case, where the fingers don't poke!"

"*You'll regret this!*"

Zara rolled her eyes. "Yeah, yeah, yeah! Why don't you just start an Andi Armstrong fan club instead? I'm sure she'd appreciate the support."

"*She's going to need some support after she reads this!*"

Zara couldn't resist one final dig. "The chances are, you're a Proud Unity freak, so I'm not at all worried about you, or your stupid stolen file, because she's leaving … for good. So you bunch of do-gooders can just go fall down a hole!"

The phone line went dead.

****

Andi squeezed on her mobile phone as the doctor and nurse began their presentation. This morning's session had been pitched as an informal, but informative introduction to the world of fertility treatment. Andi had suggested they pay for their own individual consultation session on an evening after work, but Zara had stonewalled the idea, saying it was best to just sit and listen at one of the open Saturday morning seminars, where all were welcome for Q and A. She had claimed they would be able to get more of a feel for the clinic before they actually committed to anything in particular. For Andi it was simple; they were committing to starting a family.

Andi shifted in her plastic chair and looked up at the collage of baby portraits filling the screen, aware that she should be awash with excited elation, instead of her current emotion of lonely despair. *What am I doing here?* she questioned, cross that she had been so easily sucked in. She should have insisted on a private session where they could have travelled in together after work and thrashed out the best possible options for them as a couple.

The vibrations of her phone suddenly jolted her back into the room. She looked down at the display and the small white envelope with Zara's name flashing underneath. She swiped the screen and clicked on the message. "*Stuck in traffic. Gridlocked in Marylebone. Can't be helped.*"

Andi inhaled deeply. *Can't be helped?* It could have been helped if Zara had been willing to move her 9.00 a.m. acupuncture appointment. She had gladly delayed her morning 'Go Ape' session with Pippa until the afternoon, even though it had been planned for ages. Surely Zara could have done the same? She looked back at the slide show and heard a cumulative '*ahhh*' from the people in the room. A toddler was waving out from the screen saying, '*Mama*.' Andi sighed and slid off her seat, staying low and creeping out of the double doors at the back.

Andi eased the handles back into position and stood tall as she walked down the corridor and past the main reception, pleased that the woman on the desk was deep in conversation with a heavily pregnant lady.

"Triplets!" said another woman as Andi walked past.

Andi stopped for a moment and smiled, sensing that they must be partners. "You're very lucky," she said looking back over at the woman with the huge bump.

"Sorry, I couldn't help it. You're Andi Armstrong, aren't you?"

Andi nodded.

"My wife and I are huge fans." The lady peered over her shoulder, disappointed that her pregnant wife was still engaged with the receptionist. "She'll be sorry she missed you."

Andi smiled apologetically. "Sorry, I've got to rush. Good luck with the triplets!"

"Thanks," the lady nodded and looked at Andi's stomach, "…are you?"

"Oh no!" laughed Andi. "Just here on business."

"Right, of course. Nice to have met you."

Andi nodded and scurried quickly out of the doors. She reached for her phone and dialled Pippa's number. "Can we meet up early?" she asked, "my appointment's been cancelled."

****

Pippa pulled her car onto the pavement outside the Finchley Central Tube stop. She beeped her horn and reached over the passenger's seat, forcefully pushing open the stiff door. "I'd have come and got you," she said looking up at Andi.

Andi ducked her head and climbed into the car. "Don't be daft. I've been in central London. Zara was going to give me a lift up to Trent Park, but she's stuck in traffic." Andi laughed. "But more importantly where on earth did you get this car? I assumed you'd have a Focus or a Mini or something like that." She paused. "In fact you've never even mentioned owning a car before." Andi smiled. "I like it!"

"Yeah right."

"I do," said Andi, looking around the old fashioned Morris Minor. "It's not one of the ones made out of wood is it?"

"Sure is. Gee-Gee's pride and joy. She's called Molly. I never really need a car, but when I do, Molly's here for me."

"That's so funny."

Pippa laughed and hauled the heavy steering wheel to the right, pulling out onto Ballard's Lane and starting their journey towards Trent Park. "I just can't bring myself to sell her."

Andi looked over her shoulder and admired the boot. "Spacious."

"It's a Traveller."

"It's probably worth a fortune."

Pippa shrugged. "Maybe, but money's not everything. Gee-Gee kept her in tiptop condition, and yes, I do feel a bit of a plonker driving it, but it brings back some happy memories. Plus I'm not really travelling anywhere of substantial distance at the moment, so old Molly here's the perfect fit."

"How far to Trent Park?" laughed Andi.

"Twenty minutes." She patted the brown leather steering wheel. "You'll be fine, won't you, Moll? What were you doing in London so early anyway?"

"Oh nothing, just an appointment that got cancelled. I'm so sorry to mess you around."

"It's fine."

Andi looked out of the window, aware that they were travelling very slowly. "Maybe we could go for a walk and grab a bit of lunch before the session?"

Pippa laughed. "Oh no, we won't have time for that. I contacted them as soon as you called, saying we'd be early. And guess what?" She winked. "I've booked us a pair of Segways!"

"A pair of what?"

"Segways! You know? The machines with two wheels that you stand up on? The self-balancing ones?" Pippa laughed. "We get to cruise around the forest in style!"

Andi shook her head and laughed. "You never cease to amaze me, Miss Rose."

"Good," she said with a smile. "Because I'm going to show you what real fun's all about."

"I'm starting to catch on," laughed Andi, feeling a buzz of adrenaline.

****

Andi was trussed up in a bright yellow boiler suit, bike helmet and knee pads, holding a clipboard in one hand and a pen in the other. She was sitting next to Pippa on a log outside the Segway hut at Trent Park, seemingly signing her life away. She tapped her pen under one of the statements and started to laugh. "*I acknowledge that I risk injury or death from loss of control, collisions or falls from the Segway.*" She ticked the box. "Look at me being all spontaneous! Might fall and die? Yeah, no worries!"

Pippa looked up from her own clipboard. "You'll be fine. They're really simple to drive. You just lean forwards to go and backwards to stop, but don't lean too far back or you'll start to reverse." She nodded her head back towards the car park. "Anyway, your journey here in Molly was probably more dangerous than this'll be," she grinned, "but these do go faster."

Andi laughed, "Are you like a Segway pro or something?"

"I've done it a couple of times."

Andi adjusted her helmet which had already started to itch. "With Jayney?"

Pippa nodded. "Did I tell you she called last week?"

"No! The last I heard, you were trying to contact her and find out what she was doing at my party with Melody."

Pippa placed her clipboard on the wood chipped forest floor and hugged her shoulders; it wasn't bitterly cold, but she was eager to get moving. "She phoned last week to apologise."

"Really?"

"Yep. She said she knew I'd be there, but she swore that Melody wasn't the person she'd had an affair with."

"So what was she doing with her?"

"Said they bumped into each other a few days before the party and got chatting; reminiscing about work and stuff. Apparently Melody needed a plus one and it was a bit of a spur of the moment thing."

Andi frowned. "Sounds a bit random."

"I know. Maybe she was hoping to see her *mistress* there."

"No, Zara hardly invited anyone from work."

"And how is Zara?"

Andi puzzled a smile. "She's fine. Why?"

"Just making polite conversation."

"Well don't," grinned Andi. "I much prefer it when you flirt."

"Ooo the green light!" laughed Pippa, rising to her feet and wiggling her bottom in the yellow boiler suit. "How's this for starters?"

Andi picked up Pippa's clipboard and put it on top of hers. She rose from the log and shook her head teasingly. "If we've signed up for death via Segway collision, then I'll need a bit more than that in my final moments, please."

Pippa walked provocatively forwards and entered Andi's personal space. She tilted Andi's chin up with her forefinger and looked into her eyes. "Have I ever told you that you suit a helmet?"

Andi burst out laughing and bashed her away. "Stop it!"

"Hey, you started it," giggled Pippa, rubbing her chest.

"Oh, I'm sorry," said Andi, lifting her arm over Pippa's shoulder and whispering into her ear. "Come on then, pro. Take me for a spin."

Pippa tilted her head and whispered back. "I've already done that, and you purred like a beauty!"

"That's more like it," laughed Andi.

CHAPTER TWENTY SEVEN

Pippa and Andi were in absolute fits of giggles. The ten minute instruction session in front of the Segway hut was proving one worthy of a slot on You've Been Framed. Pippa had obviously whizzed off around the small circular course with little need of assistance, only having to prove she could stop, start and turn; which she did quickly, elegantly and with flair. Andi, however, needed a helping hand to even get up onto the machine without falling. The idea that it was as simple as standing still on a pavement didn't wash with her and it was taking a lot of coaxing from the young female instructor to even get her to tilt forwards and start the Segway into motion. When the wheels did finally begin to creep forwards Andi wailed with such delight that Pippa swerved her machine to a stop to see what was going on.

"I'M GOING!" screeched Andi.

Pippa laughed. "Well done."

"And now stop," said the instructor calmly.

"HOW?!" wailed Andi leaning further forwards and picking up speed.

The instructor jogged gently alongside her machine. "You're fine. Just slowly lean backwards."

Andi squeezed the handles tighter and flung her head back.

The instructor tried not to laugh. "There's no need to look up at the sky, just lean your body backwards."

Andi's Segway was still rolling forwards. She bent her knees and pushed out her bottom. "Like this?"

"ANDI YOU LOONY!" shouted Pippa in between her laughter. "You look like you're on the toilet!"

"I CAN'T DO IT!" screamed Andi in protest.

The instructor stayed calm. "Yes you can. Keep your arms straight and just lean back."

"I'LL FALL!"

Pippa started her machine again and swerved around the bend, pulling alongside Andi's. "You're hardly moving!" she laughed. "Look, like this ... just lean back."

Andi glanced to the side at Pippa's Segway coming to a gentle stop. She tilted her body backwards slightly, surprised that her machine actually responded. "IT'S STOPPING!"

"Well done," smiled the instructor, "now just stay upright."

"WHAT?" screeched Andi as her machine began to reverse.

"Stand normally."

Andi leaned forwards and the machine jerked into motion again. "IT'S GOING FORWARDS!"

Pippa couldn't help laughing. "Just stand still!"

"I'm trying!" laughed Andi, feeling like a unicyclist wobbling forwards and backwards. Her movements, however, were not intentional.

The instructor jumped onto the machine and placed her hands on top of Andi's. "I'm not supposed to do this, but just move your body with mine." She placed her feet either side of Andi's and pressed their bodies together. "Forwards … backwards."

Andi could feel her cheeks blushing.

"Can you feel it?"

Andi was fully aware of the instructor's movements and laughed nervously. "I think so."

The instructor brought them to a vertical stance. "See. We've stopped."

"Show me once more?"

Pippa laughed. "You look like you're enjoying that far too much!"

Andi looked over at Pippa with a smile. "I respond well to physical direction."

"I'll remember that," said Pippa.

The instructor jumped off the machine. "Okay, show me again."

Andi tilted her body forwards. "I've got it!" she said.

"And stop."

Andi stopped the machine.

"Great, now go again … That's it … Gently round the corner … Perfect! … Now pick up a bit of speed … Great! ... You're a natural!"

"I think we all know that's not true!" laughed Andi as she rounded the final bend having actually completed a full circuit of the small course. "Let me do it once more to make sure."

"Probably best," teased Pippa, hiding the pride she felt at Andi's accomplishment.

"Right." The instructor spoke to Pippa, sensing she was the more sensible of the pair. "Keep to the paths and stay on the Segways. You've got forty five minutes so you can probably do both of the blue and red routes. You've got phones?"

Pippa nodded.

"The number for the hut's on the side of the machine. Any problems, give me a ring."

"Got it!" said Pippa. "We're doing the *'Go Ape'* course this afternoon."

"God help you," laughed the instructor looking in Andi's direction.

"I heard that!" shouted Andi. "I think I'll be great at falling out of trees."

"Just make sure you're attached to the zip wire!" advised the instructor in response.

****

Half an hour into their Segway session and Pippa and Andi were having the time of their life. They had already completed two out of the three clearly marked courses and were now about to embark on their final mission - the off road track. It wasn't really off road, but it allowed the rider to experience small bumps, jumps and downhill slopes. Andi held on tightly as they neared the brow of a hill, aware that there must be quite a large drop on the other side. "HERE WE GO!" she shouted, tilting her machine over the edge.

Pippa followed closely behind, watching Andi pick up speed and steer towards the moguls. "HOLD ON TIGHT!" she shouted in Andi's direction. "THEY'RE BUMPY!"

"I KNOW" wailed Andi. "LOOK AT ME JUMP!"

Pippa watched as Andi's Segway hit the first mogul, relieved to see her keeping control. "YOU'RE A PRO! YOU'RE ACTUALLY GETTING SOME AIR!"

Andi shrieked with laughter. "I'M A SPEED DEMON!"

Pippa tilted even further forwards and hit the bumps at pace, jumping two at a time and finally catching up with Andi's machine. "Race you to the bottom," she said with a nod of her head.

"You're on," giggled Andi, relishing the challenge.

Pippa could hear her approaching and swerved into a couple of shallow troughs. "AH! THEY'RE SLOWING ME DOWN!"

"YOU DID THAT DELIBERATELY!" shouted Andi keeping on the flat and taking the lead. "THAT'S SO SWEET!"

"I didn't," lied Pippa, pulling out of the final slump. "You won, fair and square."

Andi laughed. "I haven't had this much fun in ages! Let's whizz round and do it again!"

"After you … you Segway sensation!"

"Ooo you know how to flatter a girl, don't you?! Seriously though, I look good from behind, right? I think it's a great accessory and I might just ask for one for Christmas."

Pippa pulled alongside Andi and matched her steady pace. "I could just see you rolling up to work on one," she grinned, "and yes, my view for the morning has been very pleasant indeed, especially when you're jiggling over those moguls."

Andi pretended to gasp. "I hope I don't jiggle?"

"You don't *wobble*, jiggle. You *jiggle*, jiggle!"

"Oh," she smiled, "that's okay then. Now if you wouldn't mind taking the lead, I'd like to be distracted."

Pippa stood tall and rolled in front of Andi's machine. She took one hand off the handlebars and placed it on her hip, turning her head and looking seductively over her shoulder. "So, do you Segway often?"

Andi laughed. "I might start. You?"

Pippa was about to reply when her machine hit a bump. She spun back to the handle bars but it was too late. The Segway lifted onto its left wheel, and then its right, sending her completely off balance. "SHIT!" she shouted, trying to regain control.

Andi watched in slow motion, the vision of Pippa being jerked from side to side. She was clinging on with one hand, but it was obvious that it was too late. Andi panicked and lunged her Segway forwards in an attempt to be of some assistance, but at that precise moment Pippa fell from her machine, hitting the wood chipped forest floor. Andi tried to tilt backwards, but it was too late. She hit Pippa like a mogul, even managing to get some air.

Pippa screamed out in painful laughter.

****

The phone call to the female instructor at the Segway hut had been very embarrassing indeed. They had had to explain about the hit and run; Pippa had been hit, and her Segway had done a runner - eventually located in a muddy ditch fifty metres away. The instructor had assumed it was Andi who had taken the fall and was cursing herself for letting her out on the course too soon. But Andi had taken great pride in leading the procession of quad bike (driven by the instructor) and trailer (carrying Pippa) back to the hut.

Pippa had found the whole incident hilarious, if somewhat painful. The instructor had lifted her into the trailer and insisted they go straight back to the hut for RICE. Andi had tried to joke that it wasn't time for eating, whereupon the ever-so efficient instructor versed them both on the policy of Rest, Ice, Compression and Elevation. Andi and Pippa had shared a secret smile, fully aware from their recent first aid course that RICE was indeed something other than a food group.

Once in the hut, the treatment had been quick and simple. Pippa had lifted her left trouser leg and exposed a Segway tyre imprint and a slightly swollen ankle. The instructor had efficiently assessed the injury as non-life threatening and twenty minutes later the journey back to Molly had begun. Andi was under Pippa's shoulder and Pippa was perfecting her hobble.

"It's not that bad!" laughed Andi.

"You ran me over! You actually ran me over with your Segway!"

"You were already on the floor. I was trying to speed up and rescue you!"

"But you didn't though, did you?" Pippa was struggling to control her giggles. "You put your foot down and jumped me like a mogul. I bet you were seeing how much air you could get!"

Andi laughed. "I'm so sorry. I feel dreadful. You can actually see the tyre mark on your leg."

"I know! You're going to have to drive."

"Stop it. It's bad enough that you've cried off from '*Go Ape*,' but don't tease me with driving that beast."

"Shhh, she'll hear you," giggled Pippa as they made it to the car park. "Seriously the clutch is so stiff and you have to press down really hard every time you want to change gear. I'm struggling to bend my ankle."

"Really?"

"Really," nodded Pippa in earnest. "I'm also going to sit in the boot so I can keep my foot up."

"Stop it," laughed Andi again. "I'm not driving that old wagon with you in the back like Lady Muck."

Pippa hopped to a standstill. "I'm being serious. You have to drive. You're fully comp, aren't you?"

"Yes, but I've never driven anything like that before." Andi nodded towards the old Morris Minor Traveller. "Do I have to wind her up to get her going?"

"Don't you always?" said Pippa with a grin.

"Stop it. I'm going to have to concentrate. Where are the keys?"

"We're not even there yet," laughed Pippa, "and she's not got electric locking!"

Andi bent back under Pippa's shoulder and helped her hobble. "You owe me for this."

"You ran me over!"

"You were showing off and you fell off!"

"Maybe," laughed Pippa, still devastated that she had been the one to take a tumble. "It's fine. We'll go back to mine and warm up with a hot chocolate." She smiled. "Plus it means we can rearrange the *'Go Ape'* for another weekend."

"Sounds good to me," said Andi coming to a standstill next to the wooden framed car. "But remember that's all assuming we make it home alive."

"Gee-Gee wouldn't have it any other way."

"I bloody well hope so," laughed Andi, surveying the old fashioned motor vehicle and taking a very deep breath. "The Segways have a higher horse power than this thing."

"Shhh, she'll hear you!"

"Oops, sorry Molly."

"No," Pippa pointed up at the sky. "I'm talking about Gee-Gee."

Andi turned around and felt Pippa's forehead. "Oh blimey, now we've got to add concussion into the mix!"

Pippa couldn't help but laugh. "I love it when you panic."

Andi took the keys out of Pippa's bag and fumbled with the old fashioned door handle. "I'll remind you of that when we're on the A406 with an articulated lorry up our backside."

****

The short journey home had in fact been incident free, and even though Andi wouldn't admit it, she had quite enjoyed playing the role of driving Miss Daisy. Pippa had insisted on a seat in the boot, stretching her leg out and balancing her foot on the front passenger's headrest, wailing with painful giggles each time the old car hit a bump.

Andi had mocked her cries, but now, as she was sitting on Pippa's sofa with Pippa's tyre marked leg and swollen ankle on her knee, she felt dreadful. "It's really bad, isn't it?" she said. "I'm so, so, sorry."

Pippa adjusted her head on the cushion and shrugged from a horizontal position. "It's fine, I shouldn't have been wiggling around on a moving vehicle trying to get you to look at my tits."

"You only had to ask," laughed Andi, "and you didn't have to go to such extremes to get my attention."

Pippa looked serious for a moment. "Don't I?"

"No." She grinned. "I'm always looking at your tits."

Pippa pressed her head further into the cushion. "Oh how you've changed from the prim and proper Andi Armstrong on interview who looked aghast when I recited from memory an exact description of your physical attributes and choice of clothing."

Andi laughed. "It did kind of freak me out."

"Hey, I just make sure I pay attention to what's important."

Andi lowered her voice. "And what's important right now?"

Pippa lifted herself onto an elbow. "Telling you that today's been great. That I've loved every minute of it."

"Me too," whispered Andi, leaning her head back onto the sofa and closing her eyes. "I feel so alive when I'm with you." She paused. "Does that sound corny?"

"It's a good job you've got your eyes closed and you can't see the face I'm pulling."

Andi opened her eyes.

"I'm joking," smiled Pippa. "No, that's not corny. I just wanted to have your attention when I said this."

"Said what?"

Pippa pulled herself up into a seated position, stopping inches away from Andi's face. She took a deep breath and whispered quietly. "You're my one."

Andi couldn't draw her eyes from Pippa's. "What do you mean?"

"You're the one I was meant to find, and now that I've found you, I have to tell you." She said it again, only this time, louder. "You're my one, Andi."

Andi gently shook her head. "I'm someone else's."

"All I know is what I feel, and all I feel here," she touched her own chest, "is you."

Andi held her breath and closed her eyes. "Why does my heart beat faster when I'm with you?"

Pippa waited for Andi's eyes to re-open. "Because you know I'm yours too."

"My one?"

Pippa nodded. "I'm your one, too…" she smiled "…so stop counting and kiss me."

Andi laughed lightly and leaned forwards; drawn in by the warming spiel. "I want to, I just-"

"Do it." The connection was intense and their lips were just millimetres apart. "Kiss me."

Andi couldn't stop herself, the pull was too strong. She moved her head forwards and parted her lips, pressing them gently against Pippa's.

"I love you," breathed Pippa, engulfed by the soft emotion of the embrace.

Andi froze.

Pippa continued the kiss, but Andi didn't respond. "Andi?"

Andi stuttered. "You love me?"

"I've known it for a while," nodded Pippa. "I'm sorry, but I love you."

Andi reached for Pippa's head and held it gently in her hands. She looked into her eyes and kissed her slowly, for one final time.

Pippa gasped with arousal and increased the pressure, pushing Andi backwards and grabbing at her body.

Andi lifted a finger to Pippa's mouth. "Stop," she whispered, staying in control. "This has to stop. I can't let you love me."

"It's too late," murmured Pippa pushing back onto the kiss.

Andi turned her head to the side. "I can't lead you on. I'm married and I have a job to do."

"What about *you*? What do *you* want?"

"I want same-sex couples to get the same rights as everyone else. I want equal marriage. Crikey, I'm *fighting* for equal marriage." She shook her head. "I can't just walk away from my own civil partnership, Pippa. What sort of example would that set?"

"What about love?

"I *love* my job."

"But you don't love me?"

Andi closed her eyes. "Don't ask me that question."

"You could change departments and focus on the education side of things. You could work with the schools. You could-"

Andi opened her eyes and spoke slowly. "I could honour my commitment." She paused. "I know what I want, Pippa. I want to get this job done. I want us *all* to be equal. I want equal marriage rights for everyone."

Pippa shook her head. "I know what *I* want … I want you."

"You can't have me, Pippa! I'm married!" Andi shocked herself with her chastising tone of voice. She shook her head and whispered quietly. "I'm married."

"I'll wait."

Andi took Pippa's hands. "For what? Nothing's going to change. I'm bound by the commitment I made seven years ago."

Pippa said it again. "I'll wait."

CHAPTER TWENTY EIGHT

It had taken a huge amount of will power to walk out of the door and head back home; but that's what Andi had done. She had walked away from Pippa and made a vow, never to be in that situation again. Now, moments away from her own home - the home she shared with her wife of seven years - she gulped, finally aware of the enormity of the situation. She was on the brink of an affair. She was on the brink of destroying it all; her love, her commitment, and her life as she knew it. She spoke to herself once again. *You're fine. You've stopped it. There's no harm done.* She walked up the short path and stopped in front of the large front door. *You're putting the greater good before yourself, it's admirable.*

She shook her head. *You left her on her own with an injured ankle. She loves you! She actually loves you.* Andi snapped herself free from the daydream and focused on the Yale lock. *Keep calm and stay in control,* she whispered, lifting her key to the door and twisting it quickly, feeling the warmth of her home drawing her in.

Andi stepped into the large hallway and immediately grabbed the door frame, unable to stop her foot from skidding on a large discarded envelope. She hovered for a moment in a state of unbalance, looking down at the floor and the pile of post, cursing the postman, though fully aware that he wasn't at fault. Zara had clearly not been home. Andi regained her composure and bent down. She lifted the pile of leaflets and letters, and closed the door, flopping forcefully onto the velvety chaise longue.

Andi lay still for a moment and looked at the ceiling, before sighing and straightened the pile of post on her chest. *I'm a cheat*, she said to herself. *I'm nothing but a cheat.* She shook her head, feeling her fingers drawn to the oversized envelope. She lifted it up and read the name on the front. F.A.O: ANDI ARMSTRONG. That was it. Just her name. No address. No stamp. Just her name. She puzzled for a moment and sat up, shuffling backwards so she was resting, legs outstretched, in a seated position against the end of the long lounger. She dropped the rest of the post to the floor and pushed her finger under the lip of the envelope. She ripped it open and pulled out a large brown file. FOR ANDI, it said on the front.

Andi swung her legs off the chaise longue and rested her elbows on her knees. She opened the file and stared at the list of statements:

-Affair with Zara started Jan 5th 2012 - Sex in her office 3.15 p.m.
-Jan 6th - Sex after work in her car 6.00 p.m.
-Jan 10th - Sex in the lobby 7.30 a.m.

Andi scanned page, after page, after page, of non-descript meetings for sex. She stopped at the entry for Nov 3rd.

-Nov 3rd Met Jayney to discuss HER affair with Zara! October 2011 - September 2012. OVERLAP!!

Andi couldn't move. *What the hell was she reading?* She flicked to the final page.

-A record of my affair, by Melody Fickler.

Andi felt a surge of fear rising inside her. The file had started to shake and she looked down at her hands that were white at the knuckles. She closed it back over and stared at the cover, unable to comprehend exactly what it was that she was holding.

The front door swung open and Zara stepped noisily into the hall, spotting Andi and starting to rant. "You could have opened it! Didn't you hear me messing with the lock?! My new key's still too bloody stiff!"

Andi didn't move.

"Didn't you hear me?" said Zara, pulling her coat off and walking to the stand. "I should have gone to the proper key place and not the bloody supermarket! I'm sure you told me to go there. Who gets their keys cut at a bloody supermarket anyway?"

Andi dropped the brown file onto the chaise longue and walked silently into the lounge.

"Sweetie?" puzzled Zara.

"FOR FUCK'S SAKE! I'M NOT YOUR FUCKING SWEETIE!" came the screaming reply.

****

Andi waited alone in the lounge for what felt like a lifetime. She was sitting and waiting, but for what, she wasn't quite sure. All she knew was that she felt cold. Cold, numb, but surprisingly calm. She turned slowly, hearing the door creak open.

Zara was standing motionless in the doorway with the file clutched close to her chest. "Can I come in?"

Andi shrugged. "It looks like you do whatever you want anyway, so why are you bothering to ask?"

"Aren't you going to shout?"

"No. You're not worth it."

Zara walked into the room and stood in front of Andi, intent on proving her wrong. "So you believe it then? Without question?"

"You want me to ask you?" said Andi, barely able to look at her wife. "You want me to ask you if it's true?"

Zara nodded.

"Fine. Is it true?"

Zara smirked. "She's missed a couple of entries actually."

"WHAT?!" shouted Andi, absolutely raging inside.

"I thought you weren't going to shout?" grinned Zara, mission accomplished. "I thought you weren't bothered?"

"JUST FUCK OFF, ZARA! JUST FUCK RIGHT OFF!"

"No. Look at you, losing your cool! The wonderful Andi Armstrong lets rip! I knew you'd shout!"

Andi jumped up and eyeballed her wife, fuming with her nonchalance and cross at her own eruption. "You've got five seconds to leave this house, or I will."

Zara pushed Andi by the shoulders back down onto the sofa. "Look at you, Miss high and mighty! Don't pretend you didn't know."

Andi hauled herself back up. "OF COURSE I DIDN'T FUCKING KNOW! YOU'RE MY FUCKING WIFE, ZARA!" She shook her head, holding back the tears. "My wife," she uttered.

Zara dropped the file onto the coffee table and walked over to her recliner. She sat down and folded her arms. "What am I meant to say? I've been busted. I've had affairs. Sorry, I thought you knew."

"How many?" shouted Andi, angry at her own emotion and cross with Zara for taking great relish in her outburst.

"Four or five."

"BUT WE'RE FUCKING MARRIED! WHAT BIT OF THAT DON'T YOU GET?!"

"Oh Andi, listen to yourself. It was only sex and it only started a couple of years ago when things really started to take off with Proud Unity."

"So it's my fault?" she gasped.

Zara shrugged. "Partly. I thought you were turning a blind eye?"

Andi lowered herself back down onto the sofa and held her head in her hands. "Why? Why would I do that? I loved you, Zara."

"What do you mean, loved?" Zara was mocking her. "You've stopped loving me in the space that it's taken you to read that file?"

Andi paused, shocked at her own admission. "Why would I know? Why would I condone your dirty little affairs?"

Zara huffed. "If you didn't know, then you're even more absorbed in yourself and your stupid little job than I thought." She laughed. "Now that really is saying something."

"YOU'RE THE ONE WHO'S HAD THE FUCKING AFFAIRS!" shouted Andi, struggling to keep a lid on her fury. All she wanted to do was see clearly. "This isn't my fault! Fine! While you're being so open, who were they?"

"Women from work."

Andi rubbed her fingers though her short blonde hair. "And Jayney? You know who she was, right?"

Zara pressed the recliner button on her chair, lifting her feet into the horizontal position. "She was just some temp who got above her station."

"OH MY GOD, ZARA! You were fucking her! No wonder she felt above her station. Fucked by the boss of a FTSE 100 company." Andi swept her hair backwards. "She was Pippa's girlfriend. She left Pippa for you!"

Zara tutted. "No she didn't! It was *just sex*. No emotion. No dates. No chats. No feelings. Just sex … and she was pretty crap actually." Zara paused. "Jayney was delusional." She turned and looked at Andi. "I would never leave you, sweetie."

"*You'd* never leave *me*?" uttered Andi, completely flabbergasted.

"No."

"And what if I walked out of that FUCKING DOOR right now?"

"Listen to yourself! Why are you screaming?"

Andi took a deep breath, willing herself to stay calm. "Did you talk about us? When you were fucking them? Did you tell them what a shit wife I was?"

Zara looked shocked. "To them? No, of course not." She frowned at Andi. "Why would I? It was just meaningless sex. You're my wife. You're the one I come home to every night. You're the one I love. You're the one I'll be with forever."

Andi was open mouthed, unable to comprehend what she was hearing. "You've cheated on me, Zara. Prolifically!"

"I got a few cheap thrills. Nothing more, nothing less."

"So, what? Melody got pissed off at you and sent me this file?"

Zara shook her head. "No. Melody knows better than that."

"Jayney then?" Andi suddenly remembered the party and laughed. "They came to the party together to show you up, didn't they?"

Zara shrugged. "Didn't work though, did it? You showed me up more on that night than they did."

Andi was frantically shaking her head. "Melody had this file! She was holding it at my party! I remember."

"That must have been before you got pissed then? Before you showed everyone what a lightweight you are."

"JUST SHUT UP ZARA!" Andi broke down in tears, completely overcome by her pain. "Just shut up," she whispered.

"Oh stop crying! If we're going to talk about this, then let's do it properly."

"I DON'T WANT TO FUCKING TALK ABOUT IT!" Andi was visibly shaking, unable to stop the tears from coursing down her cheeks. "Just tell me. Tell me what's going on."

"With what?"

"WITH THE FUCKING FILE!" Andi rubbed her face. "Seriously, Zara, I'm so close to losing it with you."

"It looks like you're there already, sweetie."

"SHUT THE FUCK UP WITH YOUR STUPID FUCKING SWEETIE BULLSHIT!"

Zara actually looked quite concerned. "Calm down, sweetie. Swearing doesn't suit you." She huffed and started to straighten her long black hair. "Fine. All I know is that Melody kept this file of the dates and times that we met for sex. I know about it because she threatened me with it. I wasn't really bothered because I thought you knew." Zara raised an eyebrow. "And really, Melody needs to learn a little etiquette. None of the other women from work have behaved like she has. We fuck. We leave. We possibly fuck again." Zara lifted her hands. "We work in a high pressured environment. People are always looking for a spot of light relief. It happens. It's meaningless sex, but it happens. You must have known?"

Andi scrunched up her face. "I still *can't* believe you're saying that!"

"Well I thought you knew, sweetie, and if you'll let me finish?" She paused ensuring she had her silence. "Melody was bluffing. She'd never have given you the file. She loves her job too much, and unfortunately, she's very good at her job. The firm needs her. She knew she had nothing on me." Zara laughed. "I think she brought Jayney to the party to make a point; to get one over on me. But it didn't work." Zara pulled at a stray black hair and dropped it to the floor. "You got pissed and took everyone's attention and someone stole the file."

"What? What do you mean, someone stole the file? Who stole the file?"

Zara raised her eyebrows. "Whoever posted it through that letter box; they stole the file. I'm guessing that it's the same person who's been ringing me and threatening to show you." She shrugged. "But again, I wasn't bothered because I thought you knew. I thought you were turning a blind eye."

Andi rubbed the corners of her mouth, still in complete shock. "So some stranger's had access to that file? For fuck's sake they've probably made a copy. Do you realise how damaging this could be to me? To Proud Unity? To the campaign for equal marriage?"

Zara tutted. "Typical! Back to your reputation again!" She sneered. "And it won't be a stranger. It'll be someone you know."

"Why?"

"They took it from the party."

"It could have been anyone then!" Andi sniffed and tried to focus on a solution. "So where does that leave us?"

Zara shrugged. "If you want me to stop, I'll stop."

"WHAT?" Andi was shaking her head, completely dumbfounded. "I mean the file, not your stupid little affairs."

"Oh fuck the file! No one will give a shit! Are you really more bothered about that, than about us?"

Andi thought about it for a moment. "I don't know what I think. I don't know what I feel. I'm just in total shock."

"Look," said Zara, trying to come to a conclusion. "I'll stop if you want me to. I'll stop the sex," she grinned, "or you could start? I wouldn't mind."

"You disgust me, Zara. YOU ABSOLUTELY DISGUST ME!"

Zara curled her lip at the corner and raised an eyebrow. "Actually you're right. You might struggle. I don't think many people are into prudes."

"You are *such* a bitch!"

"Well you're a prude. I have to get my kicks from somewhere." Zara took a deep breath. "I'm trying to sort this out."

Andi was fuming with the tears that had started again. "Why?"

Zara exhaled. "Why what?"

"Why are you so intent on hurting me?"

"Oh get over yourself, Andi. Not everything's about you. Go take a walk or something and come back when you're ready to talk about this like an adult."

Andi bit the inside of her cheek, stopping the words from escaping.

Zara was shooing her with her hands. "Go on, go. But just remember one thing. It was sex. Just sex. A meaningless act to get myself off. I've never, ever, so much as gazed into anyone else's eyes. I've never spoken about feelings. For Christ's sake, Andi, I struggle to feel anything anymore. You know what I'm going through."

"You know what? I don't think I do!"

Zara snapped. "So whose fault's that then?"

"MINE I GUESS," shouted Andi. "IT'S ALL MY FAULT! EVERYTHING'S ALWAYS MY BLOODY FAULT!"

Zara stood up, finally losing her cool. "MAYBE I WANTED YOU TO FIND OUT!" she shouted. "MAYBE I NEEDED YOU TO KNOW!"

Andi stepped backwards, thrown by the outburst. "Why? Because I'm such a shit wife, that doesn't pay you any attention?"

Zara's bottom lip started to wobble. "It's a cry for help. I'm lost, Andi. I don't know who I am anymore." She wiped away a tear.

Andi had never seen Zara cry before. She stepped forwards and looked into her wife's eyes, aware of a vulnerability for the very first time. "You're crying? For fuck's sake, Zara, why are *you* crying?"

Zara started to sob. "It meant nothing. I love you, Andi. It was cheap and meaningless, and I thought you knew … but didn't care."

Andi shook her head and reached around her wife's shoulders, shaking her gently. "You're my wife, Zara. Of course I'd care."

Zara stepped backwards, moving away from the concern. "Tell me then. Tell me what you know about my issues."

Andi thought quickly, confused by the twist of focus. "They think it might be the early menopause, or possibly your thyroid. You're trying out different drugs to see if any improve your mood."

"But what's the latest? What did they say last week?"

Andi racked her brains. "You went in, didn't you? You were going to get my results from that blood test they took as well. The one from my birthday."

"That's right!" spat Zara, "let's talk about you again."

Andi raised her hands in exasperation. "Oh come on! You just reminded me! Zara, we've both got so much on and we've been passing like ships in the night and-"

"Save it!" snapped Zara. "It's the same old story. Your life. Your issues. I'm left to fend for myself."

"Come off it! You're the most independent woman I know!" Andi frantically fingered her short blonde hair, lost with the direction of the conversation.

"Only because I have to be," said Zara, sniffing away more emotion. "But if you're interested all of a sudden, then I'll tell you. They think it's Dysthymia."

"What's Dysthymia? Why haven't you told me?"

"You were busy."

"Zara, this isn't fair! You should have talked to me about this."

She shrugged. "I'm telling you now. They think I may have this thing called Dysthymia. It's a chronic form of depression where you have negative feelings and little enthusiasm for life."

"You don't have depression!"

"I'm just telling you what they said."

Andi frowned. "Is it common?"

"They think around three per cent of the population has it." Zara shrugged. "You lose your sense of enjoyment for life. Maybe I was trying to find it again with the affairs?"

"Are you seriously trying to use that as a form of justification?" Andi shook her head. "Did it work? Did you get yourself off and get yourself back to normal?"

Zara wiped away a tear. "I felt nothing."

"Oh for fuck's sake, Zara! Why am I the one who's feeling guilty?"

"There's some good news."

"What's that?"

"It's treatable. I've got an appointment on Monday." Zara took hold of Andi's hand and guided her to the sofa. "Sit down and let me explain."

Andi was screaming inside, cursing herself for listening and believing, but she had no choice. "Fine," she whispered, slowly lowering herself back onto the seat.

Zara coughed and closed her eyes. "Let me get this right. Dysthymia is linked to a lack of Serotonin, which is a brain chemical that governs your mood. The lack of Serotonin is caused by an imbalance of Dopamine, which is another brain chemical. There's a new type of anti-depressant out called Mirtazapine and when the doctors combine this with Cognitive Behavioural Therapy, the results can be amazing." She opened her eyes and smiled. "They can make me better, Andi. I won't have to look for false highs anymore. All of that's over with now. We're going to be fine."

Andi dropped her head into her hands. "I don't know what to think, Zara. I'm just so confused."

"I love you. I always have and I always will."

"So why would you betray me? Why would you do this with so many women?"

Zara looked at Andi in earnest. "It's not betrayal. It's just a meaningless physical act. It's a release." She nodded. "I'll stop it though, I promise. Please Andi, please tell me you understand."

Andi hugged her own shoulders. "I feel so alone."

Zara leaned in closely and rubbed Andi's back. "For better, for worse. In sickness and in health. You married me for life, didn't you? Isn't that what you always say? Married for life?"

Andi took in the enormity of Zara's statement. "You're right," she whispered, trying to hold back the tears. "I married for life."

CHAPTER TWENTY NINE

Andi, Pippa, Janet and Elizabeth, were sitting around the large conference table in the Proud Unity media suite, watching on the wide screen television as the Equalities Minister, Maria Miller, spoke live from the Houses of Parliament. It was Tuesday December 11th, three days since the weekend of Segways and sex files, and Andi had been unable to think of anything else. On the one hand she had Pippa, declaring her love, offering her a chance at a life she had always dreamed of. A life where freedom and fun took precedence over routine and duty; but it was the duty and loyalty of the commitment she had made to her wife of seven years, that had forced her to listen when Zara was explaining and examining. Crikey, she'd even apologised at one point. Andi shook herself free of the dilemma and looked back at the screen.

The UK's Equalities Minister, Maria Miller, was getting into her stride. *"Today we are setting out how the Government will extend marriage to same sex couples."*

Andi and Pippa shared a glance.

"It's happening!" shouted Janet. "IT'S REALLY HAPPENING!"

A high pitched yapping started from under the table.

"It's okay, Mimi," hushed Elizabeth, leaning down and stroking the tiny Shih Tzu dog nestled closely into her feet. "Please don't shout, Janet. Mimi doesn't like shouting, do you Mimi?"

"I'm going to shout! This is bloody HISTORIC!" wailed Janet. She stopped her fanfare and pointed at the ball of fluff under the table. "You shouldn't have her at work anyway."

Elizabeth coughed. "I've told you. She's poorly and I-"

Andi interrupted them both. "Shhh!"

All eyes were back on the television screen, watching Maria Miller continue her monumental speech in front of the green leather benches. She was talking clearly, coherently and with great confidence. "*In each century, Parliament has acted - sometimes radically - to ensure that marriage reflects our society to keep it relevant and meaningful. Marriage is not static; it has evolved and Parliament has chosen to act over the centuries to make it fairer and more equal. We now face another such moment - another such chance in this new century.*"

Andi and Pippa glanced at each other once again. Pippa smiled widely. "It's going through," she whispered. "It's actually going through!"

Janet flicked up the volume on the remote, booming out Maria Miller's statement. "*For me, extending marriage to same-sex couples will strengthen, not weaken, that vital institution, and the response I am publishing today makes it clear that we will enable same-sex couples to get married though a civil ceremony.*"

Janet jumped up from the table and punched the air. "We've got it! WE'VE BLOODY GOT IT!" She raced around to Andi's side of the table and shook her shoulders. "YOU'VE DONE IT!" She laughed. "WE'VE ALL DONE IT! All of the sane-minded people who've supported our fight, have DONE IT!"

Elizabeth shushed Mimi's loud yaps and nodded back at the screen. "She's not finished yet."

"*We will also enable religious organisations that wish to conduct same-sex marriages to do so, on a similar opt-in basis to that available for civil partnerships. That is important for the obvious reason that it would be wrong to ban organisations that wish to conduct same-sex marriages from doing so.*"

"THIS GETS BETTER!" shrieked Janet.

Andi stayed silent; torn between the historic speech on the screen and Pippa's misty eyes that were piercing her own, encouraging her thoughts, and suggesting the same: *The battle is over. The work has been done.* "It's through," said Andi in shock.

"And you've played your part," smiled Pippa. "We all have."

Andi turned back to the screen, trying to focus on the specifics of the bill's *quadruple lock* where no religious organisation or individual minister would be forced to marry same-sex couples if they didn't want to. "I'm not following this bit," said Andi, frowning back down at her notes.

"They're banning the Church of England from getting involved," nodded Elizabeth.

"Serves them right!" laughed Janet. "They don't want it? They've not got it!"

Andi looked down at the Twitter feed on her laptop. "Look! The CofE have already started to complain about a blanket ban!"

Janet bent down next to her and peered at the small screen. "Social media staggers me. The fact we can get real-time reaction from across the world in seconds is mind blowing." She pointed at the screen and all the tweets that were scrolling past with the hashtag #CofE. "Look, there's a vicar complaining!"

Andi looked back at the television, checking that the red dot was still flashing. "Right, that's recording. I'll stay here with Pippa and formulate our response. I want you two to get down to the Houses of Parliament. There'll be a real buzz going on down there and there are bound to be some members of the clergy hanging around. Get them interviewed and get their responses." She nodded. "That's where the real story's going to be."

"We've got it though!" grinned Janet. "We've actually got it! Gay people will be able to get married!"

"The MP's do have to vote," said Elizabeth.

Janet nodded. "Yeah, and the majority will be huge! I'm betting at least 400 ayes."

Andi let herself laugh for the first time that morning. "It's incredible." She stretched out her arms. "Come here you lot. We need a group hug!"

Janet flung herself into Andi's arms and Pippa jumped up from her chair, marching around the table with her thumbs up in victory. She joined in the cuddle and squeezed everyone tightly together. "Come on, Elizabeth," she laughed, "we need you!"

Elizabeth bent down to the floor and reached for Mimi, scooping her up and stroking her head. "You don't want to get squashed, do you, Mimi?" She continued her cooing. "No you don't, do you, Mimi?

You want a walk though, don't you? Get some fresh air. Yes you do, don't you? Don't you, Mimi?"

Mimi snarled.

Andi patted Pippa and Janet on the back. "Right! Stop squeezing, we've got work to do!"

"Yes boss!" saluted Janet. "Then let's go out on the lash!"

"Tonight?" questioned Andi.

"Yes!" wailed Pippa. "We have to! There's so much to celebrate."

"I'm in! I'm in! We're sorted! Plan's been made!" Janet was excitedly gathering her belongings. "Let's go and get some responses, send out our press statement, and then let's bloody well party! If a group of lesbians can't celebrate on a day like today, then we might as well just drop down dead!"

Elizabeth coughed. "Rather dramatic, Janet. But please, remember I'm of the heterosexual variety."

"No sick notes for tonight's party please!" laughed Janet.

"It's a party now?" smiled Andi, desperate to have the room to herself.

"Perfect!" screeched Janet, completely overcome with giddiness from the announcement. "Let's have an impromptu party at your house!"

Andi opened the door for them to leave. "We'll see," she said, shooing them out. "Now go and do some work."

"WITH PLEASURE!" saluted Janet once more, maintaining her high.

Andi listened to the sound of Mimi's yapping trailing down the corridor. She closed the door and turned back to Pippa. "They've gone."

Pippa smiled and walked towards her. "I know," she said, lifting her arms up and wrapping them around Andi's shoulders. She held her gently and started to sway. "The battle's over, Andi. There'll be no more debate."

Andi rested her head on Pippa shoulder and breathed deeply into the mass of brown curls. "There'll be some," she whispered.

"But it will fade out. Our focus will change. We'll have to diversify. Securing equal marriage has been your focus for so long, but it's happened now. You've won." She paused. "We've won." Pippa gently stroked her finger up and down Andi's back. "I guess we'll now spend some time working with schools on changing their curriculum to include same sex marriages. We'll do more to combat homophobic bullying in the workplace. We'll be able to focus more attention on the trans community." She paused. "But your marriage, Andi … Your marriage won't be in the spotlight."

Andi held Pippa's waist and leaned backwards, looking into her eyes and smiling with warmth. "I'm not married. I'm only civil partnered."

Pippa spotted the glint in her eyes. "That's even better then," she said smiling.

"Do you think I can do this?"

"Has Andi Armstrong really just asked me that question? You're Andi Armstrong! You can do anything. You've fought so hard for people to live the lives they desire, regardless of their sexuality, and now it's time that you fought for yourself. You've got to fight for what you believe in. Fight for what you desire." Pippa lifted her hand to Andi's cheek. "Fight for me."

The door swung open and slammed against the doorstop. "ANDI! We've got a problem." Mike, the over-weight IT guy, was sweating from all available pores, signalling for her to follow, and completely unaware of the close connection and very near kiss happening in front of him.

Andi stepped backwards. "What? What is it?"

"Follow me," he urged, "it's fucking nasty."

CHAPTER THIRTY

Andi and Pippa were racing along the Proud Unity corridor behind Mike, the IT guy, who was jogging as quickly as his oversized frame would allow. The mass of keys, loose change and Bic pens, chinking around in his pockets and weighing him down, didn't help his speed. "Here," he panted, turning clumsily into Andi's office. "I'll show you in here."

Andi and Pippa followed him towards the desk.

Mike thudded down onto Andi's padded black chair and swivelled himself into her computer. He wiggled the mouse and sure enough it flashed up again. The background image, which had previously shown the Proud Unity logo, was now replaced by a rather grotesque photograph of Andi and Zara on their wedding day. Only this time it wasn't their beautiful white suits that drew the eye, or the youthful looks on their faces. It was the knife wound slashed across their necks, and the red blood dripping to the floor, that made you stare. The graffiti artist had left the blood stained knife in the photo next to Andi's white shoes, with a trail of words, scrawled in red jagged drips, starting from the tip of the blade. "*Your campaign has destroyed the institution of marriage. Now I'm going to destroy you. Stab, by stab, by stab … starting with your wife.*"

Andi shuddered.

"It's fucking nasty, right?" Mike looked up, sliding his wire rimmed glasses back up his sweaty nose. "I've called the police liaison officer and he's on his way."

Andi reached into her pocket for her phone. She dialled Zara's number. There was no answer, so she dialled her office phone line instead. Nothing. Andi tapped the mobile against her lips, before quickly trying one final number. She listened to the instructions.

"Is she there?" mouthed Pippa, fully aware of whom Andi must be calling.

Andi continued to press the buttons on her mobile, frustrated with the automated service of G-Sterling's main reception. She returned the phone to her ear and looked at Pippa. "I've got to get past the gate keeper first! I hate calling the-" She suddenly twisted her body, relieved to hear a human voice. "Hi, it's Andi Armstrong. Is Zara in the building? I need to get hold of her as soon as possible." She paused, listening to the friendly but firm response. Andi spoke again. "Yes … I understand that she's in a meeting, but I need to talk to her … No it can't wait." Andi shook her head. "Fine, I'll come over there and wait, as long as I know she's in the building … She is? … Great." Andi dropped the phone onto her desk and looked at Pippa. "I need to know she's okay. It's probably nothing, just some lunatic responding to the announcement. But I have to show her this picture. It's only right that she's aware of this." Andi lifted her phone back up and swiped through the apps, quickly reaching the camera. She stretched out her arm and clicked on a button, taking a photo of the image on the computer screen.

"It's on all of the computers across the network," said Mike.

"That's horrible!" gasped Andi. "Why would someone do that?"

"*How* did someone do that?" he corrected, typing quickly and logging into the mainframe. "I just need to do a couple more checks and I'll be able to tell whether we've been hacked."

"It must have been pre-mediated," said Pippa. "The announcement's only just been made."

"There are some sickos out there," nodded Mike, frantically tapping away. "But I guess they figured they'd be losing today. Stupid sickos."

Andi bit her bottom lip, trying not to panic. "They might not be stupid. They might just be sickos who feel I'm responsible for destroying what they believe in. Sickos who feel they've lost. Sickos who've now got nothing to lose themselves."

Pippa took Andi's hand and squeezed it. "You've handled stuff like this before. It'll be fine."

Andi shook her head. "Nothing so personal. Nothing so threatening." She squeezed the hand once and quickly let go. "I've got to get over there. I've got to check she's okay."

"She'll be fine!"

"Please, Pippa!" snapped Andi. "She's my wife!"

****

Andi stepped out of the taxi and hopped up onto the pavement, pushing though the guarded doors of the G-Sterling building and walking into the plush lobby. She headed towards the long reception desk.

"Andi!"

The voice made her spin around. Zara was stepping out of the lift and fast approaching with a concerned look on her face. "Is everything okay? They told me you'd phoned."

Andi flung her arms around her wife's shoulders and exhaled with relief. "Can we go to your office?"

"Of course we can, sweetie. Whatever's wrong?"

Andi shook her head and held back a tear. "I'll tell you upstairs."

****

Pippa continued to look over Mike's shoulder at the computer screen and the nonsensical lines of coding, not quite following the technical point he was making. She jumped at the beep of her phone, relieved to read the message from Andi that she had arrived safely. It also said that Zara was fine. She closed the message, still cursing Andi's stubbornness to travel alone, but relieved to hear that all was well. She turned back to the screen and tried to concentrate.

"See … it has to have come from within," said Mike tapping the peculiar coding. 'Look, the firewall's are all in-tact. We've not been breached. The background change must have come from an admin account."

Pippa frowned. "What does that mean?"

"Someone with an admin password has accessed the system, either on site, or remotely, and they've changed the standard background image on the server. It's as simple as that really. Like when you change the image on your personal laptop. Well someone's changed the standard image on the server, so that all of the computers in the office show this vile picture." Mike closed his tab in the mainframe and the image flashed up again. "It's quite nasty actually."

"Where's the photo come from? Someone had to get access to the photo first."

Mike laughed. "This was the picture they used in the magazine spread. It's all over the internet." He shrugged his shoulders. "And it's easy enough to doctor the image in Photoshop, or any number of art programmes."

Pippa bent down and studied the bloodied slash embedded into Andi and Zara's necks. "So who has access to the admin passwords?"

Mike swivelled around on the padded chair and looked up at Pippa. "Me, Andi and Janet. That's all." He nodded. "I'm in IT and I never write my passwords down. EVER! I never give them to anyone else and I always make sure they're so obscure that I'd be locked up if anyone ever found out what they actually were." He paused and pushed his glasses further up his sweaty nose. "Has Andi ever given you her password? Asked you to log anything onto her area?"

Pippa shook her head. "Never."

"Well I suggest you get on the blower to Janet and ask her the same thing. Then ring Andi and ask her too."

Pippa nodded and lifted her phone.

Mike pulled himself out of the chair, causing the cushioned seat to make a strange slurping sound as it regained its plumpness. "I'll wait in reception for the PC," he grinned, "and *that* was the chair."

Pippa didn't smile. None of this was in the least bit funny. Andi had run back to Zara … Janet and Elizabeth were off cavorting with the press … and she was left staring at an image of two slashed and wounded female brides, when really she should be preparing their response to the announcement. The dial tone continued in her ear.

She was about to hang up when Janet answered the phone in a very giddy fashion. Pippa clicked it onto loudspeaker and placed the phone down on the desk. "Janet," she said, "can you hear me?"

"Yes!" giggled Janet. "It's brilliant down here! Camera crews from every station. Loads of famous faces!"

"Listen carefully. Have you shared your admin password with anyone?"

"My what?"

Pippa could hear Mimi yapping in the background and the buzz of excited news crews. "Your password for your Proud Unity admin page. Have you given it to anyone? Or have you left it lying around anywhere."

"No, why? Only me and Elizabeth use it."

"Elizabeth?" Pippa paused as the sound of a passing siren wailed in the distance. "Sorry, I couldn't hear you. You said Elizabeth has access to your admin page?"

"Yes, why?"

"It's fine, I'll tell you in a bit. Can you put her on?"

Janet laughed. "No! I'll have to hold that bloody fluff-ball dog of hers!"

"Please, it's important." Pippa listened to the hubbub of Mimi being passed from Elizabeth to Janet.

"Yes, it's Elizabeth. What's the problem?"

"Have you given anyone else Janet's admin password?"

"The one for her computer? No. Why?"

Pippa sighed. "Have you written it down anywhere? Could someone have seen it?"

"No, why?"

"Can Janet hear me too?"

"No. It's too noisy here."

Pippa increased her volume. "Tell Janet that we've been hacked. Tell Janet that Mike will have to go into all of our offices and take a look at our computers."

Elizabeth coughed. "You'll be going into my office?"

"Yes, why? Is that a problem?"

"No, no. Just don't go rooting around in my drawers. I have a number of personal items in there."

"Fine," said Pippa silently tutting Elizabeth's irrelevant concern. "Can you put Janet back on?" Pippa listened, once again, to the yaps of Mimi being passed between the two women.

"I'm back!"

Pippa tried her best to summarise. "We've been hacked and a nasty photo's been put on the system. Mike thinks it's come from one of the admin accounts. So he's going to have to go into our computers and see what's going on."

"Fine, no problem, what was the picture?"

Pippa swallowed, staring at the screen in front of her. "Andi and Zara on their wedding day with their throats slashed."

"Oh good, god," gasped Janet. "Shall we come back?"

"No, it's fine. Andi would want you to get the sound bites."

"Where is she?" asked Janet.

"She's gone to G-Sterling to check on Zara. Who's fine, by the way."

"Bloody hell, that's put a dampener on things. Maybe we should hit the gin tonight!"

Pippa smiled. "At this precise moment I'd take a shot of almost anything."

****

Mike, Pippa, and the male police liaison officer were sitting in Elizabeth's compact office, for the simple reason that it was the first one they hit on their walk from the downstairs reception. They were huddled around the small coffee table looking at a file of recorded incidents.

The PC, who was becoming a friendly face within the Proud Unity offices, wanted to clarify the events to date. "So, we've had some graffiti scratched onto Janet's car. A box of offal left in the office for Andi. A number of offensive tweets, including some particularly nasty ones from a user called Beth or Bethy at the @iWatchThemFall and @iWatchThemFall2 Twitter accounts. A threatening caller on the Six Show called…" he scanned down with his fingers, "…Lizzie." He cleared his throat and continued. "A report of graffiti on Andi's personal letterbox, but we didn't get any photographic evidence." He tapped the printed wedding image, adding it to the file. "And now this. A clear threat to her personal safety."

"She also had her drink spiked," added Pippa. "Andi did. At her party. I'm sure of it."

The police officer checked his notes. "No, I've got no record of that."

Pippa frowned. "Maybe she's still waiting for the results, I'll follow that up."

"Okay, thank you." He lifted the image back out of the file. "This is a very different level of misdemeanour. It's a threat of *actual* bodily harm. If it's the same person, then I'd worry that they felt boxed in. They may feel that Andi's won and they think they're left with no option, but to harm." He shrugged. "Whether that be psychologically, with the worry caused by the threat, or physically, with an actual attack on the body." The young officer started to blush. "I'm in the middle of a criminal minds course and I'm hoping to move into profiling."

Mike shrugged his large shoulders. "You've got me convinced."

Pippa looked at the PC in earnest. "So if we find out who's uploaded this image then we find out who's behind the rest of this shit?"

"Possibly."

Pippa jumped up. "So come on then, Mike. Look at everyone's computers, and look at all our recent activity."

Mike pulled himself out of his seat and walked towards Elizabeth's computer. "It's not as simple as that. You can remotely access the admin page." He looked at the two blank faces and decided to elaborate. "Like Andi, she could log in now from Zara's computer at G-Sterling and make changes to her page. I can only see the last logins on each individual computer." Pippa was still looking confused. "Here, I'll show you." He grabbed a piece of paper from Elizabeth's printer and pulled a Bic pen out of his pocket. He started to draw, but the pen wasn't working. He shifted some of the loose change in his pocket and pulled out another pen, quickly drawing four boxes on the top of the sheet. "Right, these are our computers." He drew another box at the bottom. "This is our server." He patted his pockets and checked behind his ear. "Grab me another pen would you? I need a different colour."

Pippa opened the top drawer of Elizabeth's desk, reaching for a variety of different coloured pens. She passed them to Mike and pushed the drawer closed with her thigh, only to have it jam, jarring painfully into her muscle. "Oww! I hate it when that happens." She pulled the drawer back out and bent down, peering into the gap and looking for the blockage. A brown file had slipped out of the back of the drawer and was wedged in the runner. She pulled at it, but it wouldn't shift. She yanked even harder and ripped it free. "Bugger," she said, standing back up and assessing the damage to the file. Half of the brown cover had ripped off, exposing the statements on the top of the white sheet inside. She read the first statement twice over before shaking her head and reading it out loud.

"*Affair with Zara started Jan 5th 2012 - Sex in her office 3.15pm.*"

Mike's pen swerved off the paper. "Elizabeth's been having an affair with Andi's missus? Our Elizabeth, with the crazy orange hair?! What the fuck?"

The police officer looked over Pippa's shoulder as she flicked through page after page of photocopied times and dates. She turned to the last page and read the final statement out loud. "*A record of my affair by Melody Fickler.*" She frowned. "What's Elizabeth doing with this?"

The police officer reached for his own file. "Does Elizabeth go by any other names? Let me see … Beth? Bethy? Lizzie?"

Pippa shook her head. "No. Come on, it can't be her!"

"She's heterosexual," suggested Mike incriminatingly. "I've always wondered what she's doing here!" He lowered himself to his knees and started shifting through the drawers. "I bet there'll be a load of evangelical coalition for marriage shit in here!" He wiped his brow. "She's a mole! She has to be!"

The police officer shook his head. "She has a file that doesn't seem to belong to her, that's all. This isn't a witch hunt." He paused for a moment and thought about it. "On the plus side, if it is her, then I don't really think there's much cause for concern. How long has she been here?"

Pippa answered quickly. "Nearly a year, same as me."

"Well then, she's had plenty of time and opportunity to do something to Andi if she'd really have wanted to."

Pippa shook her head frantically. "Unless, like you said, she's finally realised that she's lost!"

CHAPTER THIRTY ONE

Zara closed the door to the office on the top floor of the G-Sterling building. She turned to her wife, surprised that she was so close, and taken aback by the arms thrown around her shoulders. "It hasn't taken you long to thaw out, sweetie, has it?" She kissed Andi on the forehead. "I'm glad you've seen sense."

Andi kept her arms looped around Zara's neck and looked up at her wife. "I'm just pleased you're okay."

"I'm fine, sweetie. I explained it all on Saturday. The doctors think a combination of treatments will lift this constant cloud." She smiled. "But I must say, you're doing a very good job of lifting that cloud all by yourself."

Andi shook her head. "No. There's been an incident at work." She pulled away from the cuddle and reached into her pocket for her phone. She scrolled to the photos and selected the one of the computer screen. She held it up to Zara's eye line.

Zara winced. "What the fuck is that?"

"Can we sit down?"

Zara ushered them to the soft chairs near the window with the incredible view of the London skyline. "Where the fuck is that from?"

Andi took a seat. "It was uploaded to the Proud Unity server and placed as the background on everyone's desktop computer."

"What freak's done that?" snapped Zara, holding out her hand and demanding the phone once again. She clicked on the picture and zoomed in, reading the red jagged writing. "What does it say?" She squinted. "*Your campaign has destroyed the institution of marriage. Now I'm going to destroy you. Stab, by stab, by stab … starting with your wife*. Well thanks a fucking lot! What did I do?"

Andi rested her elbows on her knees and rubbed her temples. "That's just it. You've never done anything. You never asked to be in the limelight. You never brought these sickos to our door." She shook her head. "I've done it. It's my fault. All of it. I can see that now."

Zara pulled her long black hair over her shoulder. "I forgive you," she said magnanimously. "But I think you should leave."

Andi looked over with a pain in her eyes. "Work?"

"Yes of course work! What else could I possibly mean?" She stood up and walked over to her desk, lifting up a pile of glossy prospectuses. She handed them to Andi. "If not for me … then do it for them." She nodded at the collage of babies on the front cover. "I really was stuck in traffic, you know? And I *am* committed to starting a family." She smiled. "Sweetie, I've gone through the information from every single clinic and rated it on potential."

Andi looked at the number 10, hand written on the top corner of the prospectus on the top of her pile. "Potential for what?"

"Potential for fulfilling our dreams." She crouched down next to Andi's chair and stroked her arm. "Our dream of having a family." Zara shook her head. "Look at you, sweetie, you're as white as a sheet." She paused. "Andi, your job at Proud Unity's been done. I watched the announcement. It's all over. You can leave now."

Andi frowned. "I thought you were in a meeting?"

"I slipped out. The point I'm trying to make is that you've won. You've made your mark. Equal marriage is happening. You've left a great legacy at Proud Unity. Now get out while you're on top. Get out while you can. Get out before some psycho tries to slit your throat."

Andi shuddered. "I was more concerned about you actually. You don't deserve to be dragged into this. Maybe I should move out of the house, so you don't get tarred with the same brush as me."

Zara narrowed her eyes. "What? How ridiculous! There's a psycho out there. The best place for you is at home, with me and your family. Just leave Proud Unity. It's your only option."

Andi shrugged and placed the wad of information back down onto the coffee table. "I don't know, I love-"

"For Christ's sake, Andi. Our lives are at risk! I'm not bringing a family into the world with this hanging over our heads. If you were to leave Proud Unity, the nutter would think they've won."

"But someone else would just take over. The campaigning would continue."

"Exactly!" said Zara, clapping her hands. "You've finally got it! You're replaceable, Andi. The organisation will survive without you." She shook her head lightly. "But I won't. I need you. You've got a duty to stand by me. Yes, I've been difficult sometimes, and I'll apologise for that for as long as you want me to; but there were crossed wires, there definitely were. I thought you knew." Zara spoke quietly. "I won't misbehave again. I won't need to because of the new treatment. We'll start a family, we'll be a unit. Tell me you'll leave. Please, Andi, just tell me you'll leave."

Andi closed her eyes. "I'll leave."

****

Pippa jumped at the touch on her shoulder. She was leaning over the desk in Andi's office, scribbling a note as to her whereabouts. "Shit, Andi!" she shouted, dropping the pen and spinning around in shock. "Where have you been?"

"At G-Sterling."

Pippa took hold of Andi's wrists shaking her head in relief. "I've been trying to get hold of you. I've left you a billion messages. I told you not to come back here!"

"Why?" said Andi completely puzzled.

"Because it's Elizabeth!"

"What is?"

"The psycho! It's Elizabeth!"

Andi checked her pockets, suddenly having a vision of Zara looking at the image on her phone before dropping it onto the littered coffee table. "I've left it at Zara's. It's fine, she'll bring it home. What do you mean, *it's Elizabeth*?"

"If you'd have listened to my messages you'd know! I've explained this to your phone three times already, and that was much easier than this is going to be." She paused, reaching down for the ripped brown file. She looked Andi in the eye. "I'm so sorry, but it appears that Zara's been having affairs. It's all in here." Pippa looked to the floor.

"Really?"

"Yes, with Melody, and it seems she was the person Jayney left me for as well." Pippa handed over the documents. "I think Elizabeth was going to go public with this or something to discredit your marriage. It's also too much of a coincidence that all of the callers and tweeters had a variation on the name Elizabeth. Plus she has access to Janet's admin code. She could easily have uploaded that image."

Andi dropped the file back onto the desk.

"Don't you want to read it?" asked Pippa. "She's been having affairs. Zara's a cheat."

"I know," shrugged Andi. "I've got the original file. This is a copy."

"What? How long have you known?"

"Saturday, after our day out on the Segways."

Pippa was puzzled. "Why didn't you come back around? Why haven't you told me? This changes everything, Andi. You can leave her now!"

"I'm bound to her by law."

"So get a bloody divorce!" laughed Pippa, not actually finding any of it in the slightest bit funny. "Look, I need to make this call. That's what I was writing down for you in case you came back. We've got the police liaison officer in the media suite. He wants to ask Elizabeth some questions, and he doesn't want you around when she comes back. I was telling you to go home and wait until I called." She took a deep breath and carried on talking. "I've got to ring Janet now, to alert her about what's going on and make sure she brings Elizabeth back here. Let me do it quickly, so we can have some time to talk before they get back. Are you following?"

Andi ruffled her short blonde hair. "Not really."

"Right, wait a minute, let me make this call." Pippa picked up her mobile and dialled Janet's number. It rang for a good ten seconds before being picked up, and she was immediately hit with the sound of sirens and the high pitched yapping of Elizabeth's dog. Pippa started to speak. "Good, you're still there. Don't talk, just listen, really carefully. We think Elizabeth's the one behind the nasty upload and the horrible tweets and gruesome deliveries. We've found a file in her office about some extramarital affairs that Zara's been having and we think she was going to go public with it to discredit Andi's campaign. You must act normally, but you have to bring her back to the office as soon as possible. We're sending Andi home so she's not in danger. But you can't repeat any of this, do you understand?"

"Yes," came the muffled response.

Andi watched as Pippa hung up the phone. "You're acting like you're on CSI."

"This is serious! She's threatened to kill you."

Andi shrugged. "Don't you think she'd have done it already?"

Pippa was shocked by the apathy. "What's wrong? What's going on?" She took Andi's hands.

Andi shook her head. "I'm leaving. I've made my decision and I think it's time. I'm leaving Proud Unity so I can focus on my duties as a wife and hopefully in a year or so, my duties as a mother."

Pippa bent down and peered into Andi's downcast eyes. "What the bloody hell did you just say?!"

Andi lifted her head and maintained the eye contact. "I'm leaving. I'm choosing my wife."

Pippa opened her mouth in shock. "She's a cheat! She's had at least two affairs if the details in that file are correct."

"She's had five."

"What?!" Pippa couldn't believe the calm manner in which Andi was responding.

"She told me about them. About all of them. It was only sex. She's got Dysthymia and she used the affairs to try and improve her mood."

"What a load of bollocks!" Pippa threw her arms up in the air. "I've never heard of Dipstickia before!" She started to point her finger. "You're a fool if you believe it."

Andi shrugged her shoulders. "It's true. I've looked into it." She stared at Pippa. "It was just sex for her. She's never betrayed me emotionally." Andi shook her head. "It's not like I can say the same, is it? I've been a worse wife than she has. I've given part of myself to someone else."

"Which part?" asked Pippa unable to comprehend Andi's position.

"My heart." She shook her head. "You're the one with my heart."

Pippa grabbed Andi by the shoulders and actually shook her with force. "So leave her! Move in with me." She pulled her close and started to rock. "I love you, Andi, and I know you love me too."

"I have a duty to my wife." Andi was staring blankly over Pippa's shoulder. "I'm bound by law."

"No! You're playing out some weird sort of binding devotion, to a shit excuse for a wife, and a loyalty to a love that's not even there." Pippa's phone stared to ring. "Don't move. Let me get this." Pippa reached for her mobile and answered it quickly. She listened carefully and put her hand on the receiver, passing it over to Andi. "It's Nurse Sarah. Sarah Farley. The one who took your blood. She wants to speak to you."

Andi frowned and reached for the phone. "Yes, hello … Yes I do remember you, I'm ever so sorry … Oh right, did you? … No, I didn't get that message … No, we're like ships in the night at the moment, there must have been some sort of miscommunication … Yes, I'll come in tomorrow … So there was? … Oh right, what was it? … Seroquel? … Okay, I'll look forward to it … Sorry again." She hung up.

"I kept her card and phoned her this afternoon. The police officer was running through the list of issues you've had and he didn't mention the drink spiking, so I thought I'd chase it up."

Andi shrugged. "I didn't report it. I thought I was just drunk."

"And were you?"

Andi shook her head lightly. "No, it looks like I had something called Seroquel in my system. I'm going in tomorrow so they can talk to me, but she said it was a common prescription drug that notorious for making you feel drunk and limp if you take too much with alcohol."

"So not a date rape then?"

"No, just one that made me look stupid." Andi exhaled heavily. "Leaving Proud Unity is my only option. I can't be dealing with shit like this. I can't have people trying to spike my drink when I'm a mother."

"A what?!"

Andi bit her bottom lip. "Zara's finally coming round to the idea of having a family."

Pippa threw her hands up in the air once again. "You don't *come round* to the idea of having a family. You crave a family. You yearn for one. You plan one with the upmost excitement and elation." She paused for breath. "You can't have a band-aid baby, Andi!"

Andi rubbed her temples. "I've got a duty to give Zara another chance. She's been ill, but she's getting better. I promised to stay with her in sickness and in health. I'm not stupid, Pippa. I'll see how it goes for a few months. See how it feels being a stay at home housewife."

"A WHAT?!" Pippa couldn't help it. "CAN YOU HEAR YOURSELF?! You're Andi Armstrong. We need you! The campaign needs you." She lowered her voice. "I need you."

"I have to give my wife a chance. It's not like she's intentionally done anything to hurt me. She's never intentionally been cruel. She loves me."

"SHE'S HAD AFFAIRS! I'd never so much as talk to another woman if I was your wife. You deserve so much better."

"Sixty per cent of people have extramarital affairs."

"Who told you that?"

"Zara." She shrugged. "But I checked it out and she was right. No one begins a marriage expecting to cheat, but it happens. It happens all of the time. The people involved just have to make a decision about what's important. Marriage is a strong bond, Pippa."

"People should think about that bond when they're out there having the bloody affairs!"

Andi rubbed her temples. "I don't really think you're very well placed to judge."

"I'm not married!"

"No," said Andi, "but I am." She looked at the clock. "I need to get going. I don't want to be here when they get back."

"Can we talk later?"

"My mind's made up, Pippa."

Pippa shook her head. "You can't. I love you."

Andi swallowed. "I need to do what's right."

"But I love you." Pippa wiped away a tear and looked up with pleading eyes. "Please, Andi, please don't do this. I love you." She sniffed away more emotion. "I'll leave. It's fine. I'll stop work. I'll make it easy for you. Just don't give up on your job. You love your job! You've said it a million times. I might not be worth fighting for, but surely your campaign is?"

Andi gasped and reached out for Pippa's waist. "You're worth so much more than any job or campaign." She wiped away the tears creeping down Pippa's cheeks. "I just can't give up on my marriage. Yes, she can be moody sometimes, and her snipes can be mean." She paused. "But she's not abusive, and she's not vindictive, she's not malicious or sadistic. She's my wife. You don't just walk away from a marriage when something better comes along. You're committed. You're committed for life. I have to try and work through this."

Pippa stroked the side of Andi's face. "I'll never stop admiring you, no matter how much it hurts."

"I'm not sure I'll be back," said Andi holding on to her tears. "I think this is best. Everyone will understand." She smiled. "I'll say I've been housebound by the threat of a psycho."

"I'm not a psycho."

Andi laughed. "No, but you'll be the reason I'm housebound." She shook her head. "If I stay a moment longer I'll change my mind."

Pippa let her go. "I'll be waiting."

"I know you will."

CHAPTER THIRTY TWO

Pippa watched with tears in her eyes as Andi walked out of the office for the very last time. She leaned backwards against the desk and held on for support. The pain was unbearable. She closed her eyes and remembered the way Andi had pulled back the covers of her bed and ordered her in. She smiled to herself, remembering the touch of her body and the sweet smell of her breath. Pippa shook with pain. There was no point in begging or trying to make her change her mind. It had to be Andi's choice. Andi's decision. Pippa took a deep breath and opened her eyes, half expecting Andi to be back in the doorway, but she wasn't. She sighed heavily. Andi had made her decision. She'd gone.

Pippa walked around to the other side of the desk and picked up the internal phone, calling the media suite, telling them that Andi had left the building and that Janet should be back soon.

"No, I'm back now!" giggled Janet blustering into the room. "Right! What's all this drama?"

Pippa hung up the phone and looked at Janet all trussed up in her winter woollies. "Where's Elizabeth?"

"Cheers! Happy welcome back to you too! Elizabeth didn't fancy the drinky-poos, but I've got some great sound bites and we'll really be able to let loose and rock out tonight! The party's still on I hope?!"

"Where's Elizabeth?" said Pippa even louder.

"You'd think she was the life and soul!"

"Where is she?"

Janet shrugged. "I don't know. We parted ways at the House of Parliament."

"What?!"

"Why?"

"The phone call! I phoned you!"

"No you didn't."

Pippa stood up. "Shit! It's too late. Andi's gone!"

"What are you talking about?"

"I phoned you! I told you it was Elizabeth!"

"What was?"

"Oh for Christ's sake, Janet. She's the psycho! She's the one who uploaded the photo. She's the one behind all of the tweets. She had a file on Zara's affairs!"

"Zara's affairs?"

"Yes I told you!"

"I went to the loo. Elizabeth looked after my phone."

A surge of panic hit Pippa. "She heard me! She knows that we know! Oh shit, Janet! She knows that Andi's gone home!" Pippa grabbed her coat and raced out of the office. "I've got to catch her!" She shouted back down the corridor. "Go to the media suite. Get the police to come to the house."

"WHOSE HOUSE?" cried Janet.

"ANDI'S!" came the echoey reply.

CHAPTER THIRTY THREE

Andi had managed to hold it together for the short taxi ride home. She had put all thoughts of Pippa and their emotional bond, to the back of her mind, focusing instead on the task ahead - saving her marriage. She nodded in agreement at her positive plans and jumped out of the cab, rounding the corner into Wellington Place. She spotted the oversized silver Range Rover parked in the distance and felt a shiver of apprehension. Zara was home. She shook herself free of the worry, reminding herself that their discussion and parting at G-Sterling had been pleasant enough. She thought back to the brochures that Zara had ordered without prompting and remembered the promise that she had made in return. A fresh start without the distraction of work. A fresh start with the potential of children. A fresh start for them all. She veered to the left, passing through the two white pillars and walking up the short path towards their front door. Andi suddenly froze at the sight of the dog.

Mimi was tied to the drainpipe next to the front door. "Shit," gasped Andi, scurrying backwards and leaning into the bushes. She reached inside her pocket for her phone. "Shit," she gasped again, remembering where she had left it. A thousand thoughts raced through her mind, but only one jumped out. *She had to save Zara.* She popped her head back out of the white pillars and glanced up and down the street. No one was around. "Shit," she gasped again, racing back up the path to the front door, not quite sure of her plan. Mimi yapped twice and started to sniff her shoes. She looked down at her feet at the ball of fluff and noticed the pristine metal boot scraper next to the hard bristled mat. It was shaped like a rugby post and designed to clean the mud off your shoes, but it had very rarely been used and was incredibly clean. She bent down and lifted it slowly, surprised at its weight, but confident in her ability to swing it if necessary. She propped it between her knee and the wall and reached into her pocket for her house keys. She slid the key into the lock, pleased that hers hadn't been the set recently replaced. The door opened quietly and she pressed her ear into the gap, listening for movement. Nothing. She took the metal weight in both hands and slowly used her shoulder to push open the door. She listened again. Still nothing. Andi took a deep breath and stepped into the warm hall. Mimi started to whine.

Andi had no choice. She returned the weight to one hand and used the other to clip the front door closed. She froze on the hall mat, barely able to breath. The weight was getting heavier so she lifted it with both hands into her stomach. She listened. There was nothing. Just silence. No voices. No shouting. No murdering. Andi shook her head. *It's only Elizabeth,* she told herself again. She swallowed quietly and tried to formulate a plan. If she could make it to the home office she could phone for help. She took a couple of tiny steps, desperately trying to remember which floorboards squeaked. A sudden bang from the kitchen at the end of the hall, made her jump.

"That's it! Your five minutes are up." Zara's voice was loud. "I'm not telling you again. You've had your fun, now just get out of my house!"

Andi took two tiny steps on her tip-toes, desperately trying to avoid the clack of her heels.

Zara shouted again. "How dare you try and bribe me with that file? You're a disgrace. My marriage is stronger than that."

Andi jumped, catching sight of herself in the long hallway mirror. The vision had shocked her, but she noticed her reflection had been smiling; smiling at the confirmation of Zara's belief. Zara valued their marriage. She gave herself a nod in the mirror and made another tiny tip-toe step.

"I'm here for Andi." Elizabeth's voice was strained. "I'm waiting for Andi."

"Never!" snarled Zara. "You've done enough damage."

"Do you know what damage is?" Elizabeth was getting louder. "I'm not going anywhere."

"Why? So you can threaten her again. So you can throw offal in her face? Everybody knows your dirty little secret, Elizabeth. Or should I call you Lizzie, or Beth?"

"It's not-"

"The uploads, the tweets, the pretty little pictures."

"Stop it!" shouted Elizabeth.

"You started it."

Elizabeth's voice was getting higher. "Andi needs to know. She needs to know why I took that file."

"Go on then, try it out on me. Let's see if I buy it?

Elizabeth started to speak. "I took that file to protect her. I didn't want it getting into the wrong hands."

"It's you who's got the wrong hands, Elizabeth! You're the psycho with the frizzy orange hair and the stupid posh voice that you used when you phoned me and demanded I tell Andi about my crappy little sexploits." Zara clapped her hands. "You lose. I win. Andi doesn't care. She's married to me. Marriage works through shit like this!"

Andi heard Zara's confidence and felt a burst of strength. She crept the final few steps towards her office, relieved that the door was ajar and the carpet was soft. She stepped into the room and breathed properly for the first time since entering the house. She kept hold of the heavy boot cleaner and scurried towards the desk, horrified to see that the phone wasn't on the cradle. She cursed Zara, who was always answering the phone and going for a wander, never returning it to the office to be charged. Andi thought quickly. She shook her head. It was probably lying on the floor in the lounge next to the side of Zara's brown recliner. "*Shit*," she gasped, unsure if she could carry the dead weight much longer. She crept back towards the office door and stepped back out into the hall.

The voices were louder. "Sort your sad little life out, Elizabeth. You've had your fun now get out!"

"No! I need to speak to Andi. I need her to know that it wasn't me."

"No one will believe you. You're like a crazy old cat lady with shockingly dreadful hair. They were all stupid in the first place to believe you'd be pro-gay rights!"

"I am!" Elizabeth had started to flap. "I've explained this to you already. I'm here because I answered the phone to Pippa. She thought she was speaking to Janet and she reeled off how they suspected me for the upload and the tweets and the nasty packages. I can't have Andi thinking that! Thinking all of that other abuse was me. Yes, I took the file, but I took it to protect her. I'll admit it, I'm a busybody. I walk my dog a lot and I see things. I've seen you with different women."

Zara snapped. "I knew someone was following me!"

"I see things and I'm perceptive. I knew something was going on with that lady from your work and when I saw her at the party with that file I knew there must be something incriminating in it. I watched the way she was speaking to you. I watched the way her sidekick with the red hair was looking at you. It was obvious. I saw everyone get distracted by Andi falling over and I grabbed it. I gave you a chance to come clean, Zara. Marriage is precious. Marriage should be cherished. I wanted you to do the right thing. But you wouldn't. So I had no choice. I had to post it. But it seems like you and Andi are working through it, so that's great. The outcome's the right one."

"Yada, yada, yada, boring. No one will believe you. If you're capable of sending a file of extra-marital affairs to your boss, knowing it would cause hurt, then you're capable of the rest of it. "

Andi stepped onto a squeaky floorboard and froze.

There was a momentary silence from the kitchen before Elizabeth responded. "I'm not responsible for anything else. I promise. I respect Andi. I admire her. I'm fighting with her. I'm on her side. I love my job at Proud Unity. I might be heterosexual but I can assure you that I've got a passion for equality."

Andi breathed again, but stayed still, too scared to move.

"Bring out the bloody violins," scoffed Zara.

Elizabeth was firm. "I'm not responsible for the other stuff."

Zara sneered, "I know."

"How? How do you know?"

There was a long pause, before Zara laughed loudly. "Because it was me."

A gush of sudden terror raced through Andi's body, and a feeling of sheer panic drained her of her strength. The metal weight started to shake.

"I did it!" laughed Zara. "All of it. I want a wife, not a bloody deity! Everyone's obsessed with her. It pisses me off! She should be at home with me. I thought I'd start lightly. Politely even. A few angry tweets here and there. Buying some offal when I picked up my meat from the butchers. A call to a TV show." She sneered. "I thought that she'd get the message. But she's so bloody wrapped up in '*the cause,*' that nothing seemed to faze her." Zara laughed. "A promise of a family and a threat to my life did though. Sweet really. Shame I'm going to slip The Pill into her system during the fertility treatment. It's easy enough to do. I gave her some Seroquel at the party. I knew it would send her doolally. Make her show herself up. Another reason to make her contemplate leaving."

"I'll tell them everything," said Elizabeth aghast.

"Ha! It's just lucky for me that they found that file in your drawer, and it's a complete coincidence that I chose names that can be linked to Elizabeth." She sniggered. "Funny really, how things fit into place when you least expect it! And such a shame that Janet trusted you with her admin password. All the fingers are pointing your way, psycho!"

"That was you too? This photo Pippa was talking about?"

"Of course it was, sweetie. Andi leaves her passwords all over the house. Cut and paste a knife and a slash wound, and hey presto, my wife's coming home!"

"You won't get away with this," said Elizabeth with more force.

"Oh stop it, sweetie! Just get yourself out of here. I can get Andi to believe anything I want." Zara laughed. "She even thinks I've got some ridiculous form of chronic depression! A quick Google search and I'm sorted. I've got a cover story for my sex sessions and an excuse for my sniping. It's funny really … how naive she is."

"I'll tell them!"

"They won't believe you. I'm a very good actress, Elizabeth. I'll discredit you. I'll make you look unstable. Look at what you're doing now, coming round here and threatening me in my own home. Won't they be missing you at the office? Where do you think they're going to look first?"

Elizabeth was quieter. "I'm not threatening you."

Zara snarled. "No. But I'm threatening you. You quit your job and you piss off some place new. Don't you ever try and approach my wife, and don't you ever breathe my name to anyone." Zara laughed. "Do you even know who I am or what I can do? I'm untouchable, Elizabeth. I get whatever I want, whenever I want. I want a pretty little housewife who does as she's told, and that's what I've got. Andi Armstrong's mine. She's all mine." Zara laughed. "And she'll stay with me forever!"

The sudden thud in the hallway was enormous, but the cry was even louder. "OH NO SHE WON'T!" shouted Andi as she raced for the front door.

Zara ran from the kitchen, just in time to see Andi disappearing out of the house. She thundered across the parquet flooring, clattering into the piece of discarded metal and crashing straight to the floor in a scream of agony.

Andi raced down the garden path, straight into the arms of Pippa. "Take me away!" she screamed. "Just take me away from here."

"What's wrong? What's happened? Who's inside?"

Andi grabbed Pippa's hand and pulled her out onto the street. "Just take me away."

"Number six!" shouted Pippa to the police liaison officer who was racing towards them, "through the white pillars!" Pippa watched him disappear up the short path and turned her attention to Andi. "What's happened?"

Andi started to walk, quickly pulling Pippa along with her. "I've been so blind."

Pippa pulled on her hand and forced Andi to stand still. "What's going on? Talk to me!"

Andi released Pippa's hand and shook her head, turning and running towards the corner of the street.

Pippa raced after her. "What are you doing? Where are you going?"

Andi rounded the bend, leaning on the signpost for St John's Wood High Street. She pointed back around towards Wellington Place. "I'm *never*, *ever* setting foot in that street, ever again."

"Why? What about Zara? What about your house?"

Andi took Pippa's face in her hands. "How could I be so stupid?"

Pippa shook her head. "What's going on? Andi, don't do this to me."

Andi closed her eyes and held back the tears. "I gave you my heart, Pippa. I can't survive without it." She shook her head. "I'm empty. There's nothing here."

Pippa lifted her hand to Andi's chest. "You're not empty. You've got *my* heart." She pressed harder. "Just feel. It's me who's beating inside you."

Andi opened her eyes, awash with tears. "Forgive me," she whispered, "forgive me, I love you."

"I know," said Pippa, wrapping her arms around Andi's shaking body. "I know."

CHAPTER THIRTY FOUR

Three years later:

"Mama Dee-Dee, please let me watch it again."

"No!" laughed Andi. "We've watched it three times already this morning."

The chubby toddler wobbled his way to the next sofa seat. "Mama Pip, let me watch it again?"

Pippa folded her copy of the Financial Times and dropped it onto the new deep pile carpet in Gee-Gee's finally modernised front lounge. She grinned at her son. "Go and give your sister a kiss and I'll think about it."

The podgy legs started their short journey once again. "Mama Dee-Dee, lift up your jumper."

Andi lifted her jumper and smiled as her son gently kissed her rounded belly. "Come on then, my little cherub, let's watch it again."

Pippa laughed. "I thought you had to upload that article to the Proud Unity website?"

Andi smiled. "Some things are more important than others, you taught me that." She nodded towards the folded paper on the carpet. "Are you sure you don't want to re-read that article about the downfall of G-Sterling?"

Pippa laughed. "I've read it ten times and I'll never tire of seeing them lay the blame at Zara's door."

Andi pretended not to hear. "Whose door?"

"Exactly! I don't know, some crazy woman who was declared bankrupt and then skipped the country part way through her sexual harassment and public nuisance court case."

Andi frowned. "Nope, never heard of her."

"Mama Dee-Dee, Mama Dee-Dee. Press play!"

Andi smiled and reached for the remote. "How could I possibly say no to this?"

Pippa reached out and squeezed Andi's hand.

The wedding music sung out from the television.

"My Mamas' got married!" giggled the toddler.

"We certainly did," laughed Pippa and Andi in blissful unison.

THE END.

About the author:

Lambda Literary Award finalist, Kiki Archer is the UK-based author of nine best-selling, award-winning novels. She was position 51 in the Guardian newspaper's Pride Power List 2018 and position 18 in the Diva Pride Power List 2017.

Her debut novel But She Is My Student won the UK's 2012 SoSoGay Best Book Award. Its sequel Instigations took just 12 hours from its release to reach the top of the Amazon lesbian fiction chart.

Binding Devotion was a finalist in the 2013 Rainbow Awards.

One Foot Onto The Ice broke into the American Amazon contemporary fiction top 100 as well as achieving the lesbian fiction number ones. The sequel When You Know went straight to number one on the Amazon UK, Amazon America, and Amazon Australia lesbian fiction charts, as well as number one on the iTunes, Smashwords, and Lulu Gay and Lesbian chart.

Too Late... I Love You won the National Indie Excellence Award for best LGBTQ book, the Gold Global eBook Award for best LGBT Fiction. It was a Rainbow Awards finalist and received an honourable mention.

Lost In The Starlight was a finalist in the 2017 Lambda Literary Awards best lesbian romance category and was named a 'Distinguished Favourite' in the Independent Press Awards.

A Fairytale Of Possibilities won Best Romance Novel at the 2017 Diva Literary Awards and was awarded a Distinguished Favourite in the New York Big Book Awards.

Kiki was crowned the Ultimate Planet's Independent Author of the Year in 2013 and she received an honourable mention in the 2014 Author of the Year category.

She won Best Independent Author and Best Book for Too Late... I Love You in the 2015 Lesbian Oscars and was a finalist in the 2017 Diva250 Awards for best author.

Kiki's 2018 ended on an incredible high winning 'Best Author' at the Waldorf's star-studded Diva Awards.

Novels by Kiki Archer:

BUT SHE IS MY STUDENT - March 2012

INSTIGATIONS - August 2012

BINDING DEVOTION - February 2013

ONE FOOT ONTO THE ICE - September 2013

WHEN YOU KNOW - April 2014

TOO LATE... I LOVE YOU - June 2015

LOST IN THE STARLIGHT - September 2016

A FAIRYTALE OF POSSIBILITIES - June 2017

THE WAY YOU SMILE - November 2018

Connect with Kiki:

www.kikiarcherbooks.com
Twitter: @kikiarcherbooks
www.facebook.com/kiki.archer
www.youtube.com/kikiarcherbooks
www.instagram.com/kikiarcherbooks

L - #0061 - 201218 - C0 - 210/148/14 - PB - DID2397225